PATRIOTS—*Volume V*

CANNON'S CALL

Adam Rutledge

BCI Producers of **The First Americans,
The Holts** and **The Frontier Trilogy: Westward!**

Book Creations Inc., Canaan, NY • *Lyle Kenyon Engel, Founder*

BANTAM BOOKS
NEW YORK • TORONTO • LONDON • SYDNEY • AUCKLAND

CANNON'S CALL

*A Bantam Domain Book / published by arrangement with
Book Creations Inc.*

Bantam edition / October 1993

*Produced by Book Creations Inc.
Lyle Kenyon Engel, Founder*

*DOMAIN and the portrayal of a boxed "d" are trademarks of
Bantam Books, a division of
Bantam Doubleday Dell Publishing Group, Inc.*

ISBN 0-553-29203-X

Published simultaneously in the United States and Canada

*Bantam Books are published by Bantam Books, a division of Bantam
Doubleday Dell Publishing Group, Inc. Its trademark, consisting of the
words "Bantam Books" and the portrayal of a rooster, is Registered in
U.S. Patent and Trademark Office and in other countries. Marca Re-
gistrada. Bantam Books, 1540 Broadway, New York, New York 10036.*

PRINTED IN THE UNITED STATES OF AMERICA

OPM   0 9 8 7 6 5 4 3 2 1

PATRIOTS—*Volume Five*
CANNON'S CALL

DANIEL REED—Son of the Virginia aristocracy and a member of General Washington's staff, he has embarked on one of the most urgent and perilous missions of the war. But a shocking discovery about the woman he loves sends him on a journey that will prove an even greater test of his courage, his resourcefulness, and his desire.

ROXANNE DARRAGH—A beautiful spy bound to America by her love of freedom and of Daniel Reed, she is now in enemy hands and headed for foreign shores. Held captive in a luxurious prison, Roxanne will go to any lengths to survive . . . because much more than her own life is at stake.

ELLIOT MARKHAM—A member of a prominent Boston family with Tory sympathies, he has become an ardent—and secret—supporter of the patriot cause. His reputation as a pleasure-seeking scoundrel leads him into a duel with his archenemy.

SARAH CUMMINGS—Just as the revolution rages around Boston, another war rages within her heart: her love for Elliot battles her promise to the man she married. A conflict that has been fought with bitterness and betrayal, it too may ultimately be decided by bullets.

PENN SLOANE—A seasoned woodsman and former soldier with Ethan Allen's Green Mountain Boys, he has vowed to help transport Ticonderoga's cannon, powerful weapons that sound the mighty roar of rebellion and freedom.

CANNON'S
CALL

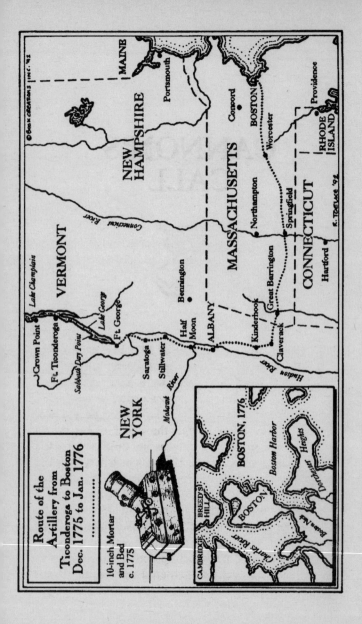

Route of the
Artillery from
Ticonderoga to Boston
Dec. 1775 to Jan. 1776

10-inch Mortar
and Bed
c. 1775

© Bear CREATIONS INC. '92

MAINE

Portsmouth

NEW HAMPSHIRE

Concord
BOSTON

Worcester

Providence

RHODE
ISLAND

Connecticut River

MASSACHUSETTS

Northampton
Springfield

CONNECTICUT

R. Teeue '92

VERMONT

Lake Champlain
Crown Point
Ft. Ticonderoga
Sabbath Day Point
Lake George
Ft. George

Bennington

Great Barrington

Hartford

Saratoga
Stillwater

Half
Moon
ALBANY

Kinderhook
Claverack

Mohawk River

Hudson River

NEW
YORK

BOSTON, 1776.

CAMBRIDGE

BREED'S
HILL

BOSTON

Charles River

Boston Harbor

Dorchester
Heights

Boston Neck

CANNON'S
CALL

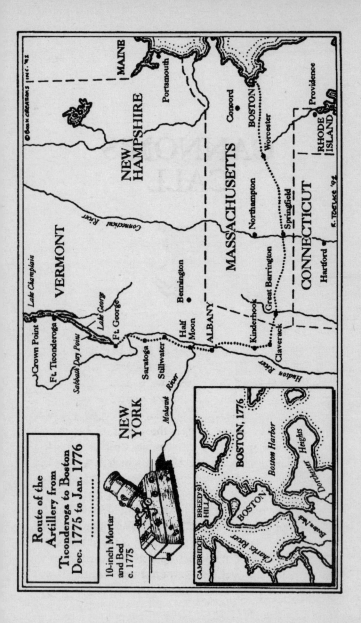

Route of the
Artillery from
Ticonderoga to Boston
Dec. 1775 to Jan. 1776
....

10-inch Mortar
and Bed
c. 1775

© Bass CREATION'S INC. '91

MAINE

Portsmouth

Concord

BOSTON

Worcester

Providence

RHODE ISLAND

NEW HAMPSHIRE

Connecticut River

Northampton

Springfield

MASSACHUSETTS

Hartford

CONNECTICUT

Great Barrington

K. TREECE '91

VERMONT

Lake Champlain

Crown Point

Ft. Ticonderoga

Lake George

Sabbath Day Point

Ft. George

Bennington

Kinderhook

Claverack

Saratoga

Stillwater

Half
Moon

ALBANY

Hudson River

NEW YORK

Mohawk River

BOSTON, 1776.

Boston Harbor

BREED'S
HILL

Dorchester
Heights

CAMBRIDGE

BOSTON

Charles River

Boston Neck

Chapter One

The hot, humid summer of 1775 had passed, and the crisp days of the New England autumn had turned cold. The trees were bare, their leaves long since fallen. Several times already, snow flurries had fallen on Cambridge. The wind forced twenty-two-year-old Daniel Reed to pull the collar of his brown cloth coat up around his ears as he strode across the courtyard in front of Vassall House, which served as the personal headquarters of General George Washington, commander-in-chief of the Continental Army.

Daniel's official rank was that of lieutenant, but he wore no uniform. His position on Washington's staff was as liaison between the general and the intelligence networks that were being set up across the colonies as the war against the British gathered momentum. It was also Daniel's duty to serve as Washington's personal representative on any assignments the commander-in-chief chose to give him, and he reported only to the tall, grim-faced military leader from Virginia.

Before Daniel could carry out his duties, however, he had to be given a job . . . and so far, there was no sign of that. He had been summoned from British-controlled Boston several weeks earlier and had hurried to Cambridge only to discover that he had fallen victim to the mentality that has pervaded every army in the history of the world: Make haste . . . and then tarry.

This evening, though, an orderly had appeared at his quarters with an order to report to Vassall House, and Daniel fiercely hoped that he was about to be given something of value to do.

A freezing wind whipped across the bleak courtyard, prompting Daniel to hold his black tricorn tighter to his head. When he reached the short flight of steps leading up to the main entrance of Vassall House, he climbed them briskly and stepped inside the impressive three-story structure that had been turned over to General Washington.

Just inside the door, a corporal in a shabby blue coat was on duty. He should have been outside, Daniel thought; standing guard behind a closed door was an exercise in futility.

"Daniel Reed to see General Washington," he said to the sentry. "I'm expected."

"Reckon you must be, at that," grunted the corporal. "Otherwise you wouldn't be out on a cold night like this 'un, would you?" The man grinned, showing rotted teeth, and jerked his head to indicate the hallway leading through the building from the foyer. "You know where to find his lordship, don't you?"

"Yes, I can find the general," Daniel said.

"Well, then, what're you waitin' for? Go ahead."

Daniel was appalled at the lack of discipline and respect shown by the corporal. The man was shirking his duty by staying inside where it was warm, and he was letting Daniel wander freely around headquarters without even checking on his identity. If the sentry was a representative example, no wonder the army's morale was so low and the war effort was in a shambles.

A moment later, Daniel knocked on the door of Washington's private office, and a voice he recognized as the general's called, "Come in." Daniel opened the heavy hardwood door and stepped into the room.

It was large and lined with bookshelves and dark oak paneling—a very masculine room, which was appropriate considering its occupant. George Washington would never be taken for a handsome man; his features were too rough-hewn, his customary expression too solemn. But as he paced back and forth across the room in his long blue coat and buff-colored pants, he gave off an air of personal power and strength that explained why he had been chosen to lead the ragtag colonial army. When Daniel entered the room, Washington stopped his pacing and greeted the young man.

"Good evening, Lieutenant Reed."

Daniel snapped to attention and saluted the general. Washington returned the salute distractedly.

"Good evening, General," Daniel said. "I was told you wanted to see me."

"That's right." Washington clasped his hands behind his back and nodded toward a chair in front of the massive stone fireplace, where a cheery blaze brightened and warmed the room. For the first time, Daniel realized they were not alone.

"Lieutenant Reed," Washington continued, "allow

me to introduce Mr. Henry Knox. You two may know each other already."

Henry Knox rose from his chair and extended a hand to Daniel. "Pleased to meet you, Lieutenant," he said in a booming voice. "I don't believe we've been formally introduced, but I've heard a great deal about your exploits."

Daniel shook hands with Knox, his own fingers all but swallowed up by the man's massive paw. If Knox had been standing when he first entered the room, Daniel reflected, he could not have missed seeing him.

Knox was a huge bear of a man, several years older than Daniel and several inches taller, easily topping six feet. General Washington was a towering figure, being three inches over six feet himself, but Knox was even taller. The civilian needed the height, however, to support his weight. His shoulders were massive, and his thighs were like the trunks of young trees. Daniel figured he had to weigh at least two hundred and fifty pounds, perhaps more; his hair was thick, fair, and curly, and his round face wore a jovial expression. Most appealing to Daniel, Knox's eyes glittered with intelligence.

"I'm glad to make your acquaintance, sir," Daniel said, even as he wondered what Knox was doing here. The big man's name was familiar, but Daniel didn't know what connection Knox had with Washington and the Continental Army.

"Do you know who Mr. Knox is, Lieutenant?" Washington asked, as though reading Daniel's mind.

Suddenly Daniel remembered him, and he exclaimed, "You're the gentleman who owned a bookstore in Boston! I've been in your shop many times with a friend of mine, Miss Roxanne Darragh."

"I remember Miss Darragh," Knox said, "and you

as well, Lieutenant Reed. Being a bookseller, I did a considerable amount of business with Miss Darragh's father. William Darragh was the best printer in Boston —before the damnable redcoats ruined things for everyone."

"What happened to your store, Mr. Knox?" asked Daniel, a faint smile on his face as he fondly recalled the times spent with Roxanne looking through the shelves of books in Knox's establishment.

For a moment, the jovial expression on Knox's face vanished, and he slowly shook his head. "Since I was known to be a colonial supporter, my wife and I thought it wise to leave Boston after the battles at Lexington and Concord. I placed my younger brother, William, in charge of the store, thinking that perhaps the Tories would leave him alone. But they wrecked and looted the place almost immediately, damn their eyes, and William had no choice but to flee. He's here in Cambridge now."

Daniel frowned, saddened by the thought of the bookstore being reduced to a shambles by a mob.

"Even though he is a civilian volunteer, Mr. Knox has become our chief engineer and commander of artillery, since he has perhaps the greatest knowledge of those subjects I have ever encountered, either in a military officer or a civilian," Washington said briskly, clearly impatient with their reminiscing.

Knox shrugged his brawny shoulders and modestly added, "I've read a few books on such matters."

"No need for self-deprecation, Henry," the general snorted. "If I didn't have the utmost confidence in you, I never would have recommended to the Continental Congress that you replace Colonel Gridley."

Daniel remembered Colonel Richard Gridley, who had been in charge of the fortifications at Breed's Hill on the Charlestown peninsula, the site of a bloody battle between British and American forces the previous summer. Daniel had been there, and despite the fact that the clash was already popularly known as the Battle of Bunker Hill, the majority of the action had taken place on Breed's Hill. He had not known, however, that Colonel Gridley, a veteran of the French and Indian War, had been replaced.

Washington turned to Daniel and went on, "You are certainly aware, Lieutenant, of the stalemate that has existed these past few months between our forces and those of the British located in Boston."

"Yes, sir. In fact, as you may know, I was in Boston not that long ago, and I've seen firsthand the effect that our siege is having on the city."

"A siege can be a tremendously effective military weapon, that is true, Lieutenant," Washington said, sighing, "but it has one major drawback: The effects of it are not easily visible to those doing the besieging. To the men of the Continental Army, it looks as though we are merely sitting here in Cambridge and doing nothing."

The general's frustration seized him again and he paced once more. "Most of the men in our army promised to stay for one year," he continued, "and that year will soon be up. They're tired, they're impatient, and they miss their families. They cannot see how they're doing anyone any good by waiting and waiting. Accordingly, morale has plummeted. We have to do something, something that will demonstrate to the lads that we mean business. Something that will show them we can win this war." The general turned around, fixed his intense gaze on Daniel and Henry Knox, and declared, "We're going to drive the redcoats right out of Boston."

Daniel's heart sank. He'd heard a great deal of talk

among the men about how they should invade Boston and force the British to leave the city. Some of the troops had even suggested that Washington lacked the courage to order such an attack. Daniel did not know Washington very well, but he had no doubts about the general's courage. What he doubted was the ability of the Americans to make good on the boast that they could kick the king's forces right into the sea.

For one thing, they were outnumbered; the British still had more men in Boston than the Continental Army did in Cambridge. For another, the Americans had never had an abundance of powder and shot; a full-scale assault on Boston would quickly exhaust their supply of ammunition. And finally, there was the matter of ability. Daniel supported the patriot cause with all his heart and soul, but his patriotism had not rendered him blind and senseless. The Continenal Army was composed largely of farmers and tradesmen. The officers had been doing their best to whip the troops into shape for months now, but the men still lacked the training and discipline to dislodge thousands of King George's crack troops from a well-defended city.

The only thing an invasion of Boston would accomplish, to Daniel's way of thinking, was the ruination of the American army and the utter failure of the movement to gain independence for the colonies.

Washington was smiling enigmatically. "I see you doubt the wisdom of our course, Lieutenant."

The last thing Daniel wanted to do was to argue with a superior officer, especially General George Washington, but he had always been one to speak his mind.

"I think it would be a grave mistake, General," he said bluntly.

Henry Knox chuckled, and Washington said, "Indeed it would be, Lieutenant . . . if it were not for the plan that Mr. Knox has presented to me this evening. It changes everything." The general smiled at the civilian. "Would you be so kind as to explain your plan to Lieutenant Reed, Mr. Knox?"

"Of course, General." Knox turned to Daniel. "Artillery is the key. Since the British withdrew from the Charlestown Peninsula, we now control the hills there once more. And for some reason known only to Howe and the other redcoat generals, they have never tried to seize control of Dorchester Heights to the south of the city. Therefore, with sufficient cannon to emplace on those heights to the north and south, we can shell the city until the British are forced to evacuate."

"That's all well and good," Daniel said. "But we don't have nearly enough cannon to do such a thing."

"Ah, but we do," Knox said, his blue eyes twinkling with excitement. "They're just . . . not here."

Understanding burst in Daniel's brain like a shell from one of the cannon Knox was talking about. "Ticonderoga!" he exclaimed.

"Exactly," Knox agreed. "Ticonderoga."

"I understand you've been there before, Lieutenant," Washington put in.

"No, sir. My brother and a friend of ours were with Colonel Allen when he and the Green Mountain Boys seized the British fort there last spring. I was supposed to be with them, but I got . . . *delayed* capturing a wagon train of British supplies."

Washington picked up a piece of paper from his desk. "According to the information we've received, there are more than enough cannon at Ticonderoga to implement the plan that Mr. Knox has proposed. All we have to do is bring them here, and that is exactly what Mr. Knox has suggested that we do."

Daniel blinked as he thought about the implications of what Washington was saying. It sounded so simple—bring the big guns from Ticonderoga to Cambridge and then use them to drive the British out of Boston.

But there were several hundred miles of countryside between Cambridge and Lake Champlain, countryside that Daniel had traveled along with Quincy and Murdoch during the spring of 1775. He remembered the rugged, wooded slopes of the Berkshire Mountains, the steep inclines, the deep valleys, the narrow, twisting roads—where there were roads at all. Not only that, but winter was coming on. Drop a thick coating of snow on those craggy hills, and they became almost impassable for a man on horseback.

How the hell does Knox plan to get dozens of heavy cannon over them? Daniel wondered.

"I'll be going along on the journey, of course," Knox was saying. "There are quite a few of our men in New York, and I'm sure we can recruit enough volunteers to bring back the artillery. I hope to be here with the cannon by just after the first of the year."

Daniel's first impulse was to declare that such a notion was impossible, but both Washington and Knox were perfectly serious about the plan. After a moment's hesitation he said, "The terrain between here and Ticonderoga is rather inhospitable, you know."

"We're aware of that, Lieutenant," Washington said.

Knox leaned forward and prodded his long, blunt finger in Daniel's chest. "Sledges, that's the answer," he declared. "We're going to load the cannon on sledges and drag them over the mountains. I promise you, Lieutenant, it can be done." He grinned broadly. "Do you mind if I call you Daniel? I'd like for us to be friends, since we're going to spend so much time together."

Daniel glanced at the general, and as if Washington had read the question in the young man's mind, he squared his shoulders and said, "I would prefer not to order you to accompany Mr. Knox, Lieutenant. An assignment of this nature should be voluntary. But since you have personally traversed much of the country involved, I'm sure you could be a great help. Moreover, on such an important mission, I'd like to have a personal representative along, and as you recall, such was our arrangement when you agreed to join my staff."

"Of course, sir." Daniel felt numb, not really paying much attention to what he was saying. He was thinking instead about how grueling and arduous such a journey as Knox proposed would be, but he added quickly, "I'd be honored to go along and help any way I can."

Knox clapped him on the shoulder with such exuberance that Daniel was staggered. "Excellent! I was hoping you would agree to go with us. We can use every good man we can get."

Daniel shook his head in an effort to clear it. He had been hoping for a mission, and now he had one. The fact that it might turn out to be a fool's errand was beside the point.

"When will we be leaving, sir?" he asked, his voice sounding slightly hollow to him.

"As soon as possible," Washington replied.

"My brother William will be going with us, too," Knox said. "We'll travel by horseback to the Hudson River and then take a boat north to Albany. From there we shall just have to see what is available."

"I can be ready to ride at first light tomorrow."

"Perhaps you will be, but I won't," Knox said with

his customary grin. "Day after tomorrow will be soon enough. William and I will be ready to depart from the courtyard at dawn."

"I'll be there," promised Daniel.

Even though Washington had smiled a few times during the conversation, he had never lost his austere look, but now, with the matter settled, his mood eased slightly.

"Thank you, Lieutenant," he said, smiling. "I've heard that you've been forced to endure several personal hardships lately. I'm afraid I may have just added another to your burden."

Daniel stood straight and tall. "Not at all, sir," he said. "I'm happy to do anything I can to help our cause."

"I'm glad to hear it, son. Now go back to your quarters and get some rest," Washington urged. "You'll need it for the trip that lies ahead of you."

Daniel saluted the general, nodded to Henry Knox, and said good night. Then he turned and left Washington's office. The same corporal was on duty when Daniel slipped out the front door of Vassall House, and he moved quietly so as not to disturb the sleeping guard, who stood leaning on his musket, his chin resting on his chest, soft snores issuing from his half-open mouth.

As he walked toward his quarters in a nearby building that had been converted into a makeshift barracks, Daniel's breath plumed in front of him in the cold night air. Judging from some of Washington's final comments, it seemed the general knew that his beloved Roxanne had disappeared from sight.

Daniel trudged on into the night. Fool's errand or not, he was glad to have the assignment from General Washington. Perhaps the journey would take his mind

off Roxanne and the horrible uncertainty of not knowing if she was dead or alive.

Daniel stirred restlessly in his bunk, sunk just deep
enough in sleep for phantom dreams to plague him, as
they so often did. Tonight, as always, Roxanne figured
prominently in his visions. Roxanne . . . the woman he
loved, the beautiful redheaded young woman whose pa-
triotic spirit was every bit as fiery as her silken tresses.
But not all Roxanne's passion had been devoted to the
cause. Some of it had been reserved for Daniel, and she
had returned his love unstintingly.

Months earlier, in late summer, they had been together at a farm outside Concord owned by their
friends Lemuel and Lottie Parsons. They had been in
the Parsons barn, making love, lost in their urgent desire for each other, when British soldiers disguised as
simple countrymen had raided the farm, searching for a
cache of patriot munitions rumored to be hidden there.
The troopers had found no guns or powder or shot, but
they had burst into the barn and one of the soldiers had
struck Daniel in the head with the butt of a musket.
Thinking him dead from the wound, they might have
left Roxanne alone—had the officer in charge not recognized her as a patriot rabble-rouser wanted by the
British on charges of treason. The soldiers had forced
her to dress hastily and then left with her as their prisoner.

That was the last anyone outside of Boston had
seen of her.

Daniel had been unconscious at the time, but he
had pieced together the story from what Lemuel and
Lottie told him, and with the help of his cousin, Elliot
Markham, who was still operating inside Boston as a
patriot secret agent, he had gotten into the city and

launched a search for Roxanne. That quest had been fruitless, however, and when the summons had come to return to Cambridge and the Continental Army, Daniel had gone, reluctantly admitting defeat.

Ever since, the events had been replaying themselves in his mind at night, and as a result, his slumber was troubled. Tonight was no different, and as he tossed and turned, he seemed to see Roxanne being dragged kicking and screaming away from him and hideously tortured at the hands of the British. Then he saw her being hanged, her limp body cut down and tossed in a shallow, unmarked grave in Boston's paupers' field.

Daniel sat bolt upright, and sweat dripped from his face despite the fact that his room was chilly and dank. He took several deep breaths and tried to calm his racing pulse, which sounded like a cacophony of hammer strikes in his head. Then he used a corner of his blanket to wipe away the beads of perspiration.

There was a very good chance that Roxanne was dead, and he knew it. But she would have wanted him to continue fighting for freedom; she would never have wanted their dream of liberty to die with her.

Maybe dragging cannon across the mountains in the middle of winter was impossible. But impossible or not, he was going to help Henry Knox do just that. And when those cannon were in place and launched their deadly cargoes toward the British, at least one of the shells arching through the sky would be for Roxanne, Daniel vowed.

He lay down, holding tight to that thought for the sparse comfort it offered, but it was still a long time before he dozed off again, and when he did, the dreams were there as always.

Chapter Two

It was no night to be traveling in an open buggy. A cold wind blew in from the sea, bringing with it a thick fog that obscured the stars and a damp chill that penetrated the clothes the travelers wore and the blankets draped over their laps. The dampness cut through to the bone.

Roxanne Darragh shivered beside the man handling the horse's reins. As usual, Major Alistair Kane had given her no choice in the matter. After all, she was his prisoner.

"I'm sorry you're cold, dear Roxanne," Kane said, feeling her tremble. "But I promise you, we'll soon be at our destination, and then you'll be warm again."

Roxanne made no reply. For one thing, she was almost too chilled to speak, and for another she had long since run out of anything she wanted to say to Major Alistair Kane. She wanted nothing to do with the man—except perhaps to see him dead.

Her lips tightened. *Dear Roxanne,* he had called her. When she had first been brought to him by the soldiers who had kidnapped her from the Parsons farm, she had been nothing to him but a potential source of information about the patriots' espionage activities. Ruthless and ambitious, he had kept her captivity a secret from his superiors, confining her in a private house in Boston rather than one of the jails. He had planned to extract the information he needed, then smash the fledgling intelligence network of the Americans. Such a coup would have undoubtedly led to a promotion for him.

But she had stubbornly resisted his efforts to interrogate her, even when he had vowed to torture her . . . a threat on which he had never followed through. And as the weeks passed he had fallen in love with her.

Thank God Kane had a sense of honor, warped though it might be at times, Roxanne had thought more than once. Otherwise he would have simply satisfied his desire for her by force, and she would not have been able to stop him. But he had decided to win her over, to convince her that she was wrong to resist him.

"I'm sure you'll like what I have planned for you," Kane said, breaking into Roxanne's brooding thoughts. "It's going to be much nicer than what you've had to endure the past few weeks."

"I hope so," she said, her voice as cold as the night air. Ever since she had accidentally discovered that Kane was in league with a criminal figure known as Lazarus, she had been shunted around the countryside and hidden in various houses belonging to British sympathizers and operatives. Kane, a clever spy, came and went as he pleased, despite the fact that the patriots controlled all of Massachusetts except Boston. She seldom saw him in uniform these days; usually he looked more like a successful businessman than a British intelligence officer.

Roxanne had heard nothing more about Lazarus since she had been smuggled out of Boston. Lazarus had wanted to kill her rather than risk exposing the link between himself and Kane, but Kane would not allow that. Instead he removed Roxanne from the city, thereby keeping the promise he had made to the powerful gang leader to keep her isolated.

Now she was being moved again, and she supposed it would be to another shabby farmhouse or small-town cottage.

She had lost track of which direction they were traveling in. Alternately defiant and depressed, she spent her time either plotting her ultimate vengeance against Kane or wallowing in the black pit of despair that swallowed her whole every time she allowed herself to think about Daniel Reed.

Daniel . . . her lover, her friend . . . the father of the child growing inside her. Daniel had wanted to marry her, to be her husband, but she had refused him, saying that while she loved him, the Revolution had to come first. Both of them would have jobs to do, she had declared, and they had to put duty ahead of personal happiness. But Daniel was dead, and now she would never have the chance to be his wife.

God, she wished she had never been so stiff-necked and stubborn!

For months the image of Daniel lying sprawled on the straw-littered ground inside the Parsons barn had never been far from her mind. In her memory, the blood that covered his face and head was an even brighter and more vivid red than it had been in real life. The British had killed him, and all her hopes and dreams had died along with him.

Well, nearly all, she added to herself. There was still the child. . . . She still had that tiny bit of Daniel to cling to.

The lane on which the buggy was traveling ended at a road that ran north and south. Kane swung the vehicle into the left-hand turn that led north. Over the sound of the horse's hooves, Roxanne heard a muffled roar, and after a moment she realized that she was hearing the ocean pounding against the rocks at the base of a nearby cliff. The thick fog in the air deadened the sound somewhat, but it was loud enough for Roxanne to know what it was.

She frowned. She had not realized they were that close to the sea. Where could Kane be taking her? Some isolated cottage overlooking the ocean, perhaps? A hovel on some rocky, windswept point? Such a place would suit her mood perfectly, she told herself.

The road wound ever closer to the sea, however, and the pounding of waves grew louder.

"Where are we going?"

"You'll see," Kane replied.

Her feeling of unease was becoming stronger with each passing moment. Kane had moved her from one hiding place to another before, but she sensed that tonight was different. Something else was afoot.

A few minutes went by, and then Kane slowed the buggy and watched the side of the road intently. It was difficult to see on this dark, mist-shrouded night, but after the buggy had traveled another hundred yards, Kane slowed the horse even more and swung the vehicle into another turn that put them on a narrow path barely wide enough for the wheels of the buggy. It followed a downhill slope, twisting and turning back upon itself, and Roxanne knew they were going down toward the water.

Fear made her heart pound heavily in her chest. Something was very wrong, and for a few seconds she considered throwing herself from the buggy and trying to escape into the fog. But if she tried to make her way up or down this steep slope, she might tumble down the rocky incline, putting herself—and the baby—in mortal danger.

No, she thought, all she could do now was wait to see what Kane had planned for her.

The descent finally came to an end, and Kane drove the buggy out onto the hard-packed sand of a small beach at the head of a tiny cove. Roxanne could barely make out the dark shape of the shoulders of land that enclosed the cove to the north and south. Waves rolled in and hissed on the sand as Kane brought the buggy to a halt.

Roxanne spotted several small points of light, and for a second she thought the fog had lifted enough for her to see stars close to the horizon. Then she realized she was looking at the lights of a ship lying at anchor just inside the cove. In fact, one of the pinprick glimmers of illumination detached itself from the others and appeared to come closer.

"What is this?" she asked Kane, hysteria threatening to edge into her voice. "What are you going to do?"

"I'm sending you someplace you'll be safe, my dear," Kane replied smoothly. "Someplace where you won't have to worry about the war or anything else. You'll be well taken care of, I promise you."

"No!" Roxanne cried shrilly. She had recognized the approaching light as a lantern in the hands of a man sitting in the bow of a small boat being rowed to shore by several other men. "I don't know where you're send-ing me, but I won't go!"

"I'm afraid you have no choice. I'm going to be quite busy in the weeks ahead, and I've run out of places for you to stay where I know you'll be safe. I'm sorry, Roxanne, but I have no choice."

The small boat was only a few yards offshore by now, and the lantern cast enough light for Roxanne to see the uniforms of the sailors manning the oars. They were the blue-and-white striped shirts, white duck trou-sers, and blue caps of common British seamen.

Kane turned toward her and reached for her arm. "Let me help you down," he murmured, "then I'll get your bag."

Panic shot through Roxanne. He planned to ship her off to England, where she would never see her homeland again. She could not allow that to happen.

Her hands were gripped together in her lap. Mov-ing with unexpected speed, she brought them up and drove them at his face with all the strength she could muster. Kane had no chance to block the blow, and it took him in the jaw and knocked his head against the wooden framework of the buggy. While he was momen-tarily stunned, Roxanne surged to her feet and leapt from the little vehicle.

"You!" shouted the man carrying the lantern in the boat. Its prow was scraping the sand of the beach now. "You there! Come back 'ere!"

Roxanne staggered as she landed on the beach. Regaining her footing, she turned to run toward the path that led to the top of the bluff overlooking the cove. The slippers she wore were not made for that ac-tivity, however, and within a few yards they were soaked and filled with cold sand.

She heard more shouts behind her as she slogged

through the wet, heavy sand. Sobs of desperation welled up in her throat, but she swallowed them, knowing she would need all her air for running. She heard booted feet slap the sand in a frantic tattoo as the pursuit was launched.

It was hopeless, and a part of her brain knew it. But she was not going to give up. If she could just get to the top of the path, where the fog was thicker, she might be able to give them the slip.

A rough hand caught her shoulder and tried to jerk her to a halt. She cried out and pulled away, but the man's scrabbling fingers found a purchase again for an instant. Then, with the sound of tearing cloth, she was free once more. But her pursuer was so close she could hear his breath rasping in his throat.

The man was not so gentle in his next attempt to stop her. He threw himself forward in a diving tackle, and as his long arms went around Roxanne's waist, he swept her to the ground. She landed heavily, the impact knocking the air from her lungs, and she tasted gritty sand in her mouth as she gulped down oxygen to replace what she had lost. The British seaman's weight was on her back, and although she wanted desperately to roll over, she did not have the strength to dislodge him. Fear for the baby flooded through her, but when she finally managed to stop gasping for breath, she realized the only pain she felt was from some mild scrapes on her elbows and knees.

"Get off her, you damned fool!" Kane shouted.

The weight lifted from Roxanne's back, and she was able to roll over and draw several deep breaths. She saw a dark shape looming over her and recognized it as Kane. The major took hold of her and effortlessly lifted her to her feet.

"Are you all right?" he asked, his tone anxious, his hands gripping her shoulders tightly.

There was still sand in Roxanne's mouth. She leaned to the side and spat it out. Under the circumstances it was ludicrous to worry about being ladylike, and with a shudder, she hawked up the rest of the sand in her throat.

"There, there, it'll be all right," Kane murmured.

Rage boiled inside Roxanne. She was wet and filthy, and rolling around on the beach fighting with the sailor could have seriously injured her child or, worse, caused her to lose it. She put her hands against Kane's chest and shoved him away, crying out as she did so, "Leave me alone, you bastard!"

In the light of the sailor's lantern, she could see Kane's features harden.

"There's no need for talk like that," he said stiffly, "just as there was no need for that ridiculous display. Now come along, Roxanne, and don't make any more trouble."

"Do I have any choice?" she asked caustically.

"None at all."

From the tone of his voice, she knew she had pushed Kane about as far as he was willing to go. He would not allow her to continue humiliating him in front of these sailors. They had surrounded her now, and any chance of escaping had utterly disappeared.

A man in the uniform of a ship's officer approached the group and gave Roxanne a disdainful look. "This is the colonial woman you want us to take to England?" he asked.

"What do you think?" snapped Kane. He took a deep breath, controlled his anger, and said, "Sorry, Captain. This is indeed the woman. Once you have her on board, I'll expect you to give her the privacy necessary to change out of these wet clothes. And I'll also expect you and your men to treat her with the respect and dignity she deserves."

"Of course. We're not *pirates*, for God's sake. We're sailors of the king, and we'll conduct ourselves as such."

"See that you do." Kane reached inside his coat and took out a piece of paper that had been folded and sealed with wax. "You're also to deliver this message to the usual destination."

The British captain nodded and took the paper, stowing it away inside his coat. It was clear that he and Kane had had dealings before, and Roxanne supposed the man was part of the spy network Kane had set up in the colonies.

"Very good," the captain said with an officious sniff. To his men, he added, "Bring her along."

"A moment, please, Captain," Kane said quickly. "I'd like to say my farewells."

"Certainly," the captain replied with a shrug. "Just don't take too long about it. I want to be well away from here before daybreak."

Along with the sailors, the captain withdrew toward the rowboat, which was beached near the buggy. Kane turned his attention to Roxanne and said quietly, "I wish you wouldn't hate me for this. It's really for your own good."

She lifted her chin defiantly as she said, "Don't worry, Major. I learned to hate you long before tonight."

"You'll feel differently someday, when this foolish rebellion has been crushed."

"No, Major. Nothing could ever change the way I feel about you."

With obvious effort, Kane assumed a lighter tone

and said, "We'll see about that. Now, come along. You've far to go."

"You know what you're condemning me to by turning me over to those sailors, don't you?"

"That's not true," Kane said sharply. "You heard what the captain said. You won't be mistreated during the voyage. You have my word on that." His features took on a grim cast as he added, "Besides, those men know that if any of them so much as lays a hand on you, I'll hunt down and kill whoever is responsible. I'm sending you to a friend and associate of mine who will let me know immediately if anything untoward has happened to you during the trip."

He stepped closer to her then and lifted a hand to cup her chin. She tried to pull away from him, but his hand on her shoulder held her fast. "I really will miss you, Roxanne," he went on. "I'll miss seeing your lovely face and hearing your voice. Even though you've stubbornly resisted me, even though you've never really understood how I feel—I shall miss you desperately."

He kissed her then. She could have jerked away, she supposed, but instead she stood there motionless, her lips as cold as her heart. Truth be told, in her deep melancholy she would have let him have his way with her before now if he had ever forced the issue, but she would have submitted with the same lack of response.

Kane took his lips away from hers and said, "Come along now. The captain is anxious to sail."

He led her to the small boat, and she went without any further struggle. The time for that had passed. Her bag was put on board the boat, and then Kane helped her into the vessel. She sat down on one of the wooden benches, and two sailors took their places on either side of her. The captain exchanged salutes with Kane and then climbed on board himself, and several of the

sailors pushed the boat off the sand and hopped into
the boat. The seamen took up the oars and sculled back
toward the ship.

Roxanne experienced it all through a numb lassi-
tude. So many things had happened to her. . . . Her
whole world had fallen apart in the past few months,
and this was just one more example of how fate had
betrayed her.

Unless the British ship fell afoul of bad weather
and sank in a storm, she would be in England within a
few weeks—thousands of miles from her home and everything that meant anything to her—a prisoner in the
stronghold of her enemies.

She looked back once with a sudden, frantic twisting of her head as she realized that her homeland was
drifting away behind her. She wanted one last look, one
glimpse of the place where she had awakened to the
cause of liberty . . . and love. But the fog had thick-
ened, and the shore could no longer be seen.

Chapter Three

Before the Revolution Boston had been known as the most elegant city in North America, but now, Elliot Markham reflected as the carriage in which he rode rolled through the almost empty streets, Boston was just another name for hell.

The American siege had taken its toll. With few ships getting through from England, supplies had become desperately scarce over the past few months. The city had begun running low on food even before the Battle of Bunker Hill, but the situation had worsened drastically since. Bread and meat were frequently not available at all, and when they were, they were strictly rationed. Buildings had been torn down to provide wood for the breastworks along Boston Neck, the narrow strip of land connecting the Shawmut Peninsula to the mainland. With the advent of cold weather, the need for firewood had prompted the destruction of even more structures. Empty warehouses along the harbor, no longer needed to hold goods that could not get through from England, were razed. Public structures were also torn down, including some of the buildings that had housed Boston's city government. With everything under the strict control of the military, there was no need for municipal authorities or the offices where they had worked.

As the carriage reached the bottom of Beacon Hill and turned onto Beacon Street, its route paralleled Boston Common, and Elliot winced when he looked out the window and saw the trenches that had been dug across the parkland. The ditches lay there like ugly scars on a once-beautiful face. But they would be necessary for defense when the rebels attacked the city, at least in the judgment of General William Howe, who had recently taken over command of the British forces in Boston from General Thomas Gage.

"Sad, isn't it?" said Benjamin Markham. "I remember taking you and your mother to the common for picnics when you were just a lad, Elliot." Benjamin sighed, and his wife, Polly, patted his arm.

Elliot looked across the carriage at his parents, who rode facing forward. His mother and father looked so much older than they should have, he thought, especially Benjamin. Elliot had grown up believing that his father was a fearsome figure, big, bluff, and hearty, a man of strong opinions and an arrogant, headstrong will. Anyone who dared to disagree with Benjamin Markham did so at his own risk.

But all of that had changed. Since the beating he had suffered at the hands of the Liberty Legion, Benjamin's health had deteriorated, and he had never regained his strength. Worse, though, was the loss of spirit that had infected him. He had seen his house vandalized, his business all but ruined, and the city he loved turned into an ugly, armed camp. The developments of the past few months had drained most of Benjamin's vitality.

Polly had suffered accordingly. Never a very strong-willed woman, seeing her husband's self-esteem fade had taken a toll on her, too. At first Elliot had hoped that they would regain their optimism, but as the situation in Boston worsened, that hope had faded.

At the moment, Elliot's parents were dressed in their best finery, Benjamin in a ruffled shirt, silk cravat, and black suit, Polly in a muted orange gown replete with ruffles and lace. They wore cloth coats lined with fur to ward off the chill, and a matching hat perched on Polly's graying brunette curls. Their outfits were at odds with the city that was slowly falling apart around them.

Elliot was well dressed, too, right down to his powdered wig. In the past he had been a veritable dandy and, attired in the latest, most expensive clothing from London, had cut a dashing figure in Boston society. Now he just felt uncomfortable and wished the ordeal facing him on this Sunday afternoon was over.

The sky had been cloudy in the morning, but the overcast had broken up around noon and the sun was out again, but it did little to warm the frigid air.

"I've heard that the order has been given to tear down the Old North Church this week," Benjamin said, shivering a little. "Avery and Sarah almost waited too long to hold their ceremony there. The city must have firewood, though, and as long as those damnable rebels have us besieged, this is no time for sentiment."

"Still, it seems rather a sacrilege to me," Polly said quietly. "A house of God should not be dismantled and burned simply for heat."

"Do you think God would rather have us freeze to death, Mother?" Elliot asked, drawing a disapproving frown from both his parents. "At any rate, they won't be able to burn the bricks—just the steeple and the pews."

"I wish there were some other way," Polly said, and Benjamin grunted in agreement.

Elliot leaned against the padded seat. Most of this carriage would burn if it was torn up, he thought. It might come to that soon enough unless there was a break in the stalemate between the Americans and the British.

It had been rumored, even among the staunchest Tories such as Elliot's father, that the British were considering withdrawing from Boston. The citizens were unsure whether that would be a boon or a disaster, because it was highly likely that the redcoats would burn the city when they left, rather than let the patriots have it. It was also quite possible that the rebels would burn it if the British didn't.

Of course some Tories, like his father, still placed their faith in the British, but Elliot feared they were doomed to be disappointed.

The horses pulling the carriage clip-clopped along the cobblestone streets until they reached the Old North Church, one of the city's most distinctive landmarks. As Elliot looked at the large redbrick building with the impressive white steeple crowning it, he hoped that the order for its destruction would be circumvented. The church had become a symbol of the Revolution, for it was from that very steeple that the sexton had signaled to anxiously watching patriots across the Charles River the previous April that British forces were leaving Boston by sea. They had been bound for the Massachusetts countryside to search out arms and powder cached by the patriot militia. That signal had sent Paul Revere, Billy Dawes, and Dr. Samuel Prescott on a desperate ride through the night to warn the colonists of the approaching redcoats.

The colonists had formed into their militia units and met the British at Lexington and Concord, turning them back and making them flee to Boston.

The echoes of the shots fired that day were still reverberating throughout the colonies.

Elliot's cousin Daniel had stood with the patriots that day, along with Murdoch Buchanan, and Elliot had learned about the battles from them. Daniel had been at Bunker Hill as well, and his brother, Quincy, and Murdoch had been at Ticonderoga. They had fought their battles out in the open, while Elliot's war had been waged in secret, and he had never been sure which was the more difficult way to fight.

He thrust that thought aside as the carriage came to a stop beside more than a dozen other vehicles, all of them painted and decorated with ornate trim. Rich men's carriages, Elliot thought. But the horses hitched to them looked hungry because grain was in short supply, too, and a horse could not eat filigreed brass trim.

The Markhams' driver hopped down from the carriage seat to open the door for his passengers. Elliot got out first and turned to help his mother. Benjamin climbed out last, moving stiffly and awkwardly; his injuries had healed, but they still bothered him on cold, damp days.

Elliot took his mother's arm and led her toward the door of the church, and Benjamin followed behind. Other guests were entering the church, and there was an undercurrent of conversation and laughter in the air. For a moment Elliot frowned. Couldn't these people see how bad things had gotten? How could they blithely ignore what was happening and carry on with a society wedding as if nothing were wrong?

He grimaced. He was being too hard on his fellow guests, and he knew it. Of course they knew the seriousness of the situation. But there was nothing wrong with putting aside the gloom for one afternoon and celebrating the union of a young man and a young woman. After all, optimism was what marriage was all about, wasn't it?

He couldn't help but feel angry and hurt because until six months earlier, he had pictured *himself* as the young man exchanging vows and promising to love and protect the bride. For the bride this afternoon was none other than Sarah Cummings, who, for several years, first implicitly and then officially, had been Elliot's fiancée.

But the groom was Avery Wallingford.

Once the best of friends, Avery and Elliot had become bitter rivals over the past few years, and Elliot knew perfectly well that the only reason Avery wanted him to attend the wedding was to taunt him with the fact that it was he, Avery, marrying Sarah. The smarmy fellow had pounced as soon as the relationship between Elliot and Sarah faltered, and he had wasted no time in getting Sarah to agree to marry him.

And it was all because Elliot had been unable to explain to Sarah's satisfaction why he had been kissing Roxanne Darragh one warm night the previous spring. He couldn't tell her that he and Roxanne were only friends and fellow espionage agents for the patriot cause. That admission would have rendered Elliot useless as an intelligence operative.

So instead he had lied to Sarah and ruined what had been between them. Perhaps they had not had the strongest relationship to begin with . . . perhaps he

hadn't been particularly faithful to her when there were
pretty tavern wenches around . . . perhaps the liaison
had been more business-oriented than romantic in the
beginning, since his father and Sarah's were partners in
the Markham & Cummings shipping line. All of that
might well be true, but it did little to lessen the pain
Elliot felt.

"My, you look grim!" Polly whispered as they went
into the church. "For heaven's sake, Elliot, I know this
must be difficult for you, but please try to smile."

"All right, Mother," Elliot nodded, forcing his lips
into a semblance of a smile.

The church was already crowded. The Markhams
were among the last guests to arrive, but a pew had
been reserved for them close to the front of the sanctuary, and an usher showed them to their seats. The or-
ganist was playing a hymn, and an air of solemnity hung
over the church. Given the season, there were no flowers decorating the altar, and as Elliot settled into the
hard wooden pew and removed his tricorn hat, he
thought that with the exception of the white ribbons
and candles that brightened the church, they might as
well be here for a funeral as a wedding.

The black-robed bishop stood up, opened the
Book of Common Prayer, and led the guests in a digni-
fied, ponderous supplication to the Lord. Then Avery
and his groomsmen filed in from a small room to the
right of the altar. Thank God Avery had not asked him
to serve as best man, Elliot thought. That would have
been carrying things too far, even for a scoundrel like
Avery Wallingford.

Elliot paid little attention as the bridesmaids entered the church, but when everyone turned to watch
the bride make her slow-paced walk up the aisle, he
turned and looked as well. As the music from the pipe

organ swelled, Sarah began her procession on the arm
of her father, Theophilus Cummings.

God, she's beautiful! Elliot thought. The long white
satin wedding gown was magnificent, but no more
lovely than Sarah herself. Her long blond curls were
swept up atop her head and covered with a lacy cowl
that also included the gauzy veil over her face. Two
strands of hair had been allowed to escape the elaborate arrangement and curl gently in front of her ears.
The gown was high-necked, but the satin fabric clung to
her body and revealed the slender, graceful lines of her
figure. Elliot had never seen her look more appealing.

He was lost from the moment he saw her, and the
rest of the ceremony passed in a blur for him. He stood
when he was supposed to stand, recited prayers along
with the rest of the guests when he was supposed to
recite. Then, almost before Elliot knew it, the bishop
pronounced Avery and Sarah man and wife, and Avery
turned to Sarah, lifted the veil, and lowered his lips to
hers in the traditional eager kiss.

Elliot wanted to scream, wanted to lunge up to the
altar and rip Avery away from her, but it was too late.
They were married. Sarah was Avery's wife, and would
be forevermore.

Elliot closed his eyes and shuddered.

When he opened them again at the insistent prod-
ding of his mother's elbow in his side, he saw that Avery
and Sarah were coming up the aisle arm in arm. There
was a broad smile on Avery's face that looked more like
a smirk to Elliot, and for a moment the two young
men's eyes met. If lightning had struck at that very moment, there could not have been more angry heat in the
air. Then Avery and Sarah walked past, and the moment was over. Elliot took a deep breath and tried to
calm himself.

"Come along," Benjamin said. "There's still the reception to attend."

Elliot would have gladly skipped the reception at Theophilus Cummings's house, but his parents had to go, of course, and he had promised them that he would cooperate. *Put on a cheerful face,* he instructed himself. The ordeal would be over sooner or later.

In better weather, the reception would have been held in the large garden behind the Cummings mansion. Today, though, since it was cold despite the sunshine, the party was indoors, in the huge ballroom.

As Elliot stood by himself at one side of the room, he looked around and wondered idly just how much firewood could be obtained from the mansion if *it* were torn down.

He sipped from the glass of brandy in his hand. Music from a string quartet filled the room as the musicians played the latest minuets from Vienna and Paris. The guests were dancing and drinking, talking and laughing—having a splendid time, in fact. Sarah had shared the first dance with her new husband; then she had entertained a succession of partners, beginning with her father. As she swept past Elliot in the arms of yet another man, he heard her laughing gaily.

They could dance and drink all they wanted to, Elliot thought glumly, but that wouldn't change the fact that the world they had known and loved was on the verge of crashing down upon their heads.

He chuckled. It was unlike him to allow his depression to get such a solid hold on him, and at the moment, he did not like himself very much. He had to shake this feeling, or he would drive himself crazy. And he tried to convince himself that he had more important things to worry about than whom Sarah Cummings had married.

Sarah Cummings Wallingford, he reminded himself. Very rich Mrs. Avery Wallingford.

Elliot tossed down the rest of his brandy. Sarah had gotten what she wanted. Now she would have to live with it.

"Elliot?"

The voice was like a hot poker jabbed into his heart. He had not seen her coming up beside him and had assumed she was still whirling merrily around the floor, as she had been only moments earlier. But when he turned toward her, Sarah put a hand on his arm, and he felt the warmth of her fingers through his clothes, and it made him shiver.

He found his tongue at last and said, "I suppose you're waiting for me to congratulate you."

"Not really." She smiled faintly. "I was wondering if you were going to dance with me."

"I'm not sure that would be a good idea."

"I'd rather dance with you than with most of these old men."

"What about your husband?" Elliot asked, placing such emphasis on the last word that Sarah blushed.

"Avery is holding court on the other side of the room," she replied in a quiet voice. "Please, Elliot. I don't think I could stand it if I thought you hated me."

That gave him pause, and he said quickly, "I don't hate you, Sarah. I never have."

"Then prove it. Dance with me."

He turned and placed his empty brandy glass on a nearby sideboard. "All right," he said, taking her into his arms as the musicians began playing another tune.

As they swirled over the glossy parquet floor, Elliot got his first good look at her on her wedding day. She was beautiful, there was no doubt about that, but now, close up, he could see something lurking in her eyes, something that put the lie to the gaiety she had been displaying.

"What's wrong?" Elliot asked, concern for her welling up inside him despite the circumstances.

"Wrong? What could be wrong? This is my wedding day—the happiest day of a girl's life, isn't it?"

He heard the desperate irony underlying the words. "Sarah, if there's anything I can do . . ."

She stopped dancing, and he had no choice but to stop as well. Still holding his hand, she said, "Come with me."

"Wait a minute. I can't—"

She was already tugging him toward a door. "You said you'd do anything you could to help me," she pleaded. "I have to talk to you, Elliot."

"But the guests—"

"Damn the guests!" she hissed, keeping her voice pitched so low that only he could hear it over the music. "Besides, no one is paying attention."

Elliot glanced quickly around the room and saw that she was right. The young men who were not dancing had surrounded Avery on the far side of the ballroom, where they were drinking and laughing heartily at whatever the groom had to say. The older men had gathered around Theophilus Cummings and Benjamin Markham, and Elliot knew from the solemn looks on their faces that they were discussing either business or the war or both. Most of the young women were dancing, and the older women were clustered in a group of their own, talking about whatever it was women talked about at a wedding reception; Elliot had no idea what that might be. But the important thing was that no one seemed to notice as Sarah opened the door and pulled him into the small room beyond.

"I thought the bride was supposed to be the center of attention at a wedding," he said as she closed the door behind them, muting the sound of the music.

"So did I," Sarah said bitterly. "I thought at least Avery would pay attention to me. But I suppose now that the ceremony is over, he thinks he has what he wants."

"Doesn't he?" Elliot challenged. "You were quick enough to agree when he asked you to marry him."

Sarah's eyes flared angrily. "Is that what he told you? It was my father who agreed right away. I struggled with the decision for a long time, Elliot. I was hoping—"

She stopped abruptly, and after waiting for a moment, Elliot asked, "Hoping for what?"

"Hoping that you'd come back to me, damn you!" Sarah's hands went to her face, covering her eyes as she started to sob.

Elliot stood there thunderstruck. When he trusted himself to speak again, he said, "You told me you never wanted to see me again, that you wanted nothing more to do with me. You gave me back my ring."

"Of course I did." Sarah looked up at him with moist, red-rimmed eyes. "What else could I do when I caught you kissing that . . . that redheaded doxy! But you could have told me that she meant nothing to you, that it was all a horrible mistake. You could have forced me to believe you and forgive you and take back your ring!"

"I had no idea," Elliot said, his voice hushed. "I thought I was doing the right thing. I thought I was doing what you wanted."

"Well, you were a . . . a fool! I waited and waited

for you, and you never came. And then Avery was so nice to me and tried so hard to comfort me. Oh, God, Elliot, I made a dreadful mistake by turning to him!"

He could have told her that from the first, he thought, but wisely kept the comment to himself. Instead he stepped closer to her. "I'm sorry, Sarah. If I had known, things might have been different, but it's too late now."

"No, it's not!" she exclaimed. "I can go out there and tell everyone the marriage was a mistake!"

This time it was Elliot who cut in. "You can't do that, and you know it. You'd humiliate your parents, scandalize all your friends, and embarrass yourself. I suppose you'd even hurt Avery." That last was hard for him to say, but he managed. "It's just too late, Sarah. I'm sorry, but there's nothing I can do to help you."

"You mean it, don't you?" she whispered as she looked up at him, tears sliding down her cheeks.

Elliot nodded grimly.

Where had this streak of morality come from, he wondered? In the past, he had never worried much about right and wrong, only about what his needs and desires of the moment were. Had the war changed him that much? He had never balked at a dalliance with a married woman before, not if she was pretty and appealing enough, and Sarah certainly fit that description. Nor did he have the least bit of respect for her husband.

Still, not wanting Sarah to see what her words had done to him, he kept his face an expressionless mask. He was shaken to the core of his being by the knowledge that he might have been able to salvage his relationship with her, had he only tried harder.

"Oh, Elliot . . ." she moaned.

He knew he was making a huge mistake, but he reached out and put his hands on her shoulders, so soft

and warm under the wedding gown. He meant to give
her only a brief hug to comfort her; then he would slip
out of the room and try to forget what had happened.
But as soon as he touched her, he felt himself drawing
her toward him, and she came willingly.

Before their lips had touched, the door of the
room slammed open, and Avery Wallingford stepped
through, his narrow face flushed brick-red with anger.
"My God!" he exclaimed. "Married less than an hour
and already you're trying to steal my wife from me!"

Elliot took a quick step backward. "Wait just a
minute," he said. "You've got this all wrong, Avery."

Avery stalked toward them, and Sarah flinched
away from him. His voice shaking with rage, he said,
"When someone told me the two of you had slipped in
here, I didn't believe it at first. But then I thought I had
better check, since I remember how it used to be between you. But I never expected to see what I saw!"

"You didn't see anything, damn it!" Elliot responded. "Nothing happened."

"I saw you about to kiss my wife!"

"No, Avery," Sarah put in. "It wasn't like that, I
promise you."

"Be quiet," Avery said, his voice cold with menace.
"I'll deal with you later. Right now, there's the matter
of this blackguard here." Fists clenched, he stepped
toward Elliot.

Elliot held his hands up, palms out. "Wait, Avery,"
he urged. "Don't do anything foolish."

"Foolish?" echoed Avery. "I'll show you foolish,
you bastard!"

He swung a wild blow at Elliot's head, and Sarah
screamed.

Elliot darted aside, letting the punch go past him

harmlessly. "Stop this, Avery!" he shouted. "I don't want to hurt you!"

Avery flailed at him again, and Elliot threw his arm up and blocked the punch. Avery was wide open, and Elliot could have finished him off with little trouble. A short, sharp left hook to the belly and then a right cross would have dropped Avery senseless to the floor. But as much as Elliot despised the man, he truly didn't want to harm him.

"Fight back, you son of a bitch!" Avery yelled, windmilling more punches that Elliot successfully blocked or backed away from. Avery had never been known as a fighter; in fact, Elliot had always considered him a coward.

The realization that Avery had to care deeply about Sarah to be doing this burst on Elliot with stunning force. It occurred to him that Avery might actually love her.

That thought distracted Elliot enough to allow one of Avery's blows to crack into his jaw, and as the punch knocked him backward, he heard Sarah scream again. Elliot's feet tangled in a rug, and he felt himself falling.

Avery would have come after him and continued the fight, but by now Sarah's screams and Avery's shouts had attracted the attention of everyone else at the wedding reception. Several men crowded into the room, among them Benjamin Markham and Theophilus Cummings.

Cummings plucked at his new son-in-law's arm and cried, "Avery! What is it, Avery? What's going on here?"

One of the guests grabbed Avery and held him back as he tried to get at Elliot again. "Let me go!" Avery howled. "I'll kill him, I swear I will!"

"Stop it!" Benjamin Markham boomed, some of

the old power restored to his voice. "Settle down, lad! I
don't know what's going on here, but I think it's time
we found out."

Benjamin looked past Avery at Elliot, who was sitting on the floor with a small trickle of blood oozing
from his lower lip. He had bitten it when Avery hit him,
he realized. That was the extent of the damage, however, and as he scrambled to his feet, he saw several
women, including Sarah's small, white-haired mother,
leading the sobbing bride from the room.

Avery leveled a taut, shaking finger at Elliot and
accused, "He tried to steal my wife!"

"That's insane," Elliot said, taking a linen hand-
kerchief from his pocket and dabbing at the blood on
his mouth. "I was merely talking to Sarah when Avery
burst in here and went mad."

"What *were* you doing in here with my daughter?"
Theophilus Cummings demanded, sounding as angry as
Avery. Cummings had never forgiven Elliot after Sarah
had broken their engagement.

"I was simply giving her my best wishes," Elliot
lied. "Sarah and I are old friends, after all."

"You swear that's all it was, son?" Benjamin asked.

"Of course."

"He's lying," Avery snapped. "And I won't stand
for it." He looked at the man holding him. "Let go of
me, blast it. I'm not going to fight anymore."

The man glanced at Benjamin and Cummings,
both of whom nodded slightly. He released Avery and
stepped back. The groom squared his shoulders and,
with a visible effort, calmed his trembling.

"I don't have a glove at the moment, so this will
have to do," Avery declared as he stepped up to Elliot
and slapped him across the face.

Elliot jerked back, more surprised than hurt.

"What the hell was that for?" he asked, although he was afraid he already knew the answer.

"I'm challenging you to a duel. We shall settle this on the field of honor."

"It's already settled—" Elliot began.

"No, it's not. I demand satisfaction. My honor demands it, and the honor of my wife demands it. What do you say, Markham?"

Elliot looked around the room, saw the dismayed look on his father's face, the anger on Cummings's sallow features, the uncertainty on the faces of men who had been his friends until now.

"This is crazy," Elliot muttered. "It's ridiculous for two men to be fighting a duel over a woman when the whole city is about to collapse into anarchy and chaos."

"Is that your way of saying that you're too cowardly to answer my challenge?"

Elliot's jaw clenched tightly. "Is there nothing else that will satisfy you?"

"Nothing," Avery snapped.

"Very well, then. We'll meet on Boston Common—and settle this once and for all."

Chapter Four

In a peaceful clearing a few miles from a settlement called Wheeling in the Ohio River valley, Quincy Reed lifted the big ax over his head and brought it down with a sweeping motion. The blade bit deep into the end of the log he was shaping, and another large chunk of wood peeled off. Both ends of the fallen tree had to be squared off before the long, heavy length of timber would be suitable for use in the walls of the nearby cabin. Construction had barely gotten under way, but already Quincy could tell that it was going to be a lengthy, difficult task.

The tall, wiry seventeen-year-old had help, however. Gresham Howard was cutting down a tree on the other side of the clearing. The burly, middle-aged former wagonyard owner from Saratoga, New York,

42

wielded an ax with surprising skill for someone who had
spent most of his life as a businessman.

Despite the coolness of the early winter day, both
Quincy and Howard had taken off their jackets, and
their shirts were damp with sweat. Quincy rested the
head of his ax against the log and leaned on the handle
for a moment, taking the opportunity to catch his
breath and wipe the perspiration off his forehead. He
and Howard had been working since early morning
without a break, but it was important to drive themselves hard. A few miles upriver, in Wheeling, they had
been told that the Indians in the area, primarily Shawnee, Wyandot, and Delaware, sometimes raided the settlers' farms. A sturdy cabin that could be well defended
was a necessity of life on the frontier.

Of course, Murdoch Buchanan had warned them
about the same thing. Murdoch, Daniel and Quincy
Reed's great friend and protector as well as Roxanne
Darragh's cousin, had spent several years wandering up
and down the great valley of the Ohio River. The big,
brawny, redheaded Scotsman had hunted and trapped
the abundant game; sometimes he had fought the Indians, and sometimes he had lived with them. Murdoch
had told his traveling companions that this was a wonderful, fertile land, and from the looks of it, he had
been right. But he had also been truthful about the dangers involved in settling in the wilderness.

Quincy doubted that the frontier was any more
dangerous at the moment than the colonies back east.
He already bore quite a few scars picked up in
skirmishes with the British and with the Mohawk Indians in New York.

Two years earlier, Quincy had dressed up as an Indian and joined the group of patriots who had dumped
tons of British tea into Boston Harbor to protest Parlia-

ment's high-handed, unfair taxation practices. The Boston Tea Party, folks called it when they talked about that night. Quincy was proud to have been a part of it, just as he was proud he had been one of the soldiers who had captured Fort Ticonderoga for the patriots. Though he was still passionately devoted to the cause of liberty, a great deal had happened since that time, and Quincy was glad he had left the war behind.

He was married and had a wife to look after now, and as if she knew he was thinking about her, Mariel Jarrott Reed appeared at the back of one of the two covered wagons parked nearby and lithely stepped down to the ground. She had just turned sixteen and glowed with the beauty of young womanhood. Her long flaxen hair was caught up in a thick braid that hung down her back, and she wore a sky-blue dress that matched her eyes and a long woolen wrap to keep out the cold. She opened one of the water barrels attached to the side of the wagon and used a wooden dipper to scoop up some water.

"I thought you looked thirsty," she said, offering the water to Quincy.

"I am," he said, returning her smile. He took the dipper and drank some of the cool water, then splashed the rest over his head, enjoying the feel of it as it dripped down his face.

"Quincy!" Mariel protested. "You will give yourself a chill. It is no longer summer, you know."

"Maybe not, and I suppose it's already pretty cold back east, but that sun is very warm today. Especially when a body's working like this." He inclined his head toward the stack of logs that had already been cut for the cabin.

"You have been working hard," Mariel agreed. "Perhaps you should stop for a while."

"Nope. Got too much to do. We've got to get a cabin up for us and Dietrich, and another one for Cordelia and Mr. Howard. Besides, Murdoch'll be back soon with some game, and we'll stop to eat then."

Out of the corner of his eye, Quincy spotted a small boy with blond hair running toward the creek which meandered through the woods about a hundred yards away. "There goes Dietrich again," he warned Mariel.

"Oh, no. Dietrich, come back here!" Mariel called. When the child ignored her, she said something under her breath in German and started after him.

Quincy grinned. Mariel's little brother was well behaved most of the time, but ever since they had reached this spot and decided to settle here, he had been a handful of trouble, constantly getting into mischief and straying away from the camp. Quincy could understand Dietrich's high spirits. This was pretty country, and the boy was glad to be released from the confines of the wagons in which they had traveled for so long.

Mariel and Dietrich were the only two left of a family of German farmers who had immigrated to New York and settled in the Mohawk Valley. Their parents as well as their other brothers and sisters had been wiped out in an Indian raid, and Mariel and Dietrich had come close to losing their lives, too. The timely arrival of Quincy and Murdoch had been all that prevented further tragedy. Not having any reason to stay in New York, they had decided to head west with Quincy, Murdoch, and their two traveling companions, Gresham Howard and his daughter Cordelia Faulkner, a young, attractive widow. During the journey, romance had bloomed between Quincy and Mariel, and they had gotten married several weeks earlier at a settlement on the Allegheny River, near Pittsburgh. Since then, the travelers had floated by raft down the Allegheny to where it joined the Monongahela to form the mighty Ohio. The big river had carried them to Wheeling, where they had driven their wagons off the rafts and started overland, following the Ohio until they found what they were looking for.

Murdoch had told them all along that they would know the place when they saw it, and he had been right. They'd found a small creek and followed it south for a mile or so from the Ohio, and then a peaceful valley, dotted with stretches of forest and large clearings that would make fine fields, had opened up before them. Quincy had taken one look and known that this was as far as they were going.

Mariel agreed with him, as did Howard and Cordelia. They were close enough to Wheeling so that they could make occasional trips into the settlement but isolated enough not to feel crowded. Of course, there was the danger from Indians, but there was no place in the world that was totally safe, Quincy told himself. And he felt more at home here than he had anywhere else since leaving his parents' plantation in Virginia, on the other side of the Blue Ridge Mountains.

Holding tightly to her brother's hand and half dragging him, Mariel returned from the creek. Dietrich would settle down sooner or later, Quincy thought with a grin as he went back to work with his ax. He just hoped the boy would get over his excitement before he ran Mariel ragged.

Ten minutes later the sound of whistling floated out of the woods on the far side of the clearing, and Quincy knew from the brisk Scottish tune that Murdoch was back. The big man, clad in fringed buckskins and a coonskin cap mashed down on his rumpled thatch of red hair, strolled out of the forest with his long-barreled flintlock rifle canted over one shoulder and the carcass of a turkey draped over the other.

Quincy and Howard stopped their work and went to meet him.

"Is that all you've got to show for over an hour of hunting?" Quincy gibed.

"No' really," replied Murdoch with a wide grin. "I got an hour o' peace and quiet in th' woods to lift me spirits and soothe me soul. Besides, there be enough meat on this bird t' last us a while." His expression became more solemn, and he added, "Where be your guns?"

With a grimace, Quincy looked over his shoulder. He'd left his rifle leaning against a log in the clearing where he had been working. Howard's rifle was several long yards away as well.

"A Shawnee could put three or four arrows in both o' ye 'fore ye could reach the weapons," Murdoch said. "I ken it seems peaceful 'round here, but dinna let tha' fool ye. Best keep yer gun where ye kin reach it all th' time."

"You're right, of course, Murdoch," Howard said, hurrying to pick up his rifle. "We won't let it happen again, will we, Quincy?"

"No, sir. Although it's hard to look at this beautiful countryside and think that anything dangerous could lurk in it."

"Tha' be when ye want t' be yer most alert, lad, when ye think there's nothin' t' worry about."

"I'll remember."

Murdoch swung the turkey off his shoulder and thrust it at Quincy, who staggered a little under the bird's weight when he caught it.

"Ye'd best get t' plucking this big fella," Murdoch said, his familiar grin returning.

"Why should I have to do that?" asked Quincy.

"I shot him, didn't I? And wi' one o' th' balls and powder provided by Mr. Howard here. 'Tis only fair tha' ye take care o' th' cleaning and cooking of him."

"All right," Quincy grumbled. He carried the turkey toward the wagon he shared with Mariel and Dietrich, confident that his wife would help him with his chore.

"But Mariel and I are going down to the creek to do the washing," Cordelia explained as she and Mariel emerged from the wagons carrying wooden baskets filled with dirty clothes. Each pile of laundry also had a flintlock pistol balanced on top of it.

Mariel added, "We won't be gone long. You'll keep an eye on Dietrich for me, won't you, Quincy?"

Gesturing at the turkey, Quincy frowned and asked, "What about this bird?"

"I'm certain you can handle it," Mariel told him, smiling sweetly.

"And why do you have to wash right now, of all times?"

"It's time we started living like civilized human beings again," Cordelia said tartly. "That means not letting our clothes go for a month or two between washings. Don't pout, Quincy. You can pluck a few turkey feathers."

"I suppose so," he sighed. He sat down on an empty barrel that had been upended to form a makeshift seat and began pulling the feathers from the carcass of the large bird.

Mariel and Cordelia were talking and laughing as they started toward the creek. Quincy cast a glance after them and grinned. The young women were happier here than anywhere else they had stopped on the long journey.

Mariel and Cordelia disappeared into the trees along the stream. Quincy settled down to pluck turkey feathers, while Gresham Howard resumed swinging his ax, and Dietrich sat in the shade under one of the wagons and happily used a stick to draw pictures in the dirt. Quincy wasn't sure where Murdoch had gone off to, but the big frontiersman was bound to be somewhere nearby.

After a couple of minutes, Murdoch strolled up, wiping the back of one hand across his mouth. Quincy knew he had a jug of whiskey stashed in a hollow stump on the edge of the woods, and he figured Murdoch had just paid a visit to that cache.

The Scotsman looked around, then asked, "Where be th' womenfolk?"

"They've gone down to the creek to wash clothes," Quincy replied. "It was either that or help me with this overgrown chicken."

"Ye let them go by themselves?"

"They were armed," Quincy told him. "They each had a pistol. I saw the guns on top of the clothes."

"Still, I tell ye 'tis no' safe enough around here for them t' be doing such a thing." Murdoch cradled his flintlock in the crook of his left arm. "I'd better wander down there and keep th' ladies company until they get through with what they be doing."

"All ri—" Quincy began.

But he was interrupted by a shot and a scream from the direction of the creek.

Mariel and Cordelia had found large flat rocks on the edge of the stream on which they could spread the shirts, pants, and dresses to dry. Both young women were watchful, but Cordelia honestly did not think they would encounter trouble this close to the clearing where the men were working.

They set their pistols on one of the rocks, near enough to be handy but not so close to the water that they were likely to be splashed. Then they waded into the edge of the stream, took the clothes from the baskets, and, with homemade yellow soap, scrubbed the garments against the rocks.

Cordelia was laughing at a comment Mariel had made about Quincy when a flicker of movement on the far side of the creek caught her eye. The trees were thicker there, and brush grew down to the edge of the stream, but she was sure she had seen something moving.

Suddenly, with a flash of buckskins and coppery-red skin, three Indians burst out of the undergrowth and leapt into the shallow creek. Water splashed around their feet, and silvery droplets flashed brightly in the midday sunshine as they charged toward the startled women. Two of the warriors carried tomahawks, while the third brandished a long, heavy knife.

Mariel screamed and tried to step back, but she tripped on one of the rocks in the streambed and sat down hard in the water. Cordelia felt terror welling up inside her, too, but she was able to control it and lunge toward the stone where they had placed their pistols. Her fingers closed around the smooth wooden grip of one of the weapons, but as she jerked it up, the barrel accidentally hit the other gun and it slid off the far side of the rock, out of easy reach. Cordelia didn't waste time going after the second pistol; she whirled around, brought up the gun she held, and cocked it with both thumbs.

The powder in the pan flashed when she pressed the trigger, and the charge in the barrel exploded with a heavy boom. The recoil traveled up her arms and stunned her, but she saw one of the Indians jerk sideways, stumble, and then catch himself. The pistol ball had taken him in the left arm, tearing away a huge chunk of muscle. Blood spurted from torn arteries as the wounded man gasped in pain and tried to stay on his feet.

"Run, Mariel!" Cordelia shrieked. The pistol shot had made the warriors hesitate, and this fleeting moment might be the only chance the two women would have to escape.

Mariel scrambled to her feet and lunged out of the creek and up the shallow bank. Holding on to the empty gun, Cordelia ran right behind her.

They dashed through the woods, and although Cordelia was afraid to look back, she did so anyway and saw to her horror that the Indians were only ten or fifteen yards behind them—almost close enough to hurl their tomahawks.

A bloodcurdling whoop sounded at their heels, and Cordelia looked frantically toward the clearing where the wagons were parked. Although she saw Quincy, Murdoch, and her father running toward them, she knew they would arrive too late.

In the next moment Cordelia heard an angry roar and the sudden pound of hoofbeats somewhere to her left. She dared to glance in that direction and saw a man on horseback thundering toward them at an angle, moving to intercept the three Indians. Her first thought was that it must take a sturdy mount indeed to support such a huge man. She caught a glimpse of his bushy black beard and a massive pistol with a barrel half as long as those of ordinary muskets. Without slowing his horse's headlong gallop, the rider held the pistol out at arm's length and touched off its charge.

It sounded like a cannon, and Cordelia looked back in time to see one of the Indians drop as though he had run headlong into a stone wall.

The horseman was almost on top of the warriors now. He left his saddle in a dive that showed incredible grace and agility for a man of his size and crashed into one of the Indians. The burly man rolled over, jumped to his feet, and flung up his left hand to stop the downward sweep of the tomahawk held by the third warrior. The Indian's arm stopped short, his wrist caught by the ironlike vise of the bearded man's fingers.

Cordelia stopped running and turned to watch as the stranger's fingers closed ever tighter on the Indian's wrist. She heard a crunching and grinding sound and knew that bones were shattering under that grip. Then the stranger slammed his fist with such force into the side of the Indian's head that he dropped to the ground and did not move again.

The surviving member of the raiding party, the Indian wounded earlier by Cordelia, turned and ran into the forest.

"Go on, run, damn you!" the bearded stranger called in a stentorian voice. "We'll meet again another day, I reckon."

At the sound of running footsteps, Cordelia looked around. Murdoch and her father hurried up, and Howard caught her shoulders. "Are you all right, Cordelia?" he asked anxiously.

"I'm not hurt," she said. "Just frightened. The Indians never got a chance to hurt us."

Looking past her father, she saw Mariel and Quincy wrapped in a tight embrace. Quincy was stroking his wife's hair, and Cordelia could see he was whispering soothing words to her, assuring her that she was safe now and everything would be all right.

The bearded stranger roughly prodded the Indian at his feet with a booted toe. Even at this distance, Cordelia could see the sunken place in the Indian's misshapen skull. Could someone have really done such a thing with a bare fist? she wondered.

Checking on the other Indian took only a glance. He had a fist-sized hole blown in his chest by the ball from the stranger's huge pistol.

He retrieved the gun from where he had dropped it when he flung himself off his horse, then strode over to the others. "Everybody all right?" he asked in his booming voice.

"Thanks to you, sir, it appears we are," replied Gresham Howard. "You saved the lives of my daughter and my friend's wife."

The man looked at Cordelia, then at Mariel, and then back at Cordelia. He grinned, even white teeth appearing suddenly in the middle of the forest of whiskers. "Always glad to help out a pretty woman," he said.

Unaccountably Cordelia felt herself blushing under his gaze. The sensation made her a little angry with herself. She had more experience with men than it was proper for a lady to admit, and she certainly had no business blushing just because some backwoods Goliath smiled at her.

"I'm Gresham Howard," the former businessman said as he extended his hand.

The stranger took it, a paw as massive as the rest of him swallowing Howard's fingers. "Name's Ulysses Gilworth. Got me a blacksmith shop in Wheeling. When I heard that some new folks had passed through and were planning to settle hereabouts, I thought I'd ride out and say howdy. Right glad I did, too."

"Aye," said Murdoch, shaking hands in turn with

Ulysses Gilworth. "'Tis glad we are, too. I'm called Murdoch Buchanan."

"Buchanan the woodsman and long hunter?" Ulysses asked.

"That'd be me," Murdoch admitted. "Heard o' me, have ye?"

"Just about everybody on the frontier has."

For a moment, the two big men sized each other up. They were of the same height, and their shoulders spanned an equal breadth. But where Murdoch had the corded muscles, lean hips, and long legs of a man who could run all day if he had to, Ulysses was just plain big all over. His legs were like tree trunks, and the muscles of his shoulders and back strained against the homespun fabric of his shirt.

"I'm Quincy Reed," Quincy said, stepping up and breaking the momentary silence. "And this is my wife Mariel. I can't thank you enough for what you've done today, Mr. Gilworth. If anything happened to Mariel—"

"Keep her a mite closer to home and she'll be a hell of a lot safer, youngster," Ulysses told him sharply. Then, to take some of the sting out of the words, he held out his hand and went on, "I'm right pleased to meet you, Quincy, and you, too, ma'am. I don't know what you ladies was doin' down yonder by the crick, but if'n I was you, I wouldn't go down there no more without the menfolk around."

Once again Cordelia felt a prickle of irritation. "We're used to taking care of ourselves," she said.

"Reckon you must be, but this here is tricky country. It looks mighty peaceful." Ulysses paused, then added heavily, "It ain't."

"Tha' be what I been telling them," Murdoch said. "Say, why don't ye come back to th' wagons with us and have some tea? Or stay t' dinner. We're having roast turkey—tha' is, if Quincy here ever gets around t' finishing his plucking."

"I'll do that," Ulysses said with a laugh. He turned to Cordelia. "Are you comin', ma'am?"

"We left our washing down by the creek," she replied. "I'll have to get it."

"I'll go with you," Quincy said quickly, "just to make sure nothing else happens."

"Nay, ye've got a turkey t' pluck," Murdoch reminded him.

"I'll go," Gresham Howard said. He shouldered his musket. "Come along, Cordelia."

"All right," she said. As she and her father headed toward the stream, she looked back over her shoulder. Murdoch and Ulysses were chuckling about something as they walked toward the wagons. She had never seen a pair of men that big and that impressive—especially Ulysses Gilworth. She blinked in surprise as that thought occurred to her. There was nothing special about the blacksmith, she told herself, except that he was so massive . . . and that he was a ferocious fighter. Other than that, he was just a big, probably uneducated, rather ugly man with a facility for annoying her, and she ought to be able to put him out of her mind with ease.

But as she gathered the clothes and quickly finished washing them under the watchful eye of her father, she found herself still thinking about Ulysses Gilworth. She wrung out the wet clothes and tossed them back into the baskets, instead of leaving them on the rocks as she and Mariel had originally intended. Then she carried one of the baskets, her father carried the other, and they returned to the wagons. A shudder went through her when they passed the sprawled bodies of the dead Indians.

"Aren't we going to bury them?" she asked in a low voice.

"We'll have to," Howard replied. "We'll get to work on the graves after we eat. That'll delay us from working on the cabins, I suppose, but there's nothing else we can do. Even a heathen deserves a burial of some sort." Howard brightened a little. "Perhaps we can get Mr. Gilworth to lend us a hand with the cabins. I imagine a man such as he can swing an ax quite well, don't you think?"

"I wouldn't know," Cordelia said curtly.

Her father frowned at her. "What's got your back up, girl?"

"Nothing. I'm fine. It's just not every day I almost get killed by Indians."

"Indeed that's true, thank God," grunted Howard.

But was she really all right? Cordelia asked herself. She looked at the big, bearded newcomer and knew that, for the moment at least, she felt secure.

When Ulysses Gilworth noticed the beginnings of the log cabins that Quincy and Gresham Howard were building, he walked around the rudimentary structures and nodded slowly. "Got 'em laid out just fine," he said in approval. "But it's goin' to take a while to finish 'em, working on both of 'em at the same time like that. Might be better off to finish one first, then build the other one."

"We'd already been thinking about that," Quincy said. He had plucked the turkey Murdoch had caught, and Murdoch had finally taken enough pity on him to take over the cooking. The big Scotsman was roasting the turkey on a spit over the leaping flames of a fire.

"Maybe I could lend a hand," Ulysses mused. "I

may be a blacksmith, but I'm a pretty fair carpenter, too."

Cordelia glanced at the man's massive shoulders and thought he looked as though he could swing an ax or a hammer all day without tiring.

"We could certainly use some help, Mr. Gilworth." She poured a cup of tea and handed it to him. "We're not exactly inexperienced woodsmen, but—"

"Not with Murdoch Buchanan around, you ain't," Ulysses broke in with a grin. "I reckon he knows this part of the country as well or better'n anybody else."

"And he did warn us about wandering off," Cordelia said. "I suppose Mariel and I were just careless."

"Like I said, this land'll fool you if you give it half a chance." He sipped the tea, then said, "Mighty good, ma'am."

Cordelia felt a surge of pleasure at the compliment. She had never been overly domestic, but it made her feel good to know that Ulysses thought she brewed a good pot of tea.

"I was just thinkin'," Ulysses went on slowly. "I got somethin' I need to do right now, but I'll drop back by here in a little while, if that's all right with you folks."

"But you said you were going to stay and eat with us," Cordelia exclaimed, hoping the others could not hear the disappointment in her voice.

Ulysses grinned again. "It'll take a while to cook that old bird. Just keep some warm for me. I'll be back in time to eat a bit."

With that he finished his tea in one gulp, handed the empty cup to Cordelia, and swung up into the saddle of his big black horse. She fought off the urge to follow him, telling herself sternly that she shouldn't be chasing after a man as though she was some sort of foolish young girl. She stood quietly and watched him ride away toward the river.

"We need to rig a line and hang those wet clothes up to dry, Cordelia," Mariel said.

"You're right," she responded, smiling. "Let's do that." She was glad to have a chore to take her mind off the Indian attack and the attractive stranger.

A few hours later, when the turkey was ready, they gathered around the campfire to eat, but Cordelia found herself glancing often toward the spot where Ulysses had disappeared down the path into the trees. He had said he would be back in time to eat, but there was no sign of him.

When they were finished eating and the fire had burned itself into embers, Murdoch lowered the spit on which the bird had been cooked. That brought the turkey close enough to the coals so that it would stay warm for a time.

Cordelia felt herself growing angry. Ulysses had ridden in, saved their lives, and then ridden out again. If that was the way he wanted it, fine. She was grateful to him for what he had done, of course, but if he did not want to be sociable, that was his business.

The clothes, stiffened by the cold, were dry now, the sun and the wind having done their work, so she and Mariel took them off the line and sat down to mend any rips and tears they could find.

Quincy and Gresham Howard returned to trimming logs with their axes, and Murdoch went to work felling a tree. The big Scotsman was more at home wandering through the woods than clearing them away, but he could wield an ax with efficiency when he needed to.

Half an hour or so had gone by when the settlers heard loud noises in the woods, and the men grabbed their guns. But Quincy suddenly said, "Well, would you look at that?"

"Who in the world—?" asked Howard.

Cordelia looked up sharply from her mending and recognized the burly, bearded figure on the big horse leading the procession toward the building site. Behind Ulysses Gilworth were several wagons and half a dozen men on horseback. The wagons carried men, women, and children—whole families of settlers.

Murdoch lowered his gun, a wide grin on his craggy face. "Looks like there's going t' be a roof raising," he said.

"You mean all those people are going to help us?" asked Quincy.

"Aye. In these parts, when a fellow needs something, 'tis common for everybody t' pitch in an' help him out."

Howard wiped sweat off his brow. "Well, we can certainly use the help," he declared. "I never realized how much work went into building a simple cabin."

"Ye'll be surprised how fast th' buildings go up," Murdoch told him. He lifted a big hand over his head and waved a greeting to Ulysses and his companions.

A few minutes later, Ulysses reined in and grinned at them. "Said I'd be back in a little while to lend a hand," he said. "These good folks I rounded up want to help, too."

Everyone dismounted from their horses and climbed down from the wagons. A couple of little boys traded stares with Dietrich for a long moment, then began playing with him. Clearly the sizing up had gone well. At the same time, Murdoch, Quincy, and Howard shook hands with the men, and Cordelia and Mariel exchanged greetings with the women. There was a warm feeling in the air as the community—loose-knit and far-flung, but still a community—welcomed the newcomers into their midst.

Then the work got under way. The visitors had brought axes and saws as well as hammers and adzes, and two of the wagons held lumber and logs that were already prepared for building. The clearing rang with the sound of construction, accompanied by laughter and shouted conversations. As they worked the men gnawed on slices of turkey and on the corn cakes and pies their womenfolk had brought along.

Cordelia was busy making more tea to wash the food down when a shadow suddenly loomed over her, and she looked up to see Ulysses Gilworth standing there, an engaging grin on his broad face.

"I told you I'd be back," he said.

"Yes, you did," Cordelia agreed.

"I'll bet you was beginnin' to wonder, though, weren't you?"

"Not at all," Cordelia replied, lowering her eyelids. "Your comings and goings are none of my business, Mr. Gilworth. But I am glad you came back and brought all these wonderful people with you. I can't believe how quickly the cabins are going up."

"Yep, and when we get done with the cabins, we'll start in on a barn. Been enough roof raisin's around here that folks know how to get it done in a hurry. They put my place up in less'n an afternoon."

"You have a house?"

"Just a little cabin, really, out behind my black-smith shop. Ain't hardly big enough for me, let alone two folks. 'Course, I'm a mite bigger'n most gents, so I take up quite a bit of room."

She wondered why he would mention to her that his cabin was not big enough for two people, but before she could say anything he went on, "Reckon I could build onto it easy enough, maybe put on another room or two. Most of these folks'd be glad to help me. Reckon I've got a lot of friends hereabouts. Makes this a good place to live."

"Yes," she said quietly, looking around the clearing full of industrious, friendly settlers. "I think it's going to be a *fine* place to live."

For a moment, Ulysses didn't say anything; then he smiled broadly at her and declared, "I'd best be gettin' back to work. Wouldn't want folks to say I was shirkin', not when I'm the one who got 'em to come over here and lend a hand. So long, Miss Cordelia. Reckon I'll see you later."

"Yes, I'm sure you will," she said, meaning every word.

Chapter Five

Daniel dipped the quill into the inkwell, then hesitated so long as he struggled with what to put on the paper before him that he had to dip the pen again before he could write. Then, settled at last on what he was going to say, he scratched the words onto the parchment, pausing occasionally to dip the quill again.

He had never been one to write a great deal. In the two and a half years since leaving Virginia, he had sent only half a dozen letters to his parents, most of them short missives to let them know that he and Quincy were all right. He had never gone into detail about the turmoil and trouble he and his brother had been caught up in, but his mother and father were not fools; surely they knew that the Revolution had had a profound effect on their sons.

Now, before setting off on the mission to retrieve the cannon from Fort Ticonderoga, Daniel was writing to Geoffrey and Pamela Reed again. He assured them that he was in good health, but he said nothing about being a member of General Washington's staff, nor did he mention the assignment with Henry Knox. Washington had given orders that no one was to put specific information about military activities in their letters, and Daniel agreed fully with that edict. It was impossible to guarantee that the letters would wind up in the appropriate hands, so the best thing to do was to avoid revealing anything that could be of help to the enemy.

Daniel wished he could tell his parents that Quincy was all right, too, but he had no idea if that was true. He had heard nothing from his brother since Quincy had set off with Murdoch, Cordelia, and Gresham Howard some six months earlier, heading west toward the frontier. Daniel felt certain that Quincy was still alive; although there was no logical basis for it, he was convinced that he would have known if Quincy had died. But more than that, Daniel couldn't say. The travelers might have run into all sorts of trouble.

The only thing Daniel could honestly tell his parents about Quincy was that their youngest son had been fine the last time he had seen him. He said as much in his letter, explaining that Quincy was bound for the frontier, then closed by saying that he hoped the message found his parents in good health and that, God willing, they would all be together again when the war was over, if not before. He waited until the ink dried, then folded the paper, sealed it with candle wax, and pressed his signet ring into it as it hardened. He would leave the letter with Washington, knowing the general would see that it was posted, but whether the message would ever reach Virginia and the Reed plantation, no one could say. The upheaval in the colonies had affected everything, including mail service.

With that burden off his mind, Daniel blew out the candle, lay down on his bunk, and curled up in his blankets. At first light he would ride out with Henry Knox and Knox's brother William, so he needed his rest. The room was uncomfortably chilly, though, and these days sleep came reluctantly to Daniel under the best of circumstances. He lay there for a long time, staring at the darkened ceiling and wondering what this winter was going to bring. Thankfully, when sleep finally came, it was dreamless.

The dawn wind was sharp and cold when Daniel swung up into the saddle of the horse. The animal's breath fogged the air in front of it. Daniel settled himself in the saddle, looked over at Henry and William Knox, and smiled. "I'm ready whenever you gentlemen are," he said.

"We'll leave in just a moment," Henry Knox replied. He was muffled in a heavy fur coat and wore a fur hat, so that he looked something like a huge bear to Daniel. "Here comes the general."

Daniel looked toward Vassall House and saw Washington's tall, erect figure striding toward them. The commander's hands were in the pockets of his greatcoat, but he took out the right one to return Daniel's salute.

"You have plenty of supplies?" asked Washington, briskly getting down to business.

"Yes, sir," Daniel said. "And we can pick up more provisions along the way if need be."

Washington smiled slightly and nodded toward the

musket lying across the saddle in front of Daniel. "And as a fellow Virginian, I'm sure you can do a little hunting if it's necessary."

"Yes, sir. Although game may be a little scarce, what with this cold snap."

Washington stepped back. "Well, be careful, gentlemen. And Godspeed to you. The future of our noble effort rides with you."

Feeling the weight of that responsibility pressing down on him, Daniel saluted again and then turned his horse around to ride west out of Cambridge with Henry and William Knox. Both civilians turned in their saddles to wave back at Washington.

"We're on our way," Henry Knox said, grinning broadly at Daniel.

"Yes," Daniel agreed. "We're on our way."

He had ridden these roads before, the previous spring, and they had not improved since then. In fact, after the autumn rains and early snows, their condition was even worse. Some stretches were fairly dry, but others were a muddy quagmire. The going was slow, and Daniel felt his impatience growing as several days passed. He would have preferred striking out across country toward Albany, rather than following the road that led through Springfield, Westfield, Loudon, Great Barrington, and several other, smaller villages. Both Henry and William had been born and raised in Boston, however, and Daniel knew they would not be accustomed to finding a path through unsettled country and living off the land.

He got along well with William Knox, who at nineteen was only two years older than Daniel's brother, Quincy. William was a slender, soft-spoken young man who sometimes tended to vanish in the shadow of his older, larger, more boisterous brother. But Daniel sensed a core of strength within him. Henry and William were the only two survivors of a family of ten sons, William had told him, and Daniel was touched by the tragic story.

The weather grew increasingly colder, but it stayed dry, and Daniel was thankful for that. The muddy patches of road began to freeze during the nights and not thaw out until the middle of the following day, which made traveling easier. The three men crossed the boundary between Massachusetts and New York, although in truth Daniel could tell no difference in the two colonies.

In another day, however, Daniel, Henry, and William came to the settlement of Castleton, on the Hudson River, and with the papers they carried signed by General Washington, they had no trouble getting a boat to Albany. The horses were left behind, turned over to the care of the small militia garrison in Castleton.

It was December 1, 1775, another cold, gray day, when the travelers reached Albany and were ushered into the office of General Philip Schuyler, the commander of the Continental Army in the north.

Schuyler, an intense man in his early forties who had been born in Albany, stood up and shook his visitors' hands. "I'm told General Washington has sent you men to me," he said as he sat down and gestured for them to sit, too. "I'm happy to extend the general the utmost courtesy and assistance, of course. What can I do for you?"

"We're on our way to Fort Ticonderoga," Henry Knox said, "to fetch all the field artillery pieces there and take them back to Cambridge."

"In December?" Schuyler's eyebrows lifted in surprise, disbelief obvious in his voice.

"Indeed," Knox said. "Washington needs those

guns, General, and I intend to deliver them to him." He leaned forward as he spoke, and his big fist came down on Schuyler's desk.

"Of course," Schuyler replied, still looking somewhat dubious. "I'm at your disposal, Mr. Knox. What can I do to help you?"

"First of all, we'll need horses to get to Lake Champlain and survey the situation. After that—men, sledges, horses, perhaps boats." Knox shook his head. "It's impossible to say for certain what we shall need until we've looked over the ground."

"Horses and men are no problem," Schuyler assured him. "We've plenty of those. Coming up with enough sledges and boats may be a bit more of a challenge, but I'm sure we can find whatever we need." The major general frowned in thought, then continued, "I imagine you're going to use the cannon to pound Boston."

"That's right," Henry Knox confirmed. "We'll drive those redcoats right out of the city."

"Damned well about time!" Schuyler stood up again, and Daniel and his companions rose as well. "Come along, gentlemen. Let's see about some saddle horses."

Daniel had enjoyed the boat ride up the Hudson to Albany, and it would have been all right with him if they had been able to take another boat up the Hudson to the lakes, but with the ice beginning to form in places along the upper reaches of the streams, to do so would be to risk getting stuck.

The mounts provided by Schuyler were good ones, but even on the best of horses the next four days would have been difficult. The cold intensified on the night of December 1, and the temperature was well below freezing the next morning when Daniel, Henry, and William set out. Mud was not a problem now; the roads were frozen as hard as rock and did not thaw out during the day.

On December 5, with a bone-numbing wind blowing, they reached Fort George, a small post at the southern end of Lake George. At the northern end of Lake George was a short, narrow strait that opened up to form Lake Champlain, and Daniel knew Fort Ticonderoga stood on the western shore at that narrow point. This was closer than he had come to Ticonderoga during his mission the previous spring, but Murdoch and Quincy had been all the way up to the fort, along with Ethan Allen, Benedict Arnold, and their forces.

Ordinarily Daniel would have looked forward to seeing the fort, but after the frigid boat ride up Lake George, he would have been happy to see any place where he could get out of the wind and sit next to a warming fire. He and William Knox were shivering when they reached Ticonderoga and were shown into the commander's quarters. Henry Knox, however, seemed unaffected by the cold.

"Good to see you, sir," Henry boomed, shaking hands with the captain. "I bring you greetings from the Continental Congress and General George Washington."

"I'd rather you'd brung a mite warmer weather, Mr. Knox," replied the captain, a lean, leathery man who looked as though he might have been one of Colonel Ethan Allen's mountaineers at one time. "What are you boys doing up here at the ass-end of nowhere?"

"We came for your cannon," Henry said, handing over the documents containing Washington's authorization.

The captain scanned the papers, then handed them back and said, "Might as well take what you can use,

Mr. Knox. We haven't seen hide nor hair of the British since they pulled out last spring. So there's nobody around for us to shoot a cannon at. Want to take a look around?"

"Very much so," Henry answered enthusiastically. He and the captain trooped out, followed by Daniel and William.

So far, Daniel reflected, he had felt like a fifth wheel on this mission. Henry Knox, though a civilian, was definitely running things. But Daniel knew that when they began the actual work of transporting the cannon, he would have plenty to do. So he trailed along silently as Henry inspected the artillery pieces.

Many of the weapons were old and worn out and had not been taken care of by their previous owners, the British. But as Henry Knox conducted his inspection, he pointed out a gun here and a gun there, until he had sixty artillery pieces that he deemed in good enough shape to use in bombarding the British in Boston. Most of the pieces were cannon, ranging in load capacity from four to twenty-four pounds. But Henry also selected half a dozen mortars, three howitzers, and enough cannonballs, flints, and powder to keep the big guns firing for a long time. Looking at the bounty once it had been assembled on the parade ground of the fort, Henry beamed with pleasure and jovially slapped Daniel and William on the back.

"Look at all of it!" Henry raved. "Did you ever see a lovelier sight? With that to back us, we'll soon have the redcoats swimming to England, lads!"

Pressing the small garrison at Fort Ticonderoga into service, they set to work, and for the next few days no one had a chance to complain about the cold weather. The artillery pieces were partially taken apart in order to lower them from their gun emplacements, and while they were broken down, they were hauled on carts across a stretch of swampy, wooded ground to the shore at the head of Lake George. The commander at Ticonderoga had managed to supply a heavy scow and two lighter, flat-bottomed boats, and the soldiers loaded the disassembled cannon, the barrels of powder, and the crates of cannonballs onto the vessels.

"I certainly pray that this weather holds," Henry declared.

"It's almost too cold to work," Daniel said. "I could do with a bit of warmth."

"Oh, no," Henry exclaimed. "Warm weather—a thaw—is the worst thing in the world for our purposes, Daniel. As long as we have snow and frozen ground, we can use sledges to transport the guns. Otherwise we'd have to use wagons, and that would slow us down considerably. No, if we want to get these field pieces to Washington in time to do him any good, we have to have cold weather."

What Henry said made sense, Daniel admitted, and from then on he kept his mouth shut instead of complaining about the frigid temperatures.

While the cannon were still being loaded on the boats, Henry took a smaller craft and went south alone, hoping to get to Fort George in time to round up the men, animals, and equipment they would need to get started as soon as the guns arrived at the fort.

Daniel and William Knox were left in charge of the boats and their precious cargo, and the next morning the heavily loaded vessels embarked on the trip down the lake. Fort George was a little over thirty miles away, and Daniel hoped to make the voyage in one day. They would have, too, he thought, had not the favorable north wind stop blowing almost as soon as the boats were well out on the water.

"Blast it!" William Knox called fervently from the scow. "That wind cuts through us like a knife for days, and now when we need it, it's gone!"

In one of the flat-bottomed boats, Daniel grimaced wearily. There was no choice now but to row.

The trip down the lake was a harrowing one. The temperature continued to plummet, and Daniel thought he could see the ice advancing from either shore toward the middle of the lake. Lake George was three miles across at its widest point, and Daniel estimated that by the afternoon of the first day, ice had formed at least a mile out from both sides. That left only a mile of open water in which to navigate. Still, they were making fairly good progress until late afternoon, when they reached Sabbath Day Point, a headland jutting into the lake about halfway to Fort George.

From his position in the bow of one of the boats, Daniel saw the scow lurch and come to a stop; several men were almost thrown off the vessel by the sudden halt. Earlier in the day the scow had almost gone aground on a submerged rock, and only some rapid maneuvering by William and his men had saved it. Now a horrible grinding sound coming from the scow told Daniel that it had hit a rock or a sandbar extending from Sabbath Day Point.

"Daniel!" William cried, a note of desperation in his voice. "We're taking on water! Bring those boats over here, but carefully. We can't have them going aground, too!"

Daniel's heart pounded with apprehension as he and his men rowed the flat-bottomed boats alongside the stranded scow.

"Start unloading the guns. Transfer them into our boats," he ordered.

As the heavy cannon were moved onto the boats,

the already laden vessels sank lower and lower in the water. If they rode much lower, Daniel thought anxiously, they would be awash.

Finally the scow was unloaded and the other two boats were still above the water. Sabbath Day Point formed a small, protected cove, and Daniel saw that ice had not formed there yet. He waved a hand toward the shore and said, "We'll go in there."

William had transferred into Daniel's boat, and he gripped his arm and said, "Wait a moment. If we go ashore and ice forms around these boats during the night, we won't be able to get out in the morning."

"I know, but we've got to risk it," Daniel replied. "We're only halfway to Fort George, less than that, really, and we can't spend the night out here on the lake. The men need a fire and some warm food."

"You're right, of course," William said slowly. "Henry will never let us hear the end of it if we get stuck here."

Daniel grinned wryly. "We'll just have to risk your brother's displeasure," he said.

Leaving the grounded scow behind, the boats made it ashore safely. As Daniel and the other men jumped from the boats onto the land, several buckskin-clad, blanket-wrapped figures appeared in the trees. Daniel snapped up his flintlock, recognizing the newcomers as Indians.

"Wait!" called out one of the Indians, holding up his hand. "We friends. See you coming in from lake, bring food." The man held up a rawhide sack.

Daniel wasn't sure whether to trust them or not, but when he looked closer he saw that they were not carrying guns. Lowering his rifle, he stepped forward. "Thank you," he said to the spokesman for the group. "We are friendly, too."

The Indian looked at him shrewdly and asked, "Got 'baccy?"

Daniel tried not to grin. "Yes, we have tobacco, and we would be glad to share some of it with our Indian brothers."

That brought smiles to their faces, and within moments, they were helping the American soldiers pull the boats safely onto the shore.

That night, as he sat beside a roaring fire and felt truly warm for the first time in days, Daniel smoked a pipe with the Indian chief, ate some of the stew that bubbled in an iron pot over the flames, and reflected that, if nothing else, this mission had accomplished one thing—he had been too blasted busy to think much about Roxanne.

Just as Daniel had hoped, there was no ice along the shore of the cove the next morning, and the boats were able to put out into the lake again. In fact, the weather was noticeably warmer due to a strong breeze from the south. However, as Daniel and the others waved farewell to the Indians on the shore, he thought that the south wind was really a curse disguised as a blessing. It created a strong headwind for them, and they had to row right into its teeth to reach Fort George.

It was one of the most exhausting days Daniel had ever known. Along with the other men, he rowed until it felt as though his arms were going to drop from his body. There was no pause for a midday meal as shifts of men kept the boats moving. For ten long hours they struggled against the headwind, and it was nearly dusk when the lights of Fort George finally came into view. A cheer might have gone up from the men at the sight, but they were too exhausted to muster the necessary energy. The trip down the lake had taken twice as long as they had expected, but at last they were here, and the big guns were safe.

Daniel spotted Henry Knox's massive figure pacing back and forth on the shore. Several other men were with him, and behind them were the sledges that Henry had acquired. It looked as though General Schuyler had made good on his word. There were at least two dozen of the long, heavy sledges resting on runners of smooth, polished wood. The cannon could be loaded onto the flat surfaces of the giant sleds and lashed down to keep them from rolling or sliding off. There was only a thin dusting of snow on the ground, however, and Daniel knew they would need more snow if the sledges were going to make good time.

William leapt ashore first, followed by Daniel. Henry shook hands with them and asked, "Where's the scow?"

"Stuck up at Sabbath Day Point," William replied. "But don't worry, Henry. We got all the guns off it and brought them along."

"Thank God for that!" muttered Henry. He turned to the men who had been waiting with him—soldiers in the uniform of the Continental Army and militiamen in the garb of mountaineers and woodsmen—and ordered them to begin unloading in the light that was left.

Daniel turned and stepped back into the nearest of the boats. He bent and picked up a crate of four-pound cannonballs. Under normal circumstances, he could have carried it without difficulty, but now as he tried to straighten, he felt his strength flowing out of him like water. He had done too much, rowed too many strokes during the long day. He was exhausted. The crate began to slip, and Daniel tried desperately to hang on to it. If he dropped it over the side of the boat, it would sink in the mud and shallow water.

Strong hands suddenly gripped the crate, and a deep voice said, "Hold on there, friend. You've done enough today. Let me handle that, while you get yourself a drink and some hot food."

It was the best offer Daniel had heard in a long time. He relinquished his hold on the crate and let the man have it. He was tall and broad-shouldered, with dark hair, a thick mustache, and several days' worth of beard stubble. He wore a fur coat with fringed buckskin leggings beneath it, and a floppy-brimmed felt hat was cuffed back on his thick dark hair. With seemingly little effort, he stepped off the boat and carried the heavy crate to one of the sledges, where he placed it with a growing pile of similar crates. Then he started back to the boat for more.

Daniel smiled his thanks to him as they passed, and the man paused and held out his hand. "Pennington Sloane," he introduced himself. "But my friends call me Penn."

"Daniel Reed. And you certainly made a new friend when you took that crate from me, Penn."

They shook hands, and then Daniel continued on to the fort while Penn Sloane unloaded the boats, along with the other men Henry Knox had assembled.

So far, so good, Daniel thought. The big guns were safe, they hadn't lost a man—and he had made a friend.

Chapter Six

To Roxanne's surprise, not one of the sailors on the British ship bothered her during the Atlantic crossing. She stayed in her cabin most of the time, seeing only the boy who brought her meals and the captain, who paid her an occasional visit to see if there was anything she wanted or needed. The captain always treated her politely, although he seemed to hold her in faint disdain.

The whole crew must have been afraid of Major Kane, she decided; otherwise their treatment of her would not have been so courteous.

At this time of year there were frequent squalls in

the North Atlantic, and two weeks out of Boston, for nearly twenty-four hours, the ship rocked and plunged on the waves as rain lashed down in torrential sheets and the wind howled. Roxanne was repeatedly sick as she rode out the gale. The constant pitching and tossing on the angry, white-capped sea had her stomach clenched in knots, and she was sure her pregnancy wasn't helping matters. Half her time was spent praying that the ship would be delivered into safety and the other half hoping that it would sink and put her out of her misery.

Finally the storm blew on and the ship emerged onto a calm sea. Roxanne had been awake since the squall hit, and now she slipped into an exhausted sleep.

Five days later the lookout in the crow's nest spotted land and cried out his news to the men below. The word spread belowdecks to Roxanne's cabin, and when the boy brought her lunch, he announced, "We'll be in Liverpool this afternoon."

"You're sure?" she asked.

"Bloody right, mum—pardon me language. I've made this 'ere crossin' a few times before, ya know."

"I'll take your word for it," Roxanne told him.

The cabin boy was right. In the middle of the afternoon, under a cloudy sky pocked here and there with a patch of blue, the ship sailed into the bustling harbor and docked.

A few minutes later, the captain opened the door of Roxanne's cabin without knocking. He grunted in surprise when he saw her sitting on her narrow bunk, her coat and bonnet on, her single bag on the floor at her feet.

"You're ready to go, then?" he asked.

"What are you going to do with me now?" she inquired, lifting her chin defiantly as she stood up. She had no idea what fate awaited her in England, but there was no point in delaying it.

"There's an officer waiting to take charge of you," the captain answered, frowning. "What happens after I hand you over to him is none of my business, and that's the way I want it, miss. Now come along."

He took hold of her arm and led her abovedecks, and the cabin boy followed along behind, carrying her bag. Roxanne got her first sight of Liverpool when she emerged from the hatchway. The busy harbor town reminded her of Boston. The docks were much the same, busy with men loading and unloading cargo from a multitude of ships. She looked along the forest of masts and saw the Union Jack fluttering proudly over the vessels. Trade with the colonies might have fallen off due to the Revolution, but there was still the rest of the far-flung British Empire to supply England's needs and provide a market for her goods.

As she and the captain started down the gangplank toward the dock, Roxanne saw a covered carriage parked nearby. Three British soldiers and an officer stood beside it, and they strode forward as Roxanne and the captain descended.

With a brisk salute for the naval commander, the officer said, "Hello, Captain. Good to see you again."

"Lieutenant," the captain said brusquely. "I have two items for you." He reached inside his jacket and brought out the letter that Kane had handed over to him in the foggy cove on the Massachusetts coast. "This is one of them. And here's the other." He urged Roxanne forward, not shoving her but not being too gentle about it, either.

"I say!" The young lieutenant's eyes widened in surprise when he looked at Roxanne. "I knew there was

a prisoner, but I didn't know . . . no one told me . . .
Well, this is just—"

"Read the letter, Lieutenant," the captain broke
in. "I'm sure it explains everything." He gestured for
the cabin boy to place Roxanne's bag in the carriage.

The lieutenant ripped open the letter and read it
quickly. The news it contained evidently did little to
lessen his confusion, but when he refolded the missive
and placed it inside his jacket, he nodded and said, "All
right, miss, if you'll just get in the carriage, we'll be on
our way."

"Where are you taking me?" Roxanne asked
coldly.

"There's a house nearby where you'll be staying for
the time being. I'm sure you'll be quite comfortable."

For a second, Roxanne considered trying to break
away from her captors, but on the crowded dock all the
lieutenant would have to do would be to cry out for
someone to stop her, and there would be dozens of willing hands to carry out the order. Although she hated
the idea of being put under house arrest again, there
was nothing she could do about it.

"All right," she agreed. Despair made her voice
dull.

The lieutenant helped her into the carriage, then
got in himself and sat down beside her, being careful
not to crowd her. One of the troopers got in the carriage, too, and seated himself on the opposite bench.
The other two soldiers climbed to the driver's box, and
one of them took up the reins.

The carriage rolled through the streets of Liverpool, having to go slowly because of the traffic. Roxanne had not seen so many carriages, coaches, and
wagons since business in Boston had been at its height.
The carriage picked up speed when it reached the out-

skirts of town, but after only a few minutes, the vehicle slowed and came to a stop in front of a whitewashed cottage.

"This is where you'll be staying," the lieutenant said to Roxanne as he hopped out of the carriage and then turned to help her down.

She looked at the place, telling herself that one prison was pretty much like another, but that wasn't true and she knew it. There could be much worse places to be confined than this neat, clean, pleasant-looking house on a knoll overlooking the city and the harbor. There were flower beds, bare at this time of year, of course, but in spring and summer she supposed it would be a very nice place.

And she might still be here next spring, she realized with a sense of desperation made worse by the unbearable thought that her child might be born in England. There was no way of knowing how long her captivity might last . . . or what waited for her at the end of it.

She never did learn the young lieutenant's name, although he was her jailer for nearly a week. Unlike Thornton Selwyn, the first man to whom Major Kane had entrusted her custody in Boston, the lieutenant was unfailingly polite. Selwyn had tried to molest her and had been killed by Kane when the major caught him in the act. If the lieutenant found her attractive, though, Roxanne saw no sign of it. He stayed in the house and saw her several times each day, but he never even met her eyes squarely, let alone looked at her with an indecent attitude.

There were other guards in the house, as well as men stationed outside. They were acting as though she was as important to the patriot cause as Samuel Adams or Thomas Jefferson or even General Washington, she thought wryly.

As the days passed, Roxanne's anxiety grew. The lieutenant and the other men seemed to be waiting for something else to happen, and the anticipation she sensed made her nerves draw taut. Three days of severe morning sickness during that time only made things worse. Roxanne knew she had been lucky so far during this pregnancy, not suffering the awful sickness some women did, but perhaps all that was beginning to catch up to her now.

The nausea passed, however, and more importantly, she was able to hide her illness from the lieutenant and the other soldiers. She was nearly four months along now, and she knew that within a few weeks she would begin to show enough that she would be unable to disguise it.

In the meantime, she ate every bit of food the British soldiers provided for her, and she asked them for milk to drink. She might be carrying this baby under the most difficult of circumstances, but she was still going to try to take care of herself and the child.

Finally, on one of the gray, drizzly days that looked like all the other days since she had arrived, the lieutenant rapped tentatively and then opened the door to her room. When he stepped inside, he looked even more nervous than usual.

"There's someone here to see you, Miss Darragh."

Roxanne was sitting by one of the windows, a shawl wrapped around her shoulders to ward off the chill. She looked over her shoulder at the lieutenant and asked, "Who?"

"I'm . . . not at liberty to say."

That caught Roxanne's attention. Even though she knew she had no choice in the matter—she was their prisoner, and they could do as they liked—she nodded and said, "All right."

The lieutenant ducked into the hall, and when he reappeared a moment later, he was accompanied by an older man wearing a white linen shirt, silk cravat, dark brown jacket, and dark brown breeches that ended at the knee. Instead of the soldiers' boots to which Roxanne had become accustomed, he wore shoes with silver buckles. His powdered wig was flawlessly in place with its short braid centered precisely down the back of his neck. For all his finery, he was a decidedly ugly man, with narrow features, small eyes, and faint pockmarks that looked to be the legacy of a childhood illness. He was slight in stature, and as he stood there regarding Roxanne with intense dark eyes, he clasped his hands together behind his back and rocked back and forth on his heels.

"Well, well," the man said. "What have we here?"

At odds with his appearance, his voice was deep and resonant, and Roxanne could imagine him addressing a roomful of people.

He obviously commanded the lieutenant's respect, because the young officer said quickly, "This is Miss Roxanne Darragh, sir. I sent word to you concerning her—"

"I know who she is, Lieutenant," the stranger said tartly. "I was merely asking a rhetorical question."

"Ah . . . of course, sir." The lieutenant looked as if he wished the floor of the room would open up and swallow him whole.

"I've heard a great deal about you, Miss Darragh," the civilian said. "It seems you're quite an important personage among that rabble of traitors who call themselves patriots."

"You have been misinformed, sir," Roxanne said,

keeping a tight rein on her temper. "I am a simple woman who happens to believe in the cause of liberty."

A humorless smile plucked at the stranger's thin lips. "No, my dear," he replied. "What you are is a lying slut."

Outrage flared up in Roxanne, and she found herself on her feet with her hands clenched into fists. "How dare you—" she began hotly.

"Sit down!" The stranger's voice lashed at her. It carried an unmistakable tone of command, and it was clear that he was accustomed to being obeyed.

Well, he was going to be disappointed this time, Roxanne thought, clinging tightly to her anger and drawing strength from it.

"I will not be quiet," she declared, sounding calmer than she felt. "I demand to know who you are, sir."

"My name is Cyril Eldridge," the man told her without hesitation. "I'm an assistant deputy minister in the Ministry of War."

"Assistant deputy minister," repeated Roxanne, her tone mocking. "The king has certainly sent an important man to question me."

Cyril Eldridge flushed, stung by her comment just as she intended.

"Don't flatter yourself, Miss Darragh. The king knows absolutely nothing of you. In fact, no one even knows you're in England except the lieutenant here, the men under his command, and myself."

That information made Roxanne nervous. Just as when she had been Kane's prisoner in Boston, her presence here was being kept a secret, and it did not bode well for her continued well-being. If no one higher up knew she was here, these men could do as they pleased with her and no one would be the wiser.

"I demand to see your superior," she said, trying to remain calm.

"Not just yet, I believe. Not until you and I have had a chance to talk at length, my dear."

So that was it, she thought. Kane had delivered her to a man who held the same opinion of her value as he did. Eldridge must think she had significant information about the espionage activities of the patriots. No doubt he was involved in the British intelligence effort along with Kane and was hoping to further his own career by coercing that information from her.

"Come along now, gather your things," Eldridge said, ignoring her stubborn, silent defiance. "We don't have a great deal of time."

"Time is all I have," Roxanne told him coldly.

"All right, if that's how you wish things to be, I'll simply have my men bind you and put you in my coach. It's all the same to me, dear girl."

Roxanne wished her cousin Murdoch was here at this very moment. He would have known how to handle someone like Eldridge. She could almost hear him threatening to tear the head off the "high-toned, fancy-pants son of a bitch!"

But Murdoch was thousands of miles away, and so were Quincy and Elliot. And Daniel was dead. There was no one to protect her, no one to whom she could turn.

"All right," she said, hating the note of defeat that crept into her voice. "I'll go with you."

"Excellent." Eldridge all but rubbed his hands together in glee at his small victory.

He had won this first encounter, Roxanne told herself as she began to gather her few belongings. But just like the conflict heating up in the colonies across the Atlantic, this war was far from over.

*   *   *

Cyril Eldridge's coach was a fine-looking vehicle made of shining wood and bright paint and polished brass, and the horses pulling it were thick-bodied and looked strong enough to haul the Rock of Gibraltar. The springs and thoroughbraces of the coach must have been new, because the vehicle took the road with a smoothness that was welcome to Roxanne.

The two-day journey across the English countryside might have been enjoyable—had it not been for Eldridge sitting across from her and glaring at her the whole way.

He did not try to question her, though, and she was thankful for that. She did not feel up to fending off a multitude of questions, and evidently Eldridge was content to wait until they got to their destination before he began interrogating her.

There were six guards traveling with the coach—two who rode on the driver's box and four who flanked the vehicle on horseback—and Roxanne knew she would be recaptured immediately if she tried to escape.

The first night on the road from Liverpool, they stayed at a small but well-kept country inn where the innkeeper seemed to know Eldridge and hold him in high esteem. Roxanne was given a comfortable room, but the door was barred on the outside, as were the shutters on the window.

She was certain they were going to London, even though Eldridge had not said a word about their destination. She had seen enough maps of England in her father's print shop to be sure they were traveling in the direction of that teeming capital city. And Eldridge had already admitted to being a minor functionary in the Department of War. Where else could they be going, if not London?

So she was surprised when, late on the afternoon of the second day, the coach turned onto a tree-lined lane that led away from the main road. The lane ran straight as an arrow through some fields, then made a sharp turn and swung into a large, circular drive. Roxanne caught her breath when she saw the mansion at the end of the drive.

It was a huge four-story manor house built of light-colored, square stone blocks. A tower rose from one end, and many high, vaulted windows covered the walls on each floor. A parapet around the top of the mansion gave it the look of a fortress, but the ivy that clung to the stone softened the appearance of the house. It was hideous and beautiful at the same time, Roxanne thought. Shrubs lined the drive, and although the lawn in front of the house and the gardens to both sides were bare and brown, she knew that during the summer they would be green and lovely. Behind the mansion were terraces and rolling hills stretching to a thick stand of trees a quarter of a mile away.

"Welcome to Ilford Grange, Miss Darragh," Cyril Eldridge said when the coach came to a stop. "I hope you enjoy your stay—since this will be your home for the duration of the war."

"What?" she exclaimed, her heart pounding with fear and anger.

"I said you're going to stay here until that treasonous rebellion in the colonies has been crushed. Your stay can be quite pleasant, if you so desire. It's entirely up to you."

She understood perfectly what he meant—if she cooperated with him and answered his questions, she would not be mistreated. The implication, then, was that if she continued to be stubborn, she would be letting herself in for some unpleasant consequences.

A man came around the mansion from the direction of a large stable. He wore boots, workingman's pants, a thick jacket, and a tweed cap mashed down on his thick brown hair. He was a little below medium height and had a broad, friendly face. Lifting his hand in greeting, he peered in through the window of the coach.

"Hallo, Mr. Eldridge. The laird did'na say anythin' aboot ye comin' oot here t'day."

"This is none of your business, MacQuarrie," Eldridge snapped. "Go tend to your own affairs."

"Aye, Mr. Eldridge," the man called MacQuarrie said quickly. "I did'na mean t'—" He stopped short when he noticed Roxanne, and then he backed hastily away from the coach.

Eldridge opened the door of the carriage, stepped out, and extended a hand to her. "Come along," he ordered brusquely.

Without even thinking about what she was doing, Roxanne shook her head. Something about this place terrified her, and she could not imagine spending even a night here, let alone months or perhaps years. "No," she said, her voice trembling. "Leave me alone."

Eldridge sighed wearily. "Come, come now. You know there's no need for this. You're not doing yourself a bit of good, Miss Darragh. If you insist on causing trouble, I'll simply have some of my men drag you into the house."

"No!" Roxanne cried.

With a grimace, Eldridge motioned curtly to one of the guards.

"Come on, girl," the soldier said with a leer. He leaned into the coach and held out a callused hand.

Roxanne screamed and clawed at the door on the other side of the coach. It came open easily, and she half fell out of it, but the guards were waiting for her. Strong arms encircled her, and she screamed again as she felt herself being dragged along the pebbles on the drive.

"Be careful with her!" Eldridge called. "I don't want her seriously harmed."

Roxanne flailed at the man, but her struggles did no good. He picked her up and carried her around the coach. Her screams made the horses nervous, and they pawed the crushed stone of the drive and tugged against the reins, which the driver held firmly.

"Careful, careful," repeated Eldridge. "Bring her along now, and one of you get her things—"

A strong, angry voice interrupted the orders. "Cyril! What the devil is going on here?"

The man carrying Roxanne stopped in his tracks as a newcomer strode from the now-open front doors of Ilford Grange.

The man appeared to be in his thirties, a robust figure who stalked forward with a distinctive athletic grace. He had a strong jaw, a slightly prominent nose, and a high forehead from which thick black hair was combed straight back. He wore boots, brown whipcord pants, and a white shirt that was open at the throat despite the cold weather. He came to a stop in front of Cyril Eldridge.

Planting his hands on his hips, the man demanded, "What's the meaning of this commotion? Who is this woman?"

"This is nothing with which you need to concern yourself, Bramwell. Government business, you understand."

"I see," the man said, and Roxanne felt her heart sink. For some unaccountable reason, she had hoped the man might help her. Then he added harshly, "And is the government in the business of hiring louts to kidnap and maul young women?" Without waiting for an answer, he swung around to glower at the man holding Roxanne and ordered, "Put that woman down. Now!"

The command would not be denied. The guard hurriedly lowered Roxanne's feet to the ground and released her.

Eldridge's thin face was mottled with rage. "You may be my cousin, Bramwell, but I tell you this is government business. You've no right—"

"This is my home, Cyril. I've every right in the world." The man called Bramwell approached Roxanne and asked, "Are you all right, madam? My man Hamish told me there was a lady out here with Cyril, but I had no idea you were being mistreated. You have my sincerest apologies." He took her hand. "I'm Bramwell Stoddard, Lord Oakley, the master of Ilford Grange. And you?"

"My name is Roxanne Darragh," she said breathlessly.

A smile split Bramwell Stoddard's face, revealing strong white teeth. "Ah, an Irish lass!"

"No. I'm an American."

Bramwell looked at Eldridge in surprise. The older man sighed and said, "That's what I've been trying to tell you, Bramwell. This woman is my prisoner. You've no right to interfere with the Crown's business."

"Your prisoner?" Bramwell seemed less sure of himself now.

"That's right. She's a spy."

"Then why haven't you taken her to London?"

"It was decided that she would be kept here for the time being while I interrogate her about the treasonous activities of the rebels."

"I'm sorry, Cyril," Bramwell said, suddenly much

more cooperative with Eldridge. "I suppose I got a bit carried away when I saw your man struggling with Miss Darragh. But now that I know the circumstances . . ."

"Quite," said Eldridge, barely making an effort to conceal the resentment he felt toward his cousin. "I'm sorry as well. I should have notified you first and asked your permission to use the estate in such a manner."

"Nonsense," Bramwell replied heartily. "I may hold the title of Lord Oakley, but after all, this is your home, too, Cyril. And I certainly wouldn't want to interfere in your affairs."

Roxanne's hopes had fled completely. Evidently this Bramwell Stoddard was not overly intelligent—a common failing of the English aristocracy, in Roxanne's opinion—and he had been easily manipulated by Eldridge. No help for her would be forthcoming from that source, she realized.

Bramwell added, "I really don't want to see Miss Darragh mistreated, however."

"She won't be, I assure you," Eldridge said. "As long as she cooperates with us, no harm will come to her."

"That's fair enough, I suppose." Bramwell looked at Roxanne again and smiled. "Welcome to Ilford Grange, Miss Darragh. I hope your stay is a pleasant one."

She wanted to call him a stupid clod, but instead she regarded him in cold silence until he shrugged his shoulders and turned to go inside.

In a low voice, Eldridge asked, "Are you going to cooperate, Miss Darragh?"

"I'll go inside," Roxanne snapped. It was as much as she would promise.

Eldridge's thin lips curved in a humorless smile. "I

suppose that will have to do for now. Come along. I'll
have the housekeeper show you to your room."

He took her arm, and although she wanted to
flinch away from him, she forced herself to go along
without protest as he led her into the big house. Just
inside the door, a young woman in a simple brown dress
and a white apron was waiting. She was a few years
older than Roxanne and rather plain, but bright red
hair and a spray of freckles across her features made
her attractive.

"Moira, take Miss Darragh upstairs and get her
settled in the east bedroom on the second floor," Cyril
snapped.

"Aye, Mr. Cyril, I'll do tha'," the woman said, and
Roxanne recognized the same Scottish burr so prominent in the speech of her cousin Murdoch. The man-
servant outside had had the same accent, and Roxanne
wondered idly if he and this woman Moira were husband and wife.

Eldridge stopped Roxanne to add one more thing
before Moira led her up the broad staircase. "I'll be up
to see you later," he said. "Until then, I suggest you
think about your situation, Miss Darragh. I know you're
an intelligent young woman. Don't make things worse
for yourself than they have to be."

Roxanne didn't trust herself to speak. More than
anything else, she wanted to spit in Cyril Eldridge's eye.

"Come along, ma'am," Moira said nervously. "I'll
show ye t' yer room now."

"Thank you," Roxanne murmured. She let Moira
lead her to the staircase, glad to get away from Eldridge, even for a little while.

Their footsteps echoed in the high, arched hallway
on the second floor as Moira led her to a heavy, or-
nately carved door with a huge brass knob. Everything

about Ilford Grange seemed so big to Roxanne. She would hate to live here, she thought; the dimensions of the place would make her feel like a child. With a shiver she realized that she *did* live here, at least until Eldridge decided to do something else with her.

With a squeal of hinges the door swung open, and Moira stepped back to let Roxanne enter.

Roxanne took a deep breath and stepped inside, but she stopped short at the sight of the man who stood there waiting for her.

"Come in," Bramwell Stoddard said. "Come in, Miss Darragh, and please be quiet. We don't want dear cousin Cyril to know about this, now do we?"

Chapter Seven

"**G**ood Lord, Elliot, this is insane! You have to put a stop to it!"

There had been a time in Benjamin Markham's life when such a statement would have issued forth in a loud, ringing voice and would have allowed no room for argument. Now, however, Benjamin's tone was tentative, and he sounded as if he were pleading.

Elliot lifted a hand and rubbed at his temples, but that did not make his headache go away. "I'm sorry," he said quietly to the familiar request that his father had made almost daily since Avery Wallingford had challenged Elliot to a duel. "I'm afraid there's no way to stop it now. Avery has left me no choice."

The two men were in Elliot's bedroom in the Markhams' Beacon Hill mansion. Elliot sat on the side of the bed, a good-sized box made of highly polished wood lying open beside him. His father stood nearby, hands outstretched as if in supplication.

"Are you afraid of being branded a coward?" Benjamin demanded. "If that's it, there's no reason to go through with this, Elliot. You can't risk your life simply because you're afraid of what someone might say!"

Elliot looked up at Benjamin and smiled faintly. "Really, Father, I'm surprised at you. You've been telling me for years that I'm always besmirching the family honor. Well, now I'm going to defend it."

He lifted one of the dueling pistols from the wooden case. It was a beautiful weapon, its stock polished to a high gloss, its fittings of German silver gleaming in the light from the lamp on the bedside table. The pair of pistols had been made by the noted Philadelphia gunsmith Richard Constable, and Elliot knew that they fired straight and true. He had bought them over a year earlier, more because they were beautiful than because he ever expected to use them.

But Benjamin was not going to give up easily. "You've explained to everyone that Avery is mistaken about your interest in Sarah. Surely matters don't have to be taken to this extreme."

"It's been almost a month, and Avery hasn't withdrawn his challenge," Elliot pointed out, "so evidently he isn't satisfied with my explanations."

"You should go see him, try again—"

"No," Elliot said forcefully. "I didn't want to tell you this, Father, but his seconds called on me today and arranged everything. I'll be meeting him on Boston Common tomorrow morning at dawn."

Benjamin passed a trembling hand over his face. "So soon?"

"There's no point in putting it off any longer."

After drawing a deep, ragged breath, Benjamin asked, "And there's no way I can talk you out of this madness?"

"None at all," Elliot assured him as he replaced the pistols in the case.

"Well, by God, I don't have to give you my blessing!"

Elliot looked up. Some of the old fire was back in his father's voice, and he was glad to hear it. But that didn't change anything.

"No, you don't," he said softly. "But you could wish me luck."

"I hope you don't get your damned fool head shot off," muttered Benjamin as he turned toward the door. He hesitated and looked back. "You'd better live through this, boy. I don't think your mother could stand it if . . . if . . ." Benjamin's voice choked, and his momentary anger disappeared. His shoulders slumped in defeat. "We've been through enough," he rasped, then stepped out of Elliot's room and closed the door behind him.

Elliot sighed and placed the dueling pistols on the bedside table, then lay back with his head on the thick pillow. He did not blow out the lamp but instead lay there and stared up at the ceiling. When had things gotten so confused that there were no good choices left? he wondered.

He had never wanted the duel with Avery Wallingford. It would have been fine with him if Avery had accepted his statement that he was not trying to steal Sarah away.

And yet, would that have been the truth? If he had drawn Sarah into his arms, as he had started to, would he have been able to stop himself from kissing her? Elliot knew better than that.

His father was right. His parents had suffered enough—more than enough!—in the past few months. The failing business, the brutal beating by the Liberty Legion, the increasingly virulent anti-Tory sentiment in the city, the deterioration of once-proud Boston. It was simply too much. The changes had wreaked havoc on Benjamin and Polly Markham, and if they lost their only child now, it would be more than they could stand.

But they were not going to lose him, he told himself. He had arranged things so that he was sure he would survive the upcoming duel.

As the challenged party the choice of weapons was his; the customary alternatives were either pistols or sabers. Elliot remembered the fencing lessons both he and Avery had taken as boys. Avery had always been better at it than he, handling the foils and épées with a grace and agility that Elliot had never been able to manage. He would be letting himself in for trouble if he agreed to face Avery with sabers, and he knew it.

But Elliot also knew that Avery's eyesight was weaker than his, and that his adversary simply wasn't a very good shot. Elliot felt confident that Avery would miss, and that confidence was going to be tested, because he intended to give Avery the first shot. Avery would miss, Elliot told himself now, and then he would deliberately miss as well, and the whole farce would be over. Avery's honor would be satisfied, and so would Elliot's, and they could put everything behind them.

At least that was the way Elliot was hoping it would work out. If he was mistaken, the outcome was simple: Someone would die.

Elliot was awake long before dawn and slipped quietly out of the house in order not to disturb his parents. Unable to relax, he had slept little, and his eyes felt gritty, as if they were coated with sand. He hoped that would not affect his aim when the time came.

He would hate to kill Avery by accident, he thought as he made his way down Beacon Hill toward Boston Common, the case with its dueling pistols tucked under his arm.

He was alone; he had asked two of his acquaintances to act as his seconds, but they had declined, and he had not asked anyone else. The realization was growing in him that he had no real friends in Boston anymore. Daniel was gone, having left to answer General Washington's summons, and Henry Grayson, the young man from Carolina who had befriended him, was dead. Quincy Reed and Murdoch Buchanan were hundreds of miles away, somewhere out on the frontier. No, he would have to face this by himself, he had decided, just as he had faced so many other things.

The orange-red glow in the sky that heralded the approaching sunrise was growing brighter as Elliot entered Boston Common. There had been a time when the streets would have been full of people even at this hour as the tradesmen got ready for the day's business, but since the siege had gone into effect there were few reasons for stirring this early. In fact, as Elliot walked across the open stretch of the common, he saw only the silhouettes of the three men who stood waiting for him near a small grove of trees.

As he drew nearer, Elliot recognized Avery and his seconds. He had considered the young men among his friends at one time, but now they were acting on Avery's behalf.

Elliot gave them a cold, expressionless glance, then nodded to Avery and said, "Good morning."

"It won't be for you," Avery snapped. "I intend to kill you, Markham."

"I know," Elliot said wearily. "Are you sure you want to go through with this, Avery?"

Avery stiffened. "Of course I do. I refuse to withdraw my challenge."

"All right," Elliot sighed. "I just wanted to be certain." He extended the wooden case to one of the young men. "If you'd care to examine the weapons, please?"

Avery frowned a little as his second opened the case and revealed the dueling pistols, but he held himself stiff and determined while the second examined them.

"They both appear to be in excellent working order," the man announced after a moment. "Shall I load them?"

"There are shot and powder in the case," Elliot told him.

The second, assisted by the other young man, loaded the weapons. Elliot stood with his arms crossed, waiting patiently. Avery began to fidget a little, and Elliot took that as a good sign. He wanted Avery to be as nervous as possible, to insure that his shot would go wild.

At the same time, Elliot had to admit that his heart was pounding. Even though he felt certain he would survive this meeting, it was nerve-racking to think that within moments he would be standing still and letting someone else shoot at him. Avery might get lucky, after all.

"The pistols are loaded. Choose your weapons, gentlemen."

Avery reached toward the pistols, then hesitated and looked at Elliot, who waved casually for him to go ahead. Avery selected one of the guns, weighed it in his hand for a moment, and then nodded his satisfaction.

"This one will do nicely," he announced, and Elliot could tell he was trying to sound unconcerned.

Elliot took the other pistol and did not bother checking it. He had watched the seconds load the weapons and knew that each pistol was charged with an equal amount of powder.

"The two of you will stand back to back, take ten paces apiece, then turn and fire at will," explained one of the seconds. He took a pistol from his belt and added, "If you turn before taking ten paces, Elliot, I shall be forced to shoot you myself."

Elliot's mouth quirked in a wry grin. "What if Avery turns too soon?" he asked.

"I would never dishonor myself in such a manner," Avery snapped.

"Indeed," Elliot said with a chuckle. Now that the moment was finally at hand, he felt almost giddy, and he wanted to laugh out loud. There was something so ludicrous about this whole thing, he thought. He and Avery were like two small boys in a schoolyard, glowering at each other over some affront, real or imagined, neither of them wanting to fight but knowing that things had gone too far to stop.

It would be over soon, Elliot told himself. It would all be over. . . .

He lifted the pistol, holding his arm cocked at his side, and looped his thumb over the hammer. "Ready," he announced.

Avery took his place at Elliot's back. "Ready," he said, his voice quivering slightly despite his efforts to keep it calm.

The seconds backed away. "Proceed," one of them called out, his voice ringing in the clear, cold air of dawn.

As Elliot took slow, measured paces away from

Avery, he saw the sun peeking over the horizon to the east. He frowned. When he turned, he would be facing away from the sun, but Avery would be staring directly into its glare. That was unfair; they should have been walking north and south, rather than east and west, and it was hard to believe the shrewd Avery had not thought of such a thing.

Elliot started to come to a halt. He could call out now, put a stop to this, and they could begin the deadly ritual again, this time facing in different directions. But instead he kept his mouth shut and continued walking. After all, it wasn't as though he was really going to try to kill Avery, he reasoned. If the sun blinded Avery a little, so much the better. Then Elliot could fire into the air and end this farce.

He had been counting silently to himself, even as those thoughts ran through his head, and now he called aloud, "Nine! Ten!" Turning smoothly, he brought the pistol down, cocking it as he extended his arm. Twenty paces away, Avery was doing the same thing.

Time seemed to freeze in that instant, except for the light of the rising sun that was washing across the common. There was no overcast today; the fiery orb was rising in all its glory. The brilliant rays engulfed Elliot, swept past him, and raced on past Avery as well, lancing into the thick stand of trees just behind and a little to Avery's left. The trees had lost their leaves, but their trunks grew so closely together they looked almost like a solid mass. And something in those trees suddenly glittered in the light of daybreak.

Instinct took over in Elliot, and he dove to the ground even as Avery was pressing the trigger of his pistol. Smoke and flame exploded from the barrel of the gun, but Elliot was still looking past Avery at the trees. He saw a puff of smoke there, too, then heard a high-pitched whine as a rifle ball passed over his head. Tightly gripping his pistol, Elliot took aim and fired, and the heavy weapon bucked solidly against his palm.

Avery cried out, but it was a shout of fear, not pain. Elliot had directed the shot past him and into the trees where he had seen the smoke. Someone howled in agony.

Avery's seconds were running toward the duelers, uncertain of what was going on. Elliot sprang to his feet, dropped his pistol, and leapt forward to intercept the two young men. He lowered his shoulder and smashed it into one of them, at the same time reaching down to pluck the unfired pistol from the man's fingers. He shouted, "Get down!" then whirled back toward the trees, lifting the man's gun in case he needed another shot.

But the one he had already fired was enough. A stranger staggered out of the trees, clutching his right shoulder. His arm hung limp and useless, and there was a rapidly spreading bloodstain under his fingers. Cursing, he stumbled to his knees, then pitched forward and passed out from the shock of having his shoulder shattered by Elliot's well-placed shot.

Elliot lowered the pistol he held and took a deep breath. Then he looked at Avery, who was as pale as milk. Elliot smiled coldly at him and said, "Sorry, Avery. Your plan didn't work."

"Plan?" exclaimed one of the seconds as they got to their feet. "What plan?"

Elliot gestured toward the trees. "Avery had a man with a rifle hiding in that grove. He fired at the same instant as Avery. That was to make sure I didn't survive this duel. Avery must have reasoned that I would choose pistols instead of sabers, and so he was prepared."

"Avery, is this true?" demanded one of the young men.

He made no reply, but Elliot gestured with the barrel of his pistol toward the unconscious man. "There's the proof. Look in the grove, and you'll find the rifle he dropped. I saw the sun reflecting off it just in time to figure out what Avery was up to. I wondered why he didn't mind facing the sun. He knew it didn't matter. His paid marksman would kill me regardless of what he did. In fact, I'm sure he fired wide on purpose, in order to avoid two wounds being found on my body."

"I'll look in the trees for that rifle," one of the seconds said grimly.

Elliot handed the pistol back to the other man. "You'd better fetch a doctor for that fellow before he bleeds to death," he advised.

Letting the pistol hang limply at his side, the man nodded. "Yes, I'll do that," he said with a contemptuous glance toward Avery. "I'm . . . sorry about this, Elliot."

"Yes, so am I." Elliot started to turn away.

At that instant, a cry of pure rage burst from Avery's lips. He had staked his reputation on this duel, and now his treacherous plan had backfired on him, ruining everything. With an inarticulate shout, he lunged forward and wrested the gun from the second's grip.

"Look out, Elliot!" the second called.

Elliot whipped around in time to see Avery bringing the pistol to bear, but before Avery's finger could tighten on the trigger, the second struck. He brought his clubbed fists down on the back of Avery's neck, and Avery hit the ground hard, and the pistol slipped from his fingers. Elliot darted forward and snatched it up. He snapped open the pan and blew out the priming charge, rendering the gun unable to fire. Then he tossed it aside.

The other second came running out of the woods carrying the rifle Elliot had known he would find there, and he joined his friend in looking down in contemptuous disbelief at Avery.

Vile profanity spewed from Avery's mouth as he pulled himself onto hands and knees and then struggled to his feet. His expensive clothes were soiled now, and he trembled as he railed and ranted at Elliot.

Elliot took the abuse in stoic silence while one of the men gathered up the dueling pistols and replaced them in their wooden case. He brought the case to Elliot and handed it to him. Elliot took it and held it tightly as he turned back to face Avery, who was running out of breath and obscenities.

"Listen to me," Elliot said sharply, his words cutting through the vestiges of Avery's outburst. "The duel is over, Avery. Go home to your wife, and for her sake, you had best treat her decently. Because if I ever hear of you mistreating her, the next time I've got you in my sights, I'll kill you."

Then he and the men turned and walked away, leaving Avery Wallingford standing alone in the middle of Boston Common.

Chapter Eight

His long rifle canted jauntily over his shoulder, Murdoch Buchanan ducked slightly to get his tall frame through the doorway of the rustic cabin that sat beside the crude road to Wheeling. There was a brisk, cold wind blowing in behind him, and he closed the door quickly.

Murdoch had seen this place a time or two before on his rambles around the area during the past month. Ulysses Gilworth had told him it was a tavern, and there had been a frown on Ulysses's face when he said the words. The big blacksmith was not a drinking man, and while that fact did not lower Murdoch's opinion of him in the least, it meant that they would never have quite as many things in common as they might have.

Murdoch had spent the morning hunting on foot

and had a couple of haunches of venison, which he had hung up outside the door of the tavern. But before he took them back to the women at the cabins, he thought he could do with a little warming up, both inside and out. The flames crackling in the big stone fireplace across the room would take care of the outer man, and the contents of the jugs arrayed on crude shelves behind the bar would do nicely for the inner man, he reflected as he walked across the room.

A big-bellied man with brown hair that stuck up about an inch all over his head stood behind a bar made of roughly hewn planks laid on barrels.

He grinned at Murdoch and said, "Howdy. What'll you have, mister?"

Murdoch jerked his chin toward the jugs. "Would ye be having some fine Scotch whiskey in any o' them vessels, me friend?"

The proprietor's grin never faltered as he replied, "No, but I've got some home-brewed panther piss, straight from the washtub out back, that'll shrivel your innards if you drink enough of it."

"Aye, that'll do," Murdoch said fervently.

The bartender took down a jug, uncorked it, and slid it across to Murdoch, who picked it up, tilted it to his mouth, and took a long swallow. The stuff tasted like liquid fire flooding down his gullet and burning holes in his gizzard, he reflected, but overall not too bad. He'd certainly had worse in his day.

He said as much as he thumped the jug back onto the bar and then threw down a few coins that were eagerly scooped up by the proprietor.

"Murdoch Buchanan," the big Scotsman introduced himself.

"Harvey Culberson," the bartender replied, shak-

ing hands with him. "Been around here long, Buchanan?"

"No' too long. I came out with some friends, been
staying with them off an' on, when I'm not in th' woods.
Name o' Quincy Reed an' Gresham Howard."

"I've heard of 'em," Harvey Culberson said.
"Heard that blacksmith fella, Gilworth, talking about
'em in the trading post in Wheeling the other day.
Sound like nice folks."

"Gilworth, eh? What do ye think o' him?"

Culberson shrugged. "He's a good blacksmith and
seems like a decent gent, even if he don't hold with
drinking."

"Aye, tha' be wha' I thought, too."

Ulysses Gilworth had been showing up at the cabins fairly often, usually on the flimsiest of excuses. It
was as plain as the nose on the man's face—which was
pretty plain indeed, Murdoch mused with an inner
chuckle—that Ulysses was interested in Cordelia Faulkner. And anybody with eyes in his head could see that
Cordelia returned that interest. Murdoch didn't think
things had gone beyond the stage of moon-eyed staring,
guilty flinches, and acute embarrassment, but it was
clear that they would eventually. Funny how falling in
love could make grown folks act like children again,
Murdoch thought.

He put the matter of Cordelia and Ulysses out of
his mind for the moment and turned to look around the
tavern. It had a low ceiling and was lit by a couple of
smoky oil lanterns that hung from the rafters. The floor
was packed dirt, and the furnishings consisted of tables
made from empty barrels and stools made from empty
kegs. Some pegs had been pounded into the wall over
the fireplace, and from them hung an old-fashioned
blunderbuss, the type with a huge barrel such as the

pilgrims had used. A powder horn hung from one peg, a beaded leather shot pouch from another. Murdoch doubted that the blunderbuss worked anymore; he would have hated to have to fire it. An old thing like that could blow up right in your hands.

Five other men were in the tavern, four of them playing cards around a barrel table and the fifth sitting by himself at a table near the fire. He looked to be in his midtwenties, wore the buckskins and coonskin cap of a frontiersman, and possessed the broad shoulders and long arms of a powerfully strong man. His face was broad, his jaw stubborn. His thick hair was the color of straw and stuck out from under his hat. Big-knuckled hands that were raw and red held a long-barreled flint-lock rifle with such ease that the weapon seemed a part of the man's body.

Murdoch wondered if the fellow would like a little company, and he was about to pick up his jug and saunter over to the table when the door of the tavern opened and three angry-looking men hurried in.

"Clark!" one of them called in a harsh voice. "By God, I thought that was your horse outside. Turn and face me, you son of a bitch!"

The newcomers had left the door open behind them, and a cold wind sliced through the room and made the flames in the fireplace jump.

The man called Clark slowly got to his feet and in a calm voice said, "I told you back in Boonesborough, Harkins, I don't want any trouble with you."

"And I told you I don't give a damn what you want! You got a debt to pay, Clark, a blood debt."

"It was your brother's own fault he went off and got himself killed," Clark said. "I told him to stay with the surveying party, but he figured he wanted to see some Indians." He paused, then added grimly, "Well, he saw 'em, all right. And they're the ones who did in your brother, not me."

"How he died don't matter," Harkins shot back hotly. "You were in charge of that expedition, and you let him get killed. Hell, Dick weren't but a boy! He was only twenty years old."

"Twenty's considered a man most places," replied Clark. "But like I said, Harkins, I'm sorry. If I'd known Dick was going to sneak off that way, I'd've stopped him, even if I'd had to tie him up. But I didn't know and there wasn't a thing I could do about it." He sighed wearily. "Now why don't you go on back to Kentucky and let this end here?"

"Oh, it'll end, all right," Harkins sneered. "Just not the way you want it to!" With that, he swung the muzzle of his rifle around to bear on Clark.

"Hold it!" barked Murdoch. His rifle was already at his shoulder, and the flintlock was cocked. "Dinna ye move, mister, or I'll put a ball in th' back o' your head."

Harkins froze, then said urgently, "Charley? Bracken?"

"He's got a bead on you, Frank," one of the men replied. "And he looks like he wouldn't mind usin' that rifle. You'd better keep still."

"Excellent advice, me friend," agreed Murdoch. "An' tha' goes for th' other two o' ye, as well."

Clark snapped his rifle into firing position. "Don't worry, mister," he said to Murdoch. "They're not going anywhere."

"Well, somebody ought to go over there and close the damned door," Harvey Culberson groused. "It's gettin' mighty cold in here. So either shut the door or get on with your killin' each other. Don't matter none to me."

"Nobody's going to kill anybody today," Clark declared. "Harkins, you and your friends put your guns down on that table there beside you. Rifles and pistols both. And throw in your hunting knives, just to make sure."

"What're you goin' to do, Clark?" Harkins demanded angrily. "Shoot us down once you got us helpless?"

"No, I'm not going to shoot you unless you force me to," Clark said, clearly hurt and angered by the question. "But I am going to ride out from here, and I want to be safe while I do it. So you boys do as I tell you, get rid of all your weapons, and then get the hell out of here."

"What?" Harkins exploded. His face was as red as a ripe tomato, Murdoch thought. "You'd send us out to face a wilderness full of wild animals and wilder Indians with only our bare hands? We won't last the night."

"I'm not sending you out to face the wilderness, you damned fool!" snapped Clark. "I want you to get on your horses and ride up on that hill about two hundred yards away on the road toward Wheeling. Then me and my friend—" he nodded toward Murdoch "— will be leaving. We won't pull out until we see you gents on top of that hill, though, and I don't want you starting down here until we're out of sight. Then you can do as you damn well please. But I'll be watching, and if you start down that hill too soon, I'll shoot you right out of the saddle, as God is my witness."

Harkins blustered, "That's mighty big talk—"

"And I can back it up," Clark said coolly. "I'd wager my friend here can, too."

"I gen'rally hit what I'm aiming at," Murdoch stated honestly.

"There you have it, gentlemen," Clark said to Harkins and his two companions. "Make your choice well, because you'll have to live—or die—with it."

The two men took no time at all to reach a decision. Moving quickly, they put their rifles, pistols, and knives on the table Clark had indicated. Harkins hesitated only a few moments, then grudgingly did the same. His features were set in a surly glare, but he did as he was told and left the tavern with his two friends.

Culberson heaved a sigh of relief. "Thought for a minute there you was goin' to have to shoot up the place, George," he said.

"So did I, Harvey," Clark told him with a faint grin. He looked at Murdoch and continued, "We'll give those hotheaded fools a little time to pull out, then we'd best be riding, too." He strode across the room and held out his hand to Murdoch. "I'm George Rogers Clark."

"Th' explorer from Kentucky?" asked Murdoch as he shook Clark's hand. "I've heard of ye. Murdoch Buchanan's th' name."

"And I've heard of you, Mr. Buchanan. In fact, listening to the stories about your exploits was one of the things that encouraged me to come out to this country from my home in Virginia. You're a genuine hero."

"Nay, just a fellow who likes t' see what might be on th' other side o' th' hill. You reckon those lads are gone now?"

"I think I can venture a look," Clark replied. He opened the door, stuck his head out for a moment, then ducked back in and grinned at Murdoch. "I saw all three of them riding up to the top of the hill. They're doing just as they were told."

"They did'na have much choice, being disarmed like tha'," Murdoch said dryly. "Wha' if I did'na want t' leave with ye?"

"Then you can go your own way," Clark shrugged and said, "but I honestly think we'll both be safer if we stay together for a little while. And I have to admit, I think I'd probably enjoy your company. I've heard you're a man who's seen and done most everything."

"Once or twice," Murdoch agreed. "Once or twice indeed, me friend."

"Well . . . are we going?"

"Aye. We're going."

The two frontiersmen stepped through the doorway of the tavern and waved farewell to Harvey Culberson. Once outside, Murdoch glanced toward the hill Clark indicated with a jerk of his prominent chin.

"There they are," Clark said.

Murdoch could see the three horsemen sitting their mounts at the top of the slope. Even though they were too far away to see their faces, he could feel the hatred and frustration coming from them.

"Those lads'll see ye again," he predicted.

Clark nodded gloomily as he gathered up the reins of a sturdy-looking brown horse and swung up into the saddle.

"You're probably right," he said. "But maybe they'll come to their senses. Charley and Bracken might, anyway. Dick Harkins wasn't blood kin to them, just a friend. I don't suppose Frank'll ever see that it wasn't my fault his little brother got killed. But without the other two to back his play, I don't think he'd come after me again. So about all I can do is hope for some good luck—and keep my eyes open."

"Including th' ones in th' back o' your head."

Clark chuckled. "Of course."

Murdoch didn't have a horse, but he walked alongside Clark's mount. With his long-legged stride the

Scotsman easily kept up with the animal, even with the heavy haunches of venison slung over his shoulder.

In reply to a question from Clark, he told about going to Boston to see his relatives, a short trip that had turned into a long one and finally culminated in heading west again with Quincy Reed, Gresham Howard, and Cordelia Faulkner. Murdoch explained as well how Mariel Jarrott and little Dietrich had joined their party. He concluded by saying, "They've all got themselves some cabins not far from here, and I stay there some with 'em, but I never was th' kind t' settle down too much."

"Nor I," agreed Clark. "I was born back in Virginia, but I came out to the Ohio Valley a few years ago to have myself a look around. Spent some time over in Kentucky, too, around the stations Boone and Harrod set up. Folks decided that since I knew the land hereabouts as well as any and better'n most, I ought to start surveying it for them. Help bring civilization out here, you know."

Murdoch heard the ambivalence in Clark's voice, and he uttered a grunt of understanding. Civilization was a fine thing, he supposed, but whenever it stretched its impatient fingers into new lands, there was a price to be paid. Murdoch had never figured out if that price was worth it.

"I was on one of those surveying trips when I had the trouble with Harkins's brother," Clark continued. "He wanted to meet some Indians, called 'em noble savages." Clark shook his head. "He found out how noble they are. We found his body after they got through with him. Wasn't a pretty sight."

"I know wha' ye mean. I've seen a few like tha' meself. But no' all th' natives are bad. I've run into some as decent an' upstanding as anybody ye'd ever want t' meet."

"That's true," Clark agreed. "There's good and bad and all sorts in between, I suppose, no matter what color you're talking about. In fact, the worst men I know are British agents who have come out here to stir up the Indians and cause trouble for the settlers."

Murdoch looked sharply at him. "Tha' sort o' thing is going on out here, too? We saw it happening in New York on th' way here. Tha' lass Mariel and th' bairn Dietrich, their folks were wiped out by a band o' Mohawks working for an Englisher name o' Sabbath. Crazy man—called himself a reverend."

"I'm not surprised to hear that," Clark said. "I'm certain the British are going to try the same thing out here. They think that if they keep the pressure on the west, the resistance in the colonies back east will crumble faster. But we're not going to let them get away with it."

Murdoch heard something in the other frontiersman's voice, and he asked, "What're ye planning t' do about it?"

"I'm going to put together a force to meet the Indian attacks when they come. We'll strike back against them and teach them that if they hit us, we'll hit back harder."

"Aye," Murdoch said slowly. "When do ye plan on doing this?"

"I don't believe the British will try anything this winter," replied Clark. "I'm going to start recruiting men next spring, and I hope to have a sizable force by the middle of summer. Then we'll be ready when the weather gets hot and the killing fever gets up."

Murdoch stopped along the side of the trail, and Clark reined in his horse. Turning and lifting his hand to Clark, Murdoch said, "If I'm still in these parts, count me in, George. I'd be happy t' give ye a hand."

"And I'll be more than happy to have you with us, Murdoch. The frontier has to be defended if the folks back east are going to have any chance of getting their freedom from England. We're all a part of the same fight."

"Aye." Murdoch shook Clark's hand, then inclined his head toward a smaller trail that led off to the south, roughly following the course of a creek that joined the Ohio nearby. "Tha' be th' way I'm going," he said. " 'Tis glad I am I ran into ye today, George."

"And I'm glad you did, Murdoch. I suppose you saved my bacon by jumping in before that fracas got started. Maybe I can return the favor someday."

With a wave of their hands, the two frontiersmen went their separate ways. Murdoch had a feeling as he strode toward his friends' cabins that the day would come when he saw a great deal more of George Rogers Clark.

Chapter Nine

Eighty oxen strained against the weight of more than a dozen sledges that had been loaded with the artillery pieces brought down Lake George from Fort Ticonderoga. The men waiting at Fort George had labored long into the night to load the sledges, and when the next morning dawned with a light snow falling, Henry Knox greeted the swirling white flakes with an infectious grin.

"Come on!" he shouted to the sky as he, his brother William, and Daniel Reed strode out of the cabin where they had spent the night. Henry waved his long arms in the air and urged the snow to fall faster.

Daniel and William exchanged a grin at Henry's exuberance as they followed along behind him. The other men were emerging from the fort's barracks, and Henry quickly called them together.

"We shall be leaving this morning with our precious cargo, men." He gestured toward the sledges, most of which were covered with canvas that had been lashed down over the weapons and the kegs of powder. "We will be carrying with us the hopes and dreams of this glorious Revolution, my friends. The cannon on those sledges will allow us to win our first great victory over the British. All we have to do is place them in General Washington's hands. So you see, we are not just transporting something so mundane as artillery pieces and black powder. No, gentlemen . . . we are carrying freedom!"

It was an inspiring speech, and the men cheered when Henry concluded. They cooked and ate their breakfast quickly, while Henry, William, and Daniel inspected the sledges and their loads to make sure everything was secure. Only then did they pause for a hurried bite to eat.

Penn Sloane approached Daniel, who was gnawing on a corn cake and a thick strip of bacon.

"Morning," the woodsman said, smiling. "Looks like we're about ready to get started."

"Henry's anxious to get those cannon to Washington," Daniel said, "and I don't blame him. He's going to be the commander of artillery once the guns are in place."

"Lots of glory for him, I reckon."

"I don't think he's doing this for the glory," Daniel said, his tone somewhat sharp. "Henry believes in the cause of liberty, and he believes that artillery is the key to forcing the British out of Boston."

"What about you?" asked Penn. "Why are you up here in the middle of winter, about to try to drag a bunch of heavy iron over the mountains?"

"I believe in liberty, too," Daniel said simply. "And

I'll do whatever is necessary to achieve it." *Including giving up the search for the woman I love,* he added silently. After a moment he said, "What about you? Why are you here, Penn?"

Shrugging his broad shoulders, Penn said, "I like the mountains. Grew up over in the New Hampshire Grants, and when Ethan Allen formed up the Green Mountain Boys to keep the blasted New Yorkers from stealing our land from us, I joined right off." A grin appeared under his thick mustache. "Reckon you could say I'm always looking for a fight, since I usually wind up wherever there's trouble. Missed out on Canada, though, when Colonel Allen and the rest of the boys went up there."

"Maybe that's good," Daniel pointed out. "From what I've heard, that campaign was disastrous. And the British made Allen a prisoner, didn't they?"

"That's right," Penn said, his expression hardening at the thought. "I should've been with 'em, no matter how things turned out. But my father was sick, so I had to go home for a spell. He's a minister over in the Grants. Never did like me tramping around the woods, but I couldn't stand to be shut up indoors all the time, like him."

Daniel understood. He had spent a lot of his childhood "tramping around the woods," as Penn phrased it, but in Daniel's case the woods had been along the Rivanna River in Virginia's Piedmont, near the Reed family plantation. Still, he had controlled those outdoor urges enough to read for the law at Harvard College, and it would have been his profession by now—if the Revolution had not intervened.

"We'll be pulling out in ten minutes, Daniel," Henry Knox said. "This is a good spot for you, since it's about midway along the train. I'll be leading, and William will bring up the rear and watch for stragglers. Your responsibility will be to keep everyone moving at the same pace."

"All right, Henry," Daniel agreed. The bacon was gone, and now he finished off the last of the corn cake and washed it down with water from his canteen. As he checked his pistol and rifle, he said to Penn Sloane, "Why don't you come along with me?"

"Sounds good," Penn agreed. "We can cuss these oxen together if they get balky."

"They'll get balky sooner or later," Daniel said, chuckling. "I can practically guarantee it."

The massive beasts cooperated well at first, as if they sensed the zeal of their human masters and drew some enthusiasm of their own from it. The long caravan left Fort George less than an hour after sunrise, and the sledges' runners slid easily along the narrow, snow-covered road.

They kept moving all through the gray, snowy morning, and although Daniel was chilled by the raw wind, the walk kept him from getting too cold. Henry Knox set a brisk pace, and Daniel was pleased with their progress by the time they stopped at midday to build some fires, heat some tea, and eat a quick meal. Then it was back on the move again, heading south toward Albany.

By nightfall they had covered at least ten miles, Daniel estimated. That was excellent by anyone's standards, and Henry was quite pleased as well.

Sitting down next to one of the campfires, the big man said, "If we can keep this up, I can easily fulfill my pledge to General Washington. I sent word to him before we left Fort George that I expect to place this train of artillery in his hands in less than three weeks."

Daniel worried that Henry might be getting too optimistic. True, the first day of the overland trek had gone well, but there were many miles to go, and even under the best of conditions, it might take longer than three weeks to haul the guns to their destination.

But the following day the burst of energy that had carried men and oxen diminished, and the pace slowed noticeably. The sledges covered only six or seven miles, and Henry Knox was downcast but still determined at that night's camp.

Snow had fallen steadily since their departure from Fort George, and it gave the road the necessary coating for the sledges, but the consistency could have been better. This was dry, powdery snow, fine little pellets that crunched underfoot and blew away easily at the slightest breeze. Some stretches of road had been swept clean by the wind, in fact, which slowed the sledges even more.

Daniel could see the impatience growing in Henry Knox as day after day passed and the miles fairly crawled beneath the sledges' runners. More than a week after the train of artillery left Fort George, it was still nowhere near Albany. Though Henry was becoming more and more frustrated, he kept it to himself, not wanting the men to think he was disappointed in them.

"My God, they're doing the best work any commander could expect of them," he explained to Daniel when the caravan paused one evening to make camp on a hilltop overlooking a small creek. "We may be going slower than I'd anticipated, but I still have no doubt we'll get the guns to Cambridge, just as I promised."

The temperature had been below freezing for several days, but now the wind picked up from the north, and it promised to drop even lower before morning. The creek at the bottom of the hill was only some twenty feet wide, and Daniel figured the ice on it would be more than thick enough to support the sledges for that distance. While the men were setting up camp, Henry, William, and he had gone down the hill to check on the thickness of the ice, and it had supported their weight without a sign of strain.

Stream crossings were what worried Henry more than anything else, Daniel knew. They would have to cross the Hudson and the Mohawk rivers, and if the ice on the streams gave way, the results could be disastrous, not to mention deadly for any men who plunged into the frigid waters. But perhaps they would be fortunate, Daniel told himself as he sipped a cup of hot tea that gave off thick whorls of steam in the cold air. Maybe they would be lucky enough to avoid such mishaps.

Just as everyone expected, the temperature continued to plunge during the night. The wind howled and raged, finding every little opening in the tents the men had pitched. Still, any shelter was better than none. At least the men, wrapped in thick blankets and quilts, huddled in their tents, had it better than the oxen. The shaggy-coated beasts suffered through the night in the open.

At dawn the wind died down and finally ceased altogether, and the gray light of day began filtering down through the thick overcast; the air was still and so cold it was brittle. Daniel thought he felt it freezing his lungs right in his body as he took a deep breath when he stepped out of the tent he had shared with William Knox. Daniel's eyes widened, and he resolved not to repeat that mistake. Until the air warmed up a bit, he would take only shallow breaths.

The camp was stirring; men clustered around small fires built where the snow had been brushed away on the ground. Several men stumbled toward the nearby bushes, and one of the drovers called after them, "Better make it quick, boys, else it's liable to freeze off in this air!" Laughter rang through the camp in response to the remark.

William Knox came out of the tent behind Daniel, and the two young men drew close to one of the fires and claimed cups of tea. Henry strode up to them, looking more massive than ever in his greatcoat and his large fur hat, which was pulled down over his ears. From the looks of him, he had already been up for a while.

"Fine day, isn't it, lads?" Henry asked with his customary enthusiasm.

Daniel just grunted and tried to warm his painfully stiff fingers on the cup of tea. Whatever warmth emanated from the steaming liquid was instantly whisked away by the frigid air.

"How are the oxen this morning?" William asked.

"Holding up well," replied Henry. "They're sturdy beasts, and I'm glad we settled on them to pull the sledges instead of mules or horses."

As usual, the men ate breakfast quickly; then Henry gave the order for them to line up at their positions. The men gripped the oxen's harnesses and prepared to lead the great beasts down the hill toward the creek. The oxen were yoked four to each sledge, and they did not vary from their slow, deliberate pace as they started down the slope. Men stationed behind each of the sledges clung to ropes tied to the vehicles, hauling back on them to keep them from sliding too fast. The last thing they needed was a pileup of oxen and sledges at the bottom of the hill.

The lead sledge reached the bank of the creek and started across it. Snow floated down on the oxen's heads, but the wind had ceased, and the flakes came down straight from the sky and did not whip around as they had during the previous days.

If Daniel had not known the creek was there, he might not have even noticed it. Snow had piled up on the ice so that there was only a faint, twenty-foot-wide depression to mark the course of the stream. The first sledge crossed without incident and lumbered up the bank on the far side behind its team. The second, third, and fourth crossed as well, and then the fifth sledge started out onto the ice. Daniel was walking beside it, holding tightly to the lead ox's harness. Usually, Penn Sloane would have been on the opposite side, guiding the other leader, but today Penn had gone ahead, and Daniel did not know the man who was helping him with the animals.

They were halfway across the stream when a loud crack suddenly sounded in the still air. Daniel and the men stood stunned for an instant; then, knowing what the sound meant, Daniel shouted, "Move, move! It's cracking! Get off the ice—now!"

More sharp sounds followed as Daniel and the man tugged frantically on the harness of the oxen. The huge animals would not be hurried, though, and their pace faltered even more when the ice began to shift under their hooves. Abruptly, the loudest cracking noise of all split the winter air, and the right front corner of the sledge dipped as the ice beneath it gave way.

Daniel slammed the stock of his rifle against the rump of the lead ox. "Pull!" he shouted. His own footing was unsteady now as more cracks ran through the ice. Even through the soles of his boots and his thick socks he could feel the vibrations as the ice shattered. He looked across the backs of the oxen and saw the

panic-stricken expression on the face of the other
man.

"We've got to get clear!" the man cried. "If we get
off this ice now—"

"The sledge will fall through!" Daniel interrupted.
He struck the near ox with the rifle butt again. "Pull,
you son of a bitch!"

On the far side of the creek, Henry Knox had
heard the commotion. He stood on the bank and called,
"Get away from there, Daniel!" William ran up on the
other bank and echoed the warning.

The sledge had come to a virtual halt now. Water
was swirling around the hooves of the oxen, and if they
stopped and let the weight of the sledge rest on the
weakened portion of the ice, the whole thing would fall
through. Knowing that, Daniel pulled and shouted and
did everything in his power to get the brutes moving
again.

Slowly they lurched into motion, and the sledge began to slide, but even as it did, the left rear corner
dropped through the ice. The support under the right
front corner, however, was a bit firmer now, and the
heavy vehicle continued its gradual progress. Several
men from the sledges at the rear abandoned their positions and ran forward onto the ice to help out. Daniel
waved them back, knowing they would place extra
weight on the frozen stream, but they disregarded his
shouts and reached the sledge and stooped to put their
shoulders against it, shoving with all their strength.

The added push got the sledge moving fast enough
to right itself as the ice firmed underneath it, and then
it slid across the few remaining feet onto the bank. Exhausted, Daniel sank to the snow-covered ground beside the sledge.

"Stay back! Stay back!" Henry Knox called to the

men still on the far side of the stream. "Don't try to cross yet!"

The whole train came to a standstill, half of it on one side of the creek, half of it on the other. Daniel hauled several deep breaths into his body, wincing at the bite of the cold air, then reached up and grasped the harness of the team to pull himself to his feet.

"That shouldn't have happened!" Henry exclaimed, staring at the creek with a look of anger on his broad face. "That ice was thick enough last evening, and it certainly shouldn't have weakened any during the night."

Standing beside Henry, Daniel remembered that no one had checked the ice this morning before the sledges started across it. In fact, the thought of doing such a thing had not occurred to him because he knew how thick the ice had been the night before and how cold the temperature had been.

"This doesn't make any sense," he muttered.

"No, it doesn't," Henry agreed gloomily. His expression brightened a little as he went on, "But with the way the water flowed through the places where the ice cracked, it'll freeze again in no time, probably thicker than before. We'll be able to get the other sledges across, but not in a timely manner."

Daniel walked carefully out onto the ice. "I don't want to wait that long to check something," he said over his shoulder.

"Daniel, come back here! That ice could still give way." When Henry saw that Daniel was not going to obey him, he muttered, "Confound it!" Then he eased his way onto the ice behind Daniel.

When Daniel neared the spot where the sledge had run into trouble, he bent over and brushed away the snow that had accumulated on the ice. The smooth grayish surface of the ice itself soon appeared, and after a few moments Daniel found what he was looking for.

"Take a look at this, Henry!" he called. "Just don't come too close."

Henry Knox frowned when he saw the places in the ice where it appeared great chunks of it had been gouged out. "What the devil!" he exclaimed.

Daniel moved away from the spot and went to join Henry where the ice was thicker. Pitching his voice low enough so that the men on both banks of the stream could not hear what he was saying, he told Henry, "Someone chopped down into that ice with an ax during the night. He was careful not to break through, so that the water of the creek would rise through the opening and just freeze again, but he weakened the ice enough so that it gave way under the continued strain of taking the sledges across. Whoever it was, he was careful enough to cover up his work with a nice thick layer of snow, too, so that we wouldn't notice it before we started across."

"You're sure of this?" Henry asked.

"Sure enough. You saw those places in the ice where it hadn't broken through yet. Nothing natural did that. It was man-made, all right."

Henry rubbed his heavy jaw with his gloved hand. "Yes, that's certainly what it looked like, all right. But why in the world would anyone want to do such a thing? My word, some of our men could have been killed, and the guns on that sledge lost!"

"I'd say that's exactly what our mysterious ice chopper wanted," Daniel replied. "That's why he crept out here last night while that cold wind was howling and went about his work. He wants to stop you, Henry." A theory was forming in Daniel's mind even as he spoke, but when the words came out, he knew they were true. "Whoever it is, he doesn't want General Washington to get his hands on those cannon."

"But that means . . ."

"Yes. There's a British agent among us."

Chapter Ten

It was not long before Roxanne Darragh knew
Moira MacQuarrie had been right. Bramwell Stoddard was sincere in his desire to make things easy
for her. After taking her meals in her room for two
weeks, she had decided to ask Moira if she could come
downstairs for dinner, and the Scottish girl had returned with the news that Roxanne would be more than
welcome to join Bramwell for dinner in the mansion's
great dining hall.

There was no mention of Cyril, and when Roxanne
was escorted downstairs by Moira that evening, the
dour-looking older man was nowhere to be seen. Bramwell was waiting alone in the high-ceilinged room with
its huge curtained windows, polished hardwood floors,
and massive mahogany table long enough to seat sev-

eral dozen people. If Bramwell were at one end of the table and she at the other, Roxanne thought, they would have a difficult time carrying on a conversation.

As Moira escorted her to a place set to the right of the table's head, Bramwell came forward to greet her. He wore a dark, elegant suit, a limp white shirt with ruffles at the throat, and a silk cravat. He was an extraordinarily attractive man, Roxanne realized. Not handsome in the strictest sense of the word, but he carried himself with an air of power and self-confidence. While her anger had kept her from noticing all that sooner, she was glad she had worn her best gown this evening, or she would have looked out of place.

Bramwell took her hand. "I'm so glad you've decided to join me," he said softly as he smiled at her. "I hope this will be much more pleasant for you than eating alone in your room."

"I'm sure it will be," Roxanne said, intending only to be polite but finding that she meant what she was saying. She looked at the two places set at the table and went on, "I'm surprised your cousin isn't joining us."

"Cyril was called back to London soon after you arrived," Bramwell replied. "He's a very busy man, you know. He has some important job in the government, although I've never been quite sure exactly what his duties are."

Roxanne could have told him. Eldridge was a spymaster, a link in the British intelligence network that spread all the way from England across the Atlantic and throughout the rebelling colonies. That was the only answer that made any sense, and it explained Eldridge's connection with Major Alistair Kane. But she said nothing, preferring not to get into a discussion with Bramwell concerning his cousin's activities.

The fact that Eldridge had been summoned to

London explained why he had not yet interrogated her. Roxanne had been expecting him to show up at any time with questions concerning the American espionage ring to which she belonged, but she would not have told him anything.

"Please, have a seat," Bramwell said, holding out a chair for her. "I'm sure you'll agree that Moira is an excellent cook."

In fact, Moira had vanished into the kitchen, but Hamish appeared a moment later, clad in butler's livery rather than the groundskeeper's outfit he had been wearing every time Roxanne had seen him from her window. She had to look twice to make sure it was the same man.

On a silver tray he balanced a bottle of wine and two crystal goblets so delicate they looked as though the slightest breeze would shatter them. He soundlessly placed the tray on the table, and Roxanne settled into her chair. Bramwell opened the bottle with a corkscrew, then poured the wine himself as Hamish retreated to the kitchen. He handed the first glass to Roxanne, then took up his own.

"To you, Miss Darragh. May this be the beginning of a rewarding friendship."

She hesitated, then clinked her glass lightly against his and smiled. This was the beginning, all right, but the beginning of what, remained to be seen.

The dinner was excellent, as he had promised, and over the next few days, Roxanne shared nearly all of her meals with Bramwell Stoddard. He was unfailingly solicitous, and she realized that his kindness, intelligence, and wit were winning her over.

Once she had gotten past some of her anger and resentment, Roxanne found herself becoming friends with Moira and Hamish MacQuarrie as well. The young married couple had been working for Bramwell for several years, Moira told Roxanne one day, and he was the best employer they had ever had.

To Roxanne's great relief, Cyril Eldridge remained away from the estate. His absence was responsible for the easing of tensions within the household, and she hoped his work would keep him in London indefinitely. Still, she was unable to forget that no matter how luxurious her surroundings, she was not free to come and go as she pleased. She was a prisoner and would remain so, whether Cyril was there or not.

One afternoon, while the wind was whipping the bare branches of the trees outside Roxanne's window and a cold drizzle was falling, Bramwell appeared at her door.

"Hello," he said, smiling. "I thought you might be rather bored today, what with this dreary weather, so I've brought you a book to read."

Roxanne reached out eagerly for the volume. Memories flooded through her when her fingers touched the smooth leather of the binding. Her father, William Darragh, had been one of Boston's leading printers, and she had known the pleasures of books since she had been a little girl.

"Thank you, Bramwell," she said sincerely.

"I believe that's the first time you've called me by my given name," he said, "although I've asked you to several times, if you recall. If I'd known that a book would please you so, I'd have brought you one sooner."

"I do appreciate it. I've missed books. . . ."

"You struck me as an educated person. But you haven't even looked to see what it is yet."

Roxanne turned the book so that she could see the gilt lettering on the spine. *"The Castle of Otranto,"* she read. She looked up at Bramwell. "By Horace Walpole? I've heard of this book, but I never had a chance to read it."

"It's rather frightening in places. I hope it doesn't upset you."

"I'm sure it won't." Roxanne smiled. "And a Gothic tale is rather appropriate for a day like this, isn't it?"

Bramwell took the book from her. "Why don't you sit down," he said, "and I'll read to you."

"That's not necessary."

"Please. I'd enjoy it."

Roxanne hesitated, then sat on the edge of the large four-poster bed while Bramwell moved to the window and settled himself in a wing chair that was turned to catch the light. He placed the book in his lap, opened it to the first page, and began to read.

His voice was deep and powerful, and he read well. At times, when the words of Horace Walpole demanded it, his tone became softer and more gentle. But there was not much of that in Walpole's tale of horror, madness, and the supernatural.

Often Roxanne found herself shivering, affected by both the story and Bramwell's reading of it. She barely noticed the passage of time, and although he had to be getting tired, his voice never flagged.

Suddenly, something must have caught his attention from the corner of his eye, because he let his voice trail off and turned his gaze toward the window beside him. A look of disappointment settled over his face.

"Blast!" he muttered.

"What is it?" asked Roxanne quickly.

"Cyril's back. I see his coach coming up the drive." He marked his place in the book, closed the thick volume, and stood up.

"I'll leave this here for you. I suppose I should go down to greet him." He sounded as disappointed as he looked.

Disappointment, however, was not the dominant emotion in Roxanne. She was filled with apprehension. To her, the return of Cyril Eldridge meant only one thing: Her ordeal was about to begin once more.

She stood up when Bramwell started toward the door, and he paused to smile at her.

"I've enjoyed this afternoon," he said quietly. "You were a fine audience."

"I enjoyed it, too," she told him.

"I'll be back another time, and we'll continue the story," promised Bramwell. He patted her tentatively on the arm, then turned and walked quickly from the room.

Roxanne, as startled by his gesture as she was depressed by the knowledge that Cyril had returned, stood very still. This was the first time Bramwell had touched her, and although it had been an innocent gesture—almost like an adult patting a well-liked child, she thought—she had the feeling it had meant more than that. Was he attracted to her?

She recalled that when Major Kane had professed his love for her, she had considered giving in to him, in order to make him think that she returned his affection. She would have allowed him to make love to her if it would have increased her chances of escaping. But if the same situation arose now with Bramwell Stoddard, what was she going to do?

Her hand softly caressed her stomach. She felt its slight roundness and knew that with each passing day, as her pregnancy advanced, it would grow more. Soon it would be obvious to anyone who looked at her that she was with child. Then the choice would be out of her

hands, since surely Bramwell would not want her once
he knew she was carrying another man's baby.

"I'm glad t' see ye're bein' nice t' Mr. Bramwell
these days," said Moira from the doorway. "'Tis a fine
man he is, and he really likes ye."

"He . . . he's been very kind to me," Roxanne
forced herself to say after being startled by the maid's
sudden appearance.

"Aye, he's kind t' just about everybody, includin'
tha' cousin o' his. Mr. Bramwell did'na have t' take
Cyril in, but he would'na hear o' doin' otherwise."
Moira shook her head sadly. "I shudder t' think o' th'
day when Hamish and meself will have t' work for tha'
man, rather than for Mr. Bramwell."

"What do you mean?" Roxanne frowned in confusion. "Work for Cyril instead of Bramwell? Why in the
world would you want to do that?"

"'Tis no' tha' we want t' work for Cyril—" Moira
fell silent suddenly and lifted a hand to her mouth as
though she thought she had said too much. As if to
confirm that, she said, "I should'na be talkin' about
this." She turned away from the door.

Roxanne hurried forward and grasped her arm.
Moira had said just enough to arouse Roxanne's curios-
ity, and now she had to know the rest.

"What are you talking about?" Roxanne demanded. "There's no reason you shouldn't keep working for Bramwell for a long time to come."

Anger flared in Moira's green eyes, and she said
harshly, "Except tha' Mr. Bramwell has'na got a long
time left!" She gasped. "Oh, Lord, now I've gone and
done it for sure!"

Roxanne's fingers slipped from Moira's arm. She
expected the housemaid to dart away, but Moira stayed
where she was, an anxious expression on her face. After

a moment, when Roxanne was able to talk again, she said, "You might as well tell me the rest of it, Moira."

"Aye, I suppose tha' be true. But ye did'na hear any o' this from me, do ye understand? I don't know what tha' devil Cyril would do t' me if he knew I'd been talkin' out o' turn."

"I'll protect your confidence," Roxanne promised.

Moira drew a deep breath. "All right. He does'na look it, but Mr. Bramwell is a sick man. A verra sick man. He has these spells, and th' doctor says one of 'em's goin' t' carry him off one o' these days. 'Tis his heart, you know."

"But he seems so . . . so robust."

"Aye, ye'd never know he was ill t' look at him. Th' last time th' doctor was here, not long before ye came, he told Mr. Bramwell he had six months, maybe a year at most. Then . . . well, then I guess we'll be workin' for Cyril, whether we want to or not. He'll be Lord Oakley then."

"Bramwell has no other relatives?"

"Not a one."

"How horrible," Roxanne murmured. "To have to spend your last days alone except for . . . for that man."

"But he's no' alone now," Moira said. "Ye're here, miss. And I've never seen Mr. Bramwell lookin' better than he has th' last few days, since ye decided to be friends with him."

A part of Roxanne was still stunned by what Moira had told her, and she asked, "Does Cyril know about this?"

"Oh, aye, he does. I reckon him knowin' tha' Mr. Bramwell does'na have long t' live is th' only thing tha' has kept an accident from happenin' around here."

"You don't mean you think Cyril would murder his cousin just to inherit his title and estate, do you?"

"There's nothin' I would put past tha' man!" Moira said with sudden savagery. "He's evil, and th' only reason Mr. Bramwell can'na see tha' is because Cyril's his blood kin. Mr. Bramwell likes t' believe th' best of everybody, he does. He's too good a man for his own well-bein', if ye ask me."

"I'm so sorry to hear all of this, Moira. I like Bramwell, I really do. He seems to be an admirable man."

"Well, like I said, ye did'na hear any of it from me—" Moira turned her head sharply when footsteps sounded on the stairs. "I'd better be goin'," she said breathlessly and hurried down the corridor.

Roxanne leaned out from the door and looked toward the stairway. The lamps downstairs cast a flickering shadow on the second-floor landing, and she could tell from its shape that Cyril Eldridge was on his way up. Quickly, she ducked into the bedroom and shut the door.

Maybe he wasn't coming to see her, she told herself. Maybe he was going to his own room to rest after the trip from London to Ilford Grange. But she knew it was a futile hope, and a moment later the footsteps halted outside the door and a loud rapping sounded on it. Eldridge opened the door and stepped inside without waiting for a reply.

"Good afternoon, Miss Darragh," he said, a scowl on his narrow face, his clothes damp from the rain. "I hope you didn't think I had forgotten about you."

"I might have," Roxanne said, "if I had given you any thought at all."

"We'll let that pass," Eldridge grunted. "I've come to see if you'd be agreeable to giving me the names of

everyone else who worked with you in that nest of traitors you left behind in the colonies."

"You know better than that," snapped Roxanne.

A faint smile creased Eldridge's features; the expression made him uglier. "Yes, Major Kane said that
you could be quite intractable. Well, he may have put
up with such stubbornness for whatever reasons, but I
assure you, I won't. You will tell me what I want to
know, Miss Darragh."

"Go to hell, *sir,*" she said caustically.

"Perhaps I shall," said Eldridge. "But if you fail to
cooperate with me, you may wish you had gone there
first, Miss Darragh." He stiffened his spine and clasped
his hands together behind his back. "I'm tired and
damp after my trip, so I'm in no mood for this now. But
I'll be back another time, and then you'd be well advised to answer my questions. Until then, Miss Darragh."

She stood silently, her own back ramrod stiff, as he
left the room and shut the door behind him. Only when
he was gone did Roxanne allow her fear to well up and
take over. She threw herself onto the bed, and while
she felt like crying in rage, no tears would come.

And neither did Bramwell Stoddard. Nor did Roxanne go downstairs for dinner. When it was time to eat,
Moira appeared with a tray for her.

"Mr. Eldridge has told me ye're not t' leave yer
room again without his permission," she said, her eyes
downcast.

"What about Bramwell?" Roxanne asked. She was
sitting in the chair by the window and staring out at the
misty twilight.

"He did'na tell me otherwise."

Roxanne felt her heart sink. Bramwell was accustomed to bending to his cousin's will, and it looked as

though that was going to continue despite the friendship that had grown up between the lord of the manor and her.

For the next two weeks, no one came to see Roxanne but Cyril Eldridge and Moira, who continued to bring her meals. During that time, 1775 came to an end and 1776 began, but there were no celebrations of Christmas or the new year's arrival.

Eldridge visited her at least once a day, spending an hour or so asking questions that Roxanne steadfastly refused to answer. First in Boston and now in England, she had to endure the questioning of Major Kane and Cyril Eldridge, and in neither case would she give the men any information they could use against the patriots.

More than once, Eldridge lost his temper, screamed at her, and threatened her with torture, but Roxanne did not waver. She also noticed that Eldridge only lost his temper whenever Bramwell was outside of the mansion and could not hear the shouted threats and abuse.

For all his anger, Cyril never touched her. Was he afraid of what might happen if Bramwell found out that he beat her? As things stood, Bramwell was easily manipulated, but that might change if he found out just how despicable his cousin really was.

But what if Bramwell's weakened heart stopped working? Then Eldridge would become Lord Oakley, and he would have a free hand on the estate. He would not have to fear any repercussions, no matter what he did.

She was going to have to tell Bramwell what was going on, Roxanne thought, while she still had the chance. But would he believe her?

One afternoon, after a particularly trying session with Eldridge, Roxanne felt sick to her stomach. Listening to Eldridge's bluster was enough to make anyone queasy, she thought, but this was more than that. Lately her morning sickness had returned, but the horrible feeling was no longer confined to mornings. It would come on her at any time and frequently last all day. She reached for the chamber pot under the bed and vomited, the violent spasms racking her whole body. She was so sick that she did not notice Moira enter the room until the Scottish girl rested her hand lightly on Roxanne's forehead.

"There, there," she said soothingly. "'Twill be all right. Everything will be fine, ye'll see."

Roxanne was ashamed for anyone to see her like this, but at the same time, Moira's presence was a comfort. Gradually, the sickness passed, and when Roxanne sat up in the bed and leaned against pillows Moira had fluffed and placed behind her, the maid wiped her face with a wet cloth.

"Thank you," Roxanne whispered. "I . . . I'm sorry to be so much trouble."

"'Tis no trouble," Moira assured her. "But I be wonderin' . . . when will th' bairn be here?"

"You . . . you know?" Roxanne blinked at her in surprise.

"How could I not ken wha' be happenin' t' ye, miss? 'Tis true I've never had a bairn o' me own, but I watched me mother carry me seven brothers and sisters."

There was no point in denying it. "It'll be another four months or so. I . . . I thought I was over being sick, but it's started again recently. That's why I haven't been eating much." She smiled wearily. "The food you bring me is wonderful. I always hate to waste it."

"Ye keep eatin' as much as ye can. 'Tis good for ye and th' babe both." Moira hesitated, then ventured, "Maybe 'tis none o' me business, but th' bairn's father? . . ."

"He's dead," Roxanne said flatly. The image of Daniel's bloody form lying on the floor of Lemuel Parsons's barn flashed through her mind before she could force it away.

"Oh. I'm sorry, miss. I did'na mean t' make ye feel worse."

Roxanne caught Moira's hand and squeezed it. "That's all right," she said. "I'm just glad you're here. I'm in need of a friend right now."

"Ye should tell Mr. Bramwell about this."

"I would, but I never see him anymore. You're the only one Eldridge allows up here."

"Well, we'll just see about tha'," Moira declared, and Roxanne felt a surge of hope. If the housemaid talked to Bramwell and told him about her pregnancy, he might intervene with Cyril.

Another thought occurred to Roxanne, and she said quickly, "You should be careful, Moira. You don't want to make an enemy of Cyril. After all, he . . . he's going to be your employer sooner or later. I'm sure he could make life miserable for you if he thought you were conspiring against him."

"I'm no' worried about Cyril Eldridge," she said, her voice full of contempt when she spoke the man's name. "When th' time comes, maybe Hamish and meself'll just up and leave Ilford Grange. I would'na want t' work for a man like tha', no matter how much he paid us." She patted Roxanne's hand. "Just ye rest a bit now. Maybe things will get better."

Roxanne wanted to believe that, but after everything that had happened to her in the past six months, it was difficult. She smiled wearily at Moira and then let her eyes slide shut. A few moments later, she heard the door open and close quietly as Moira slipped out of the room.

Roxanne drifted off to sleep, and she had no idea how much time had passed when she awoke suddenly. All she knew was that she had felt someone's weight on the bed, and then as her eyes started to open, a hand clamped down roughly on her mouth to keep her from crying out.

Her eyes opened wide, and as she stared up in the dim light of late afternoon, she saw Cyril Eldridge crouched on the bed next to her.

"I told you that you should answer my questions," he hissed. "Now you're going to pay for your stubbornness, you traitorous bitch!"

Eldridge grabbed her breast and squeezed, and his fingers dug cruelly into her soft flesh. There was nothing lustful in the attack, however; it was simply a way of inflicting pain on her so that he could force her to tell him what he wanted to know.

He pulled his hand away from her mouth, but before she could scream his palm cracked across her face in a vicious slap. "I warned you!" he snarled.

"Bramwell!" she gasped, but that was all she had time to say before he slapped her again. He laughed disdainfully.

"It won't do you any good to call Bramwell," he said. "That simpering cousin of mine is in the wine cellar, and he can't hear a thing going on up here! Besides, he knows this is none of his business. He's a nobleman, and he wouldn't dare interfere in the affairs of the Crown!"

Eldridge was putting more and more weight on her as he assaulted her, and fear for her baby welled up inside Roxanne. She balled her fist and swung it at his head, but he saw the blow coming and jerked aside so quickly that she barely grazed his temple.

"You shouldn't have done that," he growled.

His weeks of frustration had reached the boiling point, and now he was half insane with anger.

Just as he was about to jam his balled fist into Roxanne's face, a hand reached out and fingers clamped like iron around Cyril's wrist.

With a shout of surprise, Eldridge was yanked off the bed, and Roxanne gasped in relief when his weight was lifted from her. She rolled onto her side and stared in wonderment as Bramwell Stoddard lifted his cousin completely off the floor solely by his viselike grip on Cyril's wrist.

"How dare you?" Bramwell shouted furiously.

"Let me go, damn it!"

Eldridge was thrashing around violently, but Bramwell seemed to be holding him effortlessly.

"You've no right to interfere!" Eldridge cried. "This is the king's business, not yours!"

"This is my house!" thundered Bramwell. "And no guest will be assaulted in my house, especially not a woman!" He shook his cousin like an angry terrier holding a mouse. "Do you understand me, Cyril?"

Without waiting for an answer, he flung Eldridge away from him.

Eldridge crashed against the wall, hung there for a moment, then slid down into a sitting position. In a choked voice, he said, "You can't . . . you've no right . . . affairs of the Crown . . ."

"Oh, shut up, Cyril," Bramwell said disgustedly. "Just remember one thing: If you ever again lay a hand on my future bride . . . I'll kill you."

With that, he swung around to face Roxanne, a worried expression on his face.

She stared at him in shock, her emotions in a turmoil. What had he just said? Future bride? Had those been Bramwell's words?

"I . . . I don't understand," she said.

With one long stride he crossed the room to the side of her bed, where he knelt and caught one of her hands in his.

"I know this is terribly sudden," he said, "but I was on my way up here to ask you to marry me when I heard Cyril shouting. I'm sorry I didn't get here sooner, Roxanne."

"You want me to . . . marry you? But we hardly know each other—"

"That doesn't matter. I know enough about you, and I think you know enough about me."

Something in his eyes told her he meant more than the simple words he had just said, and suddenly she realized that Moira must have told him not only about the pregnancy, but also that she had revealed his medical condition to Roxanne.

Hamish came puffing into the room, clearly winded from running up the stairs in response to the commotion. Bramwell glanced over his shoulder at the groundskeeper, then jerked a thumb toward Cyril and said, "Get him out of here, please."

"Yes, sir," Hamish said breathlessly, grasping Eldridge's arm and lifting him to his feet. "Come along, Mr. Cyril. I'll fetch ye some brandy downstairs." Over Eldridge's muttered objections, Hamish led him out of the room and down the hall.

"I can speak frankly now, Roxanne," Bramwell said as he lowered himself onto the edge of the bed beside her. "But first, are you all right? Did Cyril hurt you? Do you need medical attention?"

"No, I'm all right. Say what you came to say, Bramwell."

He took a deep breath. "Very well. You know the crux of it already. I want you to marry me. You see, Moira told me about . . . about . . ."

"About the fact that I'm going to have a baby."

Bramwell nodded.

"And she told me about your illness," Roxanne went on, sensing that this was a moment for truth. "I'm so very sorry, Bramwell."

A smile tinged with sadness touched his face. "So am I, but there's no point in raging against the workings of fate. However, I want to make as much of the days I have left as I possibly can."

"Is . . . is that why you want to marry me?"

He lifted his hand and stroked her cheek, his touch feather-light. "Dear Roxanne," he murmured. "You're a lovely woman, and I have the greatest affection for you, but I'm afraid given the circumstances I . . . I wouldn't have much to offer to a normal marriage. However, I can provide a great deal for you and your child in the way of material comforts. And when I'm gone . . . well, you'd inherit the entire estate, my dear."

"What about Cyril?"

Bramwell's features hardened. "Cyril is my cousin, but that doesn't mean he's not also a despicable worm. I've suspected as much for a long time now. His behavior today was the final bit of proof I needed. I suppose I was blinded for a time by his position in the government and the fact that he's my only living relative, but I'm through fooling myself." He smiled again, and his hand cupped her chin. "Besides, if you'll agree to marry me, you'll be my closest relative, and we won't have to worry about Cyril anymore, now will we? He won't dare touch you once you're Lady Oakley."

"But . . . the baby."

"I don't care about that. Or rather I should say I care very much." A broad smile lit up his face. "I'll have an heir, and that's something I had given up on." He stood up and began to pace back and forth across the room, his enthusiasm no longer allowing him to remain still. "I've thought about the entire matter. I'm a wealthy, important man, you know. I can arrange things with the local officials so that all the dates on the marriage documents will insure that the child is legitimate. I daresay I can even come to an agreement with the local clergyman."

"You . . . you'd bribe a minister?" Roxanne laughed at his audacity.

Bramwell joined in her laughter. "Why not? I'm sure the child will grow up to be much more generous to the church than Cyril ever would be." He returned to the side of the bed and dropped on his knees so that he could take her hands again. "Well, Roxanne? What do you say? Will you do it?"

"This is awfully sudden," she said. "I like you, Bramwell, I really do, but this—"

Thoughts raced through her mind as she considered his proposal. She was genuinely fond of him, but by no stretch of the imagination was she in love with him. The only man she had ever loved was buried across the Atlantic, far beyond her mortal reach.

Besides, Bramwell had professed nothing but fondness for her, too. It was a . . . business arrangment he was suggesting, Roxanne told herself, and nothing more. She would provide him with an heir, and Cyril

Eldridge would be denied an estate that he surely did not deserve.

And if she did marry Bramwell, it would certainly throw a snag into whatever plans Cyril and Major Kane had for her. That was the final, deciding factor.

She smiled at him and said, "Yes, Bramwell. I'll marry you."

Chapter Eleven

O nce the news of what had happened on Boston Common between Elliot Markham and Avery Wallingford had made its way through the city, Avery was disgraced, and for once he could not lie, bribe, or intimidate his way out of trouble. The man he had hired to murder Elliot had revealed the whole story, and if not for the siege that was squeezing the city in a tighter and tighter grip, Avery might have been questioned by the authorities and had criminal charges brought against him. However, due to the uncertain political circumstances of the times, the matter had been allowed to drop.

But Benjamin Markham was still blustering about it several weeks later. "That young scoundrel ought to be horsewhipped, at the very least," Benjamin said one day. "He has no concept of honor, no concept at all."

Although Elliot was tired of hearing about Avery, it was good to see his father working up some emotion about something. Anytime the subject of the war, the situation in Boston, or the shipping line came up, Benjamin retreated into himself, falling silent in his chair. He often wore a dull, empty expression and was still losing weight, primarily because food no longer interested him. His once powerful body was only a shell of its former self.

There were but a few parties around town to celebrate the arrival of the new year. Once, New Year's Eve would have been one of the most gala nights of the year, but not many people were in the mood for celebrating as 1775 made way for 1776. The previous year had seen a tremendous amount of change, upheaval, and turmoil in the colonies, and most people prayed the the new year would bring peace and calm.

Elliot, for one, did not believe for a second that that would happen. The Revolution was just getting well under way; there was a long, bloody road stretching in front of them, Elliot feared.

A few days into the new year, he was looking over some documents spread out on the massive desk in his father's study. Most of the records from the offices of Markham & Cummings had been brought to the mansion on Beacon Hill because the building that had housed the business had been taken over by the British. The offices had been gutted, the walls and furnishings torn out for firewood. British troops were using the building as a barracks now, sleeping in bedrolls on bare floors.

There was no real reason for him to be poring over the business records, Elliot knew, but it kept him busy.

And someday, after the war was over, Markham &
Cummings might become a viable enterprise again. If
that ever happened, he would likely be running it, so it
wouldn't hurt him to learn as much about the business
as he could, he had decided.

A soft rapping sounded on the study door, and Elliot glanced up in surprise. His mother and father were
upstairs resting, as far as he knew, and neither one of
them would have knocked.

"What is it?" he called.

The white-haired housekeeper stuck her head in
the door. "You've got a visitor, Mr. Elliot, but I didn't
know if you'd care to—"

Elliot was about to ask who had come to see him,
but before he could voice the question the door was
pushed open and a young woman stepped past the elderly servant.

"Elliot!" Sarah Wallingford cried. "I have to see
you."

"Hello, Sarah," Elliot said, his eyes wide with surprise.

"Please," she said, approaching the desk. "It's very
important that I talk to you." She inclined her head
toward the housekeeper, who was still standing in the
open doorway. "A word in private. I beg of you, Elliot."

He stood up and told her gruffly, "Begging isn't
necessary." For a second, he debated the wisdom of allowing himself to be alone with her, then nodded to the
housekeeper and added, "That will be all, Rose."

"Yes, sir," the servant muttered, reluctantly back-
ing out of the room and closing the door. Elliot noticed
that she did not shut it completely, however, leaving a
gap of an inch or two, so he came around the desk,
strode across the room, and sharply pushed the door
shut. He chuckled as he imagined the housekeeper in

the corridor outside, walking away and mumbling in frustration that her plans to eavesdrop had been spoiled.

"What can I do for you, *Mrs. Wallingford?*"

Sarah stiffened, and he thought for a moment that she was going to slap him. But then her tension eased slightly.

"I'd rather you didn't call me that, Elliot. You don't need to remind me what a horrible mistake I've made."

She looked so miserable that he wanted to reach out and touch her, but he knew better than that. Instead he asked, "Has Avery been mistreating you?"

"Not . . . physically," she replied after a momentary hesitation. "But I've been subjected to all sorts of humiliation since that . . . that duel he staged with you."

"That was no duel. That was an attempt to murder me, nothing more or less."

"I know. And so does everyone else in Boston, everyone who matters, at any rate." Her fingers tightened on the knitted reticule she clutched in her hand, and her voice trembled as she went on, "We've been shunned, Elliot. No one visits us, and no one invites us to their parties."

"There aren't many parties in Boston these days anyway," Elliot pointed out.

"Perhaps not, but the ones that are held go on without us. I . . . I feel so embarrassed."

"I'm sorry," Elliot said dryly. "Maybe I should have let Avery's man kill me, so that you would've been spared all this embarrassment."

She looked up, her blue eyes flaring with anger. "You bastard!" she hissed. "You know what I mean.

There's no need to add to my humiliation with your sarcasm."

Elliot shrugged but said nothing.

Sarah stalked across the study toward the window, her long blue skirt swirling around her legs. Her hair was pinned up in its usual elaborate arrangement of curls, and a feathered hat that matched the shade of her jacket and skirt was perched on her head. She looked as lovely as he had ever seen her, Elliot thought, even as angry as she was.

God, if only things had worked out differently! If only, Elliot thought. *Perhaps the two most useless words in the English language.*

He rested a hip on the corner of the desk. As he crossed his arms on his chest, he asked, "Just what is it you want of me, Sarah?"

"I want you to *do* something—"

"What?" he cut in. "You made your decision, all those months ago when you broke off our engagement and turned to Avery for comfort. Now you're unhappy and you're coming back to me. But there's nothing I can do, Sarah. Do you understand? Nothing! You have to live with the decision you made."

She faced him squarely, moving so that she was only a couple of feet from him. He could see the moisture shining in her eyes, the faint quiver of her bottom lip as she said, "You could tell me you're sorry."

"I am," he whispered. "More than you'll ever know."

"You could hold me. You could make me feel for a moment that I'm not . . . not worthless."

"I can't do that, and you know it. It's over between us, Sarah. It has been for a long time."

Her tongue wet her lips. "It doesn't have to be." She was leaning close to him, and he could smell the sweetness of her breath when she spoke. His heart was hammering in his chest.

"Damn it, no!" he exclaimed, jerking away from her and moving around the desk to put the massive piece of furniture between them. This was ludicrous! Questions of morality had seldom bothered him in the past, especially where attractive women were concerned, and it was not as though he had never bedded married women. There had been several such occasions, in fact. Why was he worried about right and wrong now, when Sarah was so blatantly offering herself to him? And wouldn't it serve Avery Wallingford right for Elliot to sample the charms of his wife? Hell, Elliot thought, Avery had tried to have him killed! It would be only just for Elliot to enjoy the fine soft flesh that Sarah wanted to give him.

She followed him around the desk, and he did not move away this time.

"Elliot? . . ." she said softly, her voice little more than a whisper.

"Shut up," he said, his hands involuntarily closing on her shoulders. "Just don't say anything." And then he pulled her roughly against him, and his mouth came down hungrily on hers.

Sarah melted into his embrace; her body surged forward. His arms went around her and tightened as her lips opened eagerly under his questing tongue. He tasted the sweetness of her mouth, drinking deeply of the sensation. She was all soft, wet heat, and he groaned as he felt his response. She felt it, too, pressing urgently into the softness of her belly, and a moan of passion came welling up from somewhere inside her.

In the recesses of Elliot's brain, he wished something would happen to interrupt this. If his mother or father were to come into the room, he could push Sarah away and force her to leave. But if this kiss continued much longer, he would be utterly lost, unable to turn back from the course on which he had embarked.

He could lock the door, he thought wildly, and shove all the useless business records off the desk. That would be suitably sordid, to take her right where his father had spent so many long hours working over the years.

Sarah reached behind her, caught one of his hands, and pressed his fingers to her breast. He squeezed, feeling the nipple hardening against his palm through the fabric of her dress.

"Oh, yes, Elliot, yes! Hold me, just hold me."

They were two lonely people, he told himself. Not saints, not sinners, just human beings caught up in a world that was far beyond their control. There was nothing wrong with them turning to each other for a few brief moments of comfort—*just as he and Roxanne had done, all those months ago.*

The memory shot through Elliot like a physical shock. Those were the exact thoughts that had gone through his head when he and Roxanne Darragh had yielded to their loneliness and misguided passion. That decision had haunted him for months, torturing him with the knowledge that they had made an awful mistake. It had almost ruined the friendship and genuine affection he and Roxanne felt for each other, and he still lived with the worry that someday Daniel would find out what had happened. Roxanne was gone, perhaps for all time, but Elliot did not want Daniel's memory of her sullied.

On the other hand he cared nothing at all for Avery Wallingford, but still Elliot's instincts cried out to him that this was as wrong as what had happened with Roxanne. Somehow he found the strength to push

Sarah away. He had to stop touching her, had to put some distance between them, or he would never be able to think straight.

"I can't do this, Sarah," he said as he stepped back, his voice sounding as wretched as he felt. "You had better leave."

"Elliot!" Disbelief was etched on her lovely face. "You can't mean it, you just can't—"

"I do mean it," he told her. "This won't make things better between you and Avery. It'll just make the whole bloody situation worse, and I won't be a party to that. Go home—" His voice was as cold as he could possibly make it. "Go home and stay with your husband."

Sarah's features flushed with rage. "You . . . you devil!"

Slowly, sadly, Elliot shook his head. "Would that I were. That would make things simpler for all of us, wouldn't it?"

"Oh!" She turned and stalked to the door, still trembling with anger. Slamming the door open, she stalked out of the study.

"I think you can show yourself out," Elliot said to the empty room.

A moment later, the front door crashed shut, and he winced a little at the sound. His parents would probably come downstairs now and want to know what was going on, but he couldn't very well tell them the truth, he decided.

But neither Benjamin nor Polly Markham put in an appearance. Elliot drew a deep, ragged breath and sat down behind the desk. That had been close, he thought, too damned close.

And Sarah Wallingford was trouble. No doubt about it.

*   *   *

She was much on his mind for the next few days, and he was tortured by moments when he thought he should have given in to the temptation she had offered. Surely, after all he had gone through, he deserved some pleasure in life. But despite the way he felt about Avery Wallingford, he hoped Avery and Sarah could work out their troubles.

There were other things to worry about besides Sarah's restless nature and troubled marriage. There was also the matter of getting enough food to eat, and a week after Sarah's visit to the Markham house, Elliot walked down Beacon Hill and along Common Street to one of the few bakeries that was still operating. Even though it was quite early, not long after dawn, there was already a line nearly a block long of people waiting to buy their daily ration of bread.

Elliot took his place at the end of the line. Not that long ago, it would have been almost beyond comprehension that a Markham would have to stand in line for food like any common man. The servants had taken care of things like that. Now, all the servants, with the exception of the elderly housekeeper who was serving double duty as the cook, had been let go. The family would have run out of cash before now if that step had not been taken. As it was, funds were running low. Benjamin was still a wealthy man, it was true, but owning ships in the harbor did not mean there was enough money in Elliot's pockets to buy bread.

While he leaned against the wall of an abandoned building three doors from the bakery, Elliot looked at the people around him. Some wore threadbare clothes and clearly had not had enough money for anything better for a long time. Others sported finery that had been expensive when new but was now starting to show its age, like his own. War and hardship, he mused, made everyone the same—miserable.

Suddenly he felt a tug on the sleeve of his coat and looked over to see an elderly man standing there. The old-timer had several clumps of white whiskers jutting from his chin and jaws, but the hair didn't form an actual beard. The trembling hand he lifted toward Elliot was covered with liver spots, and his clothes were as ragged as any in the crowd; his faded brown tricorn was covered with stains.

"I'm sorry," Elliot said curtly to the old man, "but I've nothing for you, and if you want to get ahead of me in line, I'm afraid you can't. You'll have to go to the rear like everyone else."

"Don't want to cut in line, sonny," the man said in a raspy voice. "And I got somethin' for *you,* not the other way around." His gnarled, grimy fingers held a piece of paper that had been folded several times.

Elliot frowned. "Is that a message of some sort?" he asked.

"Naw, it's the bleedin' Magna Carta," the old man said with a glare. "O' course it's a message. Now, are you goin' to take it or not?"

"How do I know it's for me?"

"You was pointed out to me. Your name's Elliot, ain't it? Now take the paper, so's I can earn me money."

"Are you saying someone paid you to give this to me?"

"Smart as a whip, ain't you?"

Annoyed by the old man's tone, Elliot snatched the paper away from him. "Well, if you've already been paid, don't expect a coin from me for doing your job," he said.

"Wouldn't hurt a gent like you to be a little generous to a fella who's down on his luck," said the old man, his voice an insincere whine.

"This whole city is down on its luck," Elliot snapped. "Now go on. Tell whoever gave this to you that you delivered it."

"Aye, I'll do that. Maybe that gent'll find it in his heart to be a little kinder to one who's less fortunate."

Elliot grunted and turned his attention to the note, which he unfolded and read as soon as the old man shuffled away. As he read, he felt his pulse quicken.

At first glance, the words were nothing but gibberish, but Elliot understood the coded message that he was to go to the Green Gryphon, a local tavern he often visited, as soon as possible. There was no signature.

Elliot's frown deepened as he considered the message. No one would have known that he could decipher this particular code other than someone who had used it to communicate with him before. That meant the message had to have come from either Benjamin Tallmadge or Robert Townsend, the two young men who had organized the espionage ring to which he belonged. Tallmadge and Townsend had been classmates of Daniel Reed's at Yale, and it was through him that they had recruited both Elliot and Roxanne to their service. Now Roxanne was gone, and Elliot had not heard from Tallmadge and Townsend for quite some time, not since the affair with the Liberty Legion, in fact.

Well, they might want to see him, but he wasn't going to give up his place in line. Espionage could wait until he had bought bread for his family.

Knowing that he had an appointment to keep made the time pass even more slowly as he waited in line, and when he finally reached the bakery his frustration had grown to the point where it felt as if every nerve and sinew in his body was stretched taut. He bought a loaf of bread from the baker, who then sold the final loaf of the day to the man behind Elliot in line. Elliot heard the commotion begin as the baker announced that the bread was gone, and he broke into a run, wanting to get away from there before someone in the disappointed mob got the idea of jumping him and stealing his bread.

Lord, to think that things had come to this in Boston!

Elliot made his way to the Green Gryphon, clutching his loaf of bread wrapped in brown paper. Despite the fact that it was still quite early, there already were men drinking in the tavern when he entered the building. One type of business had prospered during these hard times, and that was any place that offered a man a chance to forget his troubles, even temporarily. Many of the dramshops had customers at all hours of the day and night.

With a nod of greeting to the man behind the bar, Elliot sat in one of the dark wooden booths at the rear of the room. A moment later, a familiar, sleepy-eyed serving girl in a low-cut dress brought him a mug of ale, and Elliot glanced appreciatively at the inviting cleavage displayed at the neckline. But he put all inviting thoughts out of his mind when he noticed the girl yawn. She wanted a bed, all right, but only for sleeping.

"You'd best go home and get some rest, Faye," Elliot told her. "You look exhausted."

"'Twas a long night," the girl agreed. "And you're in here mighty early, Mr. Markham."

"These days it's never too early for a good stiff drink." He lifted the mug to his lips and swallowed gratefully. His narrow escape from the bakery had left him unnerved.

Faye returned to the bar, and Elliot placed the bread on the table and then proceeded to nurse the ale for ten minutes. He wondered how long it would be before someone showed up to meet him. Whoever had sent the message probably had someone watching the tavern, waiting for his arrival. Each time the door opened, Elliot looked up, but he recognized no one, and no one approached him.

An uneasy feeling was growing in him. Had the message been some sort of ruse or trap? Surely not, but where was the person who wanted to meet with him? His thoughts were so preoccupied that the girl beside the table had to ask her question twice before he looked up with a start.

"What was that you said, Faye?" he asked with a sheepish grin. "I'm afraid my mind was elsewhere."

"And a far piece away at that," Faye said tartly. She was no longer carrying a serving tray, and she had wrapped a heavy shawl around her shoulders. "I asked if you'd mind if I sat down for a minute or two before I left, Mr. Markham. I'm mighty tired, and I've got a long walk home."

"Of course," he replied, somewhat puzzled by the request. If Faye wanted to rest her feet before heading home, there were plenty of other places in the tavern besides Elliot's booth. Maybe she just wanted a little company, he thought. Perhaps she was attracted to him. He had never dallied with her in the past, although it was an appealing prospect. She was attractive enough, with short blond hair and a scattering of freckles across her intriguingly tilted nose.

She ran her fingers through her hair for a moment and then said, "You're a real gentleman, Mr. Markham. I appreciate this." She leaned toward him across the table and went on, "And a couple of gents named Tallmadge and Townsend said to tell you hello. Now laugh like I just said something a bit naughty."

The experience Elliot had gained as a secret agent kept the shock from showing on his face. He laughed rather raucously, as she had instructed him, then said quietly, "You, Faye? I never would have suspected—"

"Good," she cut in. "Because you were never meant to. Besides, I ain't much. I run an errand every now and then, deliver a message, pass one along, things like that. Just like I've got a message for you this morning."

"I'm anxious to hear it."

She put her head even closer to his, and to anyone watching what was going on in the booth, it would have appeared that one of them was trying to seduce the other.

"It's about a woman," Faye said, "a redheaded woman. I don't know her, but I'm told you do."

Roxanne! Elliot's heart thudded heavily in his chest. She had to be talking about Roxanne. Tallmadge and Townsend had promised to find out anything they could about what the British had done with Roxanne after the redcoats had taken her prisoner during the raid on the Parsons farm.

"Go on," Elliot said hoarsely.

"This redheaded woman's gone on a long trip, all the way across the sea," Faye continued. "Somebody saw her being put on a ship that was flying the Union Jack. It was a couple of months ago, on a dark, foggy night, but nobody noticed a fisherman just outside the head of a cove where the warship sent in a small boat."

"England," breathed Elliot. "They've taken her to England."

Faye laughed merrily, a wide, false smile on her pretty face. "That's right. And that's all I know, Mr. Markham." She reached out, caught his hand in both of hers, and squeezed. "I'll be seeing you." Then with a saucy flip of her hips, she slipped out of the booth and headed for the door.

Elliot leaned back and watched her go, a silly grin on his face. It was part of the pose he was trying to maintain. As attractive as it might be, he had no real interest at the moment in Faye's backside. Instead he was thinking about Roxanne being put on a British ship in the dead of night.

She was still alive . . . she had to be! If the British had wanted her dead, they would have hanged her or put her in front of a firing squad while she was still in Boston.

Elliot considered that for a few seconds, then shook his head. Not likely at all, he decided. This was the Tories' war, and there was widespread opposition to it in England from the Whigs and others who believed it was a mistake. Executing a young, attractive woman would only increase that opposition, Elliot thought.

He knew he had to cross the Charles River to Cambridge as soon as possible to try to locate Daniel somewhere around the American military headquarters. It would be a dangerous trip and full of risks. But every time Elliot left Boston it was dangerous, and news such as he had just received made the risk worthwhile.

Elliot drained his mug of ale, dropped a coin on the table to pay for it, and picked up his loaf of bread. His step was jaunty as he left the tavern, and anyone who noticed the change in him would attribute it to his flirting with Faye, he thought. No one else needed to know what he had just discovered. It was news for Daniel alone: *Roxanne was alive!*

Chapter Twelve

If Henry Knox had not passed around a bottle of brandy so that the men could have a short drink in celebration, Daniel might not have known that the new year had come. 1776 began the way 1775 had ended: cold, gloomy, muddy, and filled with hard work.

There had been no more sabotage, and Daniel Reed had been watching closely as Henry had requested after the incident at the frozen creek. But deliberate or not, there had been more trouble. The group had attempted to cross the Hudson River at Lansing's Ferry, and the ice had given way completely, causing one of the sledges to sink. The disaster was an accident, due not to sabotage but to an unfortunate warming trend that had weakened the ice. Luckily, the river was fairly shallow where the sledge had broken through, and the men were able to retrieve the cannon. Unable to cross the Hudson, the group had backtracked and crossed the Mohawk instead, at a place called Klaus's Ferry. One cannon was lost there, when the ice broke yet again, but once more the accident had been due to the weather.

"Drat the luck!" Henry Knox exclaimed as he glared at the spot where the cannon had sunk in water too deep to recover it. "This weather is just cold enough to be miserable and not cold enough to allow us to proceed properly."

"I don't think the weather's going to bend to your will, Henry," Daniel told him with a tired grin. "No matter how much you complain about it."

"You're right, of course," Henry said, slapping the young man on the back. "We just have to make the best of the situation. We'll stay here on the west side of the Hudson until we reach Albany. Surely we can get across there."

But by the time the caravan reached Albany on January seventh of the new year, the weather had warmed even further. "A cruel thaw," Henry called it in a letter to Washington he sent on ahead with a rider. They had no choice but to wait until a new freeze strengthened the ice on the Hudson.

Henry Knox chafed at the delay. Daniel and William Knox watched the big man pace up and down the riverbank during the next few days, but the men welcomed the enforced rest after the rugged trip from Fort Ticonderoga.

Finally, on a crystal-clear, windless dawn, the temperature plunged, and Henry, Daniel, and William were

out on the ice, testing its thickness. Henry deemed it
strong enough for the sledges to cross, and Daniel and
William hurried to get the men and the oxen ready to
travel, while Henry waited impatiently at the river.

Should they be needed, there were extra men on
hand provided by General Schuyler from Albany's military garrison, but the crossing went off without incident.
One at a time the sledges negotiated the broad river,
and by midafternoon the entire long line of transports
was on the eastern side of the Hudson.

They would tarry here the rest of the day, Henry
ordered, then get a fresh start in the morning.

Unbelievably, the worst part of the journey was
still to come. For the next few days, the caravan was
plagued by broken equipment, muddy roads, and sudden storms that dumped several inches of snow on the
travelers. Unfortunately, the weather was still rather
warm, and the snow melted quickly and added to the
quagmire through which the sledges were being pulled
and shoved, often only inches at a time.

And ahead of them were the mountains.

The military trail leading east over the Berkshires,
through Great Barrington, Otis, and Springfield, was
long, winding, and steep. It was also the quickest route
to eastern Massachusetts, Daniel knew. But the next
few days, while the caravan crossed the mountains,
would be fraught with more danger than they had already faced, and the saboteur, whoever he was, would
have some excellent opportunities to strike.

Other than the military advantage the patriots
would gain if the cannon were successfully delivered to
General Washington, the best thing about the trip as far
as Daniel was concerned was his growing friendship
with Penn Sloane. The rugged mountaineer usually
tramped alongside the same sledge as Daniel, and they

had long conversations during the cold, dank days. Daniel talked about growing up in Virginia's rugged Piedmont region, and Penn told him about life in the New Hampshire Grants. Penn had plenty of stories about the clashes between Ethan Allen's Green Mountain Boys and the colonists from New York who also claimed the Grants. The conflict had almost turned into a small-scale war between the two colonies, but to Penn it had all been a grand adventure.

"What are you going to do once the war's over?" Daniel asked him one day as they wrestled with the oxen in an attempt to keep the sledge moving over the slushy crust of ice on the road.

"You're assuming I'm going to live through it," Penn said with a smile.

"No point in assuming otherwise, is there?" asked Daniel.

"I reckon not. And to answer your question, I've given that some thought. I'm going to do like that friend of yours you told me about, that fellow Buchanan. I'm going west."

"Really? I figured you'd go back to the Green Mountains."

"Maybe for a visit, but not to stay. Nope, the future of this land lies in the west, Daniel. Once we've won our independence from England, folks are going to be looking to grow. And there's only one direction for that—west."

"What about the French and the Spaniards? I've heard that they're already out there on the frontier."

"Might be some trouble with them, all right," Penn said. "But that won't stop Americans. Never has, never will. You mark my words, Daniel. Destiny only travels in one direction."

"You're doing some assuming now. There's no guarantee we'll become an independent nation."

"After all that's happened, would you be satisfied with anything less?"

Daniel only had to think about that question for a moment before shaking his head. "No, I wouldn't."

"There are plenty of people who feel the same way. The day's long past when we could have worked out some sort of peace with England. Now we either win—or lose. And I don't intend to lose."

Daniel grinned. "You like to be on the winning side, eh?"

"Always," Penn answered.

The group pushed on slowly, following the winding trail through mountain valleys and over high passes. Tall, forbidding evergreen forests closed in on both sides of the narrow road, increasing the gloom. This was some of the most ominous territory Daniel had ever seen, and it did not take much imagination to think that the entire British army could have been lurking in the woods, and the men on the road would not even know it.

Finally, there was only one major peak left to be negotiated, but it was the most hazardous of all. Glasgow Mountain was steep and rugged, and there was no pass to lead them around it. Getting up the mountain would be difficult, but getting down the other side would be a real challenge.

The slope was steep enough so that the sledges had to be belayed down it by means of ropes looped around trees. The oxen were unhitched from the sledges and led down the mountain first; then one by one the heavily laden vehicles were lowered. Gravity did all the work, and it took teams of several men on each rope to keep the sledges from plunging out of control down the slope.

Daniel spent the day moving up and down the mountain, making sure everything was proceeding smoothly. Henry was at the bottom to see that each sledge was hitched up again to its team of oxen once it was safely off the mountain. William was up at the crest of the slope, supervising the belaying operation.

Daniel was moving through a large clearing several hundred yards wide and heading toward the top of the mountain when he saw one of the sledges coming toward him. Two ropes stretched out taut behind it and disappeared into the woods on the upper side of the clearing. Up there, out of sight in the trees, were the men holding the belaying ropes, slowly letting off the tension and allowing the sledge to creep down the slope. One man walked beside the sledge to monitor its progress, and when he spotted Daniel, he lifted a hand in a wave of greeting. Daniel recognized the tall, buck-skin-clad figure of Penn Sloane.

Suddenly Daniel thought he heard a gunshot, and the big sledge jerked. An instant later, another sharp pop sounded, and the sledge lurched again. But this time it slid forward, and as Penn yelled out a warning, the sledge began to pick up speed and plummet through the clearing—straight at Daniel.

There was something hideously fascinating about watching the out-of-control sledge race toward him. It crossed the clearing faster than Daniel dreamed it could travel, throwing up spumes of snow from its runners like a ship cutting wakes through deep water. Vaguely he heard Penn shouting in alarm, but his full attention was focused on the sledge.

It veered back and forth slightly, changing course to follow the easiest path down the mountain. If Daniel tried to run to one side or the other, he might avoid the sledge or dart directly into its path. Although panic hammered wildly in his head, he forced his feet to stay rooted to the ground. He had to wait until the last possible instant to leap aside, he realized.

The runaway sledge loomed in front of him like a stampeding beast, and suddenly Daniel threw himself to his right, landed heavily on his shoulder, and rolled frantically over the hard, snowy ground. The sledge rocketed past him with a whooshing sound, and as Daniel lay on the ground trying to catch his breath, he heard a loud crashing noise behind him. The sledge had reached the trees on the far side of the clearing.

Running footsteps pounded up beside him, and Penn Sloane grabbed his arm and hauled him to his feet.

"Are you all right?" Penn demanded anxiously.

"I'm fine," Daniel said slowly.

"I thought you were never going to get out of its way! Good Lord, Daniel—"

"I'm all right, Penn," Daniel cut in. "No harm done, at least not to me." He turned and looked down the slope. The sledge had come to a grinding halt in the trees, but only after leaving jagged stumps behind. Had the sledge hit him head-on, Daniel thought, it would have left even less than that.

"What happened?" Daniel asked, turning to Penn.

"One of the belaying ropes broke," he replied. "I didn't see it, but I heard it happen. Then when the full weight of the sledge hit the other rope, it gave way, too. I saw both broken ropes trailing behind it as it was sailing down the hill."

Daniel had heard the noises, too, and figured they were the sound of breaking ropes. "Head back up the mountain," he told Penn. "Tell the men that two belaying ropes on each sledge aren't enough. I want four on each one. We can't risk this happening again. And send some men down to help me retrieve that sledge from the trees. Maybe it's not damaged too much."

"Right," Penn said. He turned and loped up the mountainside.

Daniel went the other way, into the forest on the lower side of the clearing. He made his way through the brushy debris left by the runaway sledge and after a moment reached the massive vehicle itself. A quick inspection told him that one of the runners was badly cracked, but the cannon it carried could be unloaded and the sledge turned over and repaired. This accident would cost them some time, but abandoning the sledge would slow them down even more.

Daniel walked to the rear of the vehicle, picked up one of the trailing ropes, and found it to be badly frayed on the end. Then he picked up the other rope to examine it. A coldness that had nothing to do with the weather prickled along his spine.

There was no doubt that the end of the rope in his hand was also frayed. It had snapped under the weight of the sledge, but not every strand of the rope looked the same. Some of the ends of the strands were smooth . . . as if they had been cut.

The saboteur had struck again. Daniel was sure of it. Like the ice on the frozen creek, the rope had been weakened so that it would give way under the strain of holding a sledge. Only this time the British agent, whoever he was, had not gone to great pains to conceal his handiwork. The man must have figured that no one would examine the broken ropes as closely as Daniel was now doing. Or perhaps it had gotten to the point where the man no longer cared. The important question now was—who had done this? Who was trying to stop them from reaching Washington with these guns?

Daniel's jaw tightened. Penn Sloane had been alone beside this sledge, walking down with it while the other men handled the belaying ropes in the woods up above. It would have been a simple task for Penn to slip the hunting knife he always carried out of its sheath and take a few slashes at the rope. That was all that would have been required to weaken it sufficiently.

And Penn had said that he always tried to wind up on the winning side of any fight. Maybe he had decided that in this case that was going to be the British, regardless of what he said about supporting the patriot cause.

Daniel didn't want to believe that. Penn had become a good friend in the short time Daniel had known him. Yet he had to admit he did not know him well enough to say for sure what the man was capable of. Even though it pained him, he had to accept the possibility that Penn might have been behind the two incidents of sabotage . . . both of which had come perilously close to taking Daniel's life.

There were still a lot of miles to cover before the big guns were safely in Washington's hands. And until then, Daniel vowed, he was going to keep an eye on Penn Sloane every step of the way.

Deep winter had come to the Ohio River valley, and each time the cutting wind howled outside and the cold rain fell, Quincy Reed was grateful for the snug cabin he shared with Mariel and her little brother, Dietrich. When he sat in front of the fireplace with his arm around his wife and watched the dancing flames, he knew he was a lucky man. And he owed much of that good fortune to Ulysses Gilworth, who had proven to be a steadfast friend. Along with Murdoch, Ulysses had

taught the newcomers about the land, pointing out its
beauties as well as its dangers.

And Ulysses was becoming more than a friend to
Cordelia Faulkner. He regularly visited the cabin
shared by Cordelia and her father. Murdoch kept them
well supplied with meat from his hunts, but Ulysses frequently brought flour or salt or sugar, sharing what he
had been paid in barter for his services as a blacksmith.
At first Cordelia had insisted that he should not be giving them such things, but her reluctance to accept them
wore down quickly under his persistence. Quincy had
thought more than once that before the next summer
was over, there would likely be a wedding to celebrate.

Two months into the new year, unseasonably warm
weather arrived, and the settlers took advantage of the
opportunity to do outside chores that had been post-
poned during the cold, icy days. Seeing the blue sky and
warm sunshine, Quincy had climbed onto the roof of
the cabin to chink some small holes where rain had
been dripping through. Cordelia and Mariel had gotten
together to wash clothes in big pots of water that had
been filled with buckets carried from the creek by Murdoch and Gresham Howard. The pots were hung over
the fires and the young women were talking about using
the hot water for baths once the clothes washing was
done.

"A bath . . . in th' middle o' winter?" Murdoch
had asked dubiously, shaking his head. "'Tis no' natural, if ye ask me."

"No one did," Cordelia said with a laugh as she
put more clothes to soak in one of the pots. "But the
rest of us might like to be clean for a change."

"Ye want t' be careful about such things as tha',"
Murdoch advised. "Too much bathing is bad for a man's

health. Robs him of all his natural protection from th' elements."

"We will see about that," Mariel told him. "And don't you run off, either, Dietrich. You'll be getting a bath just like the rest of us. We may even let you go first."

Up on the roof, Quincy grinned as he listened to the exchange. The idea of taking a bath in the middle of winter seemed as odd to him as it did to Murdoch. But the thought of sinking down into a tub of hot water with a willing companion—his lovely young wife, say—well, that didn't seem to be such a bad notion. No, sir, not a bad notion at all.

The sound of hoofbeats made him look up, and he was not surprised to see Ulysses Gilworth approaching along the creek. It had been several days since he had visited them, and the burly blacksmith seldom let even a week go by without coming to see Cordelia.

"Mornin', folks," Ulysses said as he reined in his horse and swung down from the saddle.

"Hello, Ulysses," Quincy called down from the roof. "What brings you out here?" As if he didn't know already, he added silently.

"Just thought I'd see how you were all doin'." Ulysses tugged off his shapeless felt hat and nodded to Cordelia. "Mornin', ma'am. If I may say so, you're lookin' as pretty as the first flowers of spring."

"The first flowers of spring are still a considerable time off, Mr. Gilworth," Cordelia replied as she pushed back a lock of blond hair that had fallen over her face while she was working. "But thank you for the compliment, whether it's true or not."

"Oh, it's true, Miss Cordelia," insisted Ulysses.

Looking down from his perch on the roof, Quincy thought that Ulysses was right. Cordelia's face was flushed from the work she had been doing, and her hair was a bit disheveled, but she was indeed beautiful.

Murdoch had been sitting in a chair leaned back against the wall of the Reed cabin, whittling on a length of wood in his big, knobby fingers, and Dietrich had been watching him intently, waiting to see what shape would emerge from the wood under Murdoch's deft touch. Now he handed the boy the whistle he had just carved and stood up to shake hands with Ulysses.

"Good t' see ye again," the big Scotsman said. "I was out hunting th' last couple o' times ye stopped by."

"I know," Ulysses replied, meeting the force of Murdoch's grip with equal strength. They made quite a matched pair, Quincy thought.

"Been meaning t' talk t' ye about something," Murdoch went on. He looked up at the roof and added, "Quincy, come on down from there. I want ye and Mr. Howard in on this, too."

Puzzled by what might be on Murdoch's mind, Quincy climbed down the ladder he had lashed together out of saplings and branches. By the time he joined Murdoch and Ulysses on the ground, Murdoch had motioned Gresham Howard over, and the four men strolled toward the barn in order to speak in private.

"I been thinking," Murdoch said, in a quiet voice, "tha' it might be a good idea t' put up a stockade 'round th' cabins and th' barn before spring gets here. I was talking to a fella named George Rogers Clark a while back, and he thinks th' Indians are going t' be raiding more this year than ever before."

"I've met Clark," said Ulysses, "and I reckon he knows more about the Indians around here than anybody else. I'd believe just about anything he says about them. And I was thinkin' myself that maybe a stockade wouldn't be a bad idea."

Gresham Howard nodded slowly. "I'd feel better if we had a little more protection. It's a ways to Wheeling, and we're pretty exposed out here."

"There's a good-sized bunch of Shawnees down-river a ways, just past where th' Muskingum joins th' Ohio," Murdoch said. "Leastways tha' be th' rumor. I'd be almighty surprised if they did'na start raiding as soon as th' weather gets better and stays tha' way."

"I'll bring some men out in a day or two, and we can get started on the stockade," offered Ulysses. "In the meantime, you folks could start fellin' some more trees. We'll need plenty of logs for the fence."

"We'll do that," Howard agreed. He looked over at Quincy. "What about you, lad? Don't you have anything to say about this?"

"I wouldn't even pretend to know as much about the frontier as Murdoch or Ulysses," Quincy replied. "If they think a stockade is a good idea, then it's fine with me." He looked around at the other men. "But shouldn't we tell Mariel and Cordelia about this?"

"I did'na want t' worry 'em," Murdoch said, and Ulysses grunted agreement. "Tha' be why I wanted t' speak t' ye in private."

"Well, they live out here, too," Quincy said, a note of stubbornness entering his voice, "and I think they have a right to know what we're talking about."

"You're right, lad," Ulysses said. "Come along, and we'll tell them."

Mariel and Cordelia agreed with the notion of building a stockade, and neither seemed overly disturbed by the idea, but Quincy thought he saw a little unease in his wife's eyes when Murdoch mentioned the possibility that the Indians might be a problem when spring arrived. After what Mariel had gone through in New York and on the journey out here, Quincy couldn't blame her for being nervous when the subject of Indian attacks arose. She had already lived through enough trouble to last any woman a lifetime.

Ulysses accepted Cordelia's invitation to stay for the midday meal, and after everyone had eaten, Quincy climbed back onto the roof to finish the job of patching holes. Keeping the rain out of the cabin was a never-ending job, and he knew he could chink every hole, but the next bad storm would create more of them. Still, all a man could do was try to keep ahead of trouble as much as possible.

Dietrich got the first bath, and although Quincy could not see what was going on, he could hear the little boy's howls of protest as Mariel stripped him, dumped him in a washtub of warm water, and began scrubbing. Cordelia pitched in to help, and from the laughter he heard, Quincy figured the two young women were getting just about as wet as Dietrich. Murdoch, Ulysses, and Howard appeared to be enjoying the spectacle.

The bucket of mud Quincy was using to chink the holes sat on the roof next to him, balanced carefully on the slope so that it wouldn't overturn or fall off. He got a handful of mud and worked it into tiny cracks between the logs.

Suddenly something brushed past the back of his neck, and there was a thudding sound beside him. He looked around to see an arrow protruding from the roof and knew that it had almost hit him before embedding itself in the wood.

"Indians!" he howled and let himself roll toward the edge of the roof, knocking over the bucket of mud with his leg as he did so. When he reached the edge, his hands shot out and grasped the rough surface of the last log. His feet and legs swung out and down, and he

caught his weight with his hands and arms just enough
to slow his fall before letting go and dropping to the
ground.

He landed with a jolt that shivered through him,
but he stayed on his feet and recovered his balance in a
matter of seconds. His rifle was leaning against the wall
of the house, and he snatched it up. More arrows
whipped through the air around him and hit the cabin.

A few feet away, he saw Mariel and Cordelia duck
through the door, a naked and struggling Dietrich
tucked under Mariel's arm. Murdoch and Ulysses had
each dropped to one knee behind the big iron pots in
which the women had washed the clothes.

Murdoch's long rifle and Ulysses' musket blasted
at the same instant, creating a tremendous roar and
sending a cloud of grayish smoke into the air as they
fired at the Indians charging from the trees at the edge
of the clearing.

"Get inside, lad!" Gresham Howard called to
Quincy. Howard was standing near the doorway, covering the retreat of the women. He held his rifle ready but
had not fired yet. Suddenly he grunted in pain and staggered back against the wall of the cabin. An arrow pro-
truded from his coat, high on the left shoulder.

"Mr. Howard!" Quincy cried, leaping toward the
older man.

"That arrow's got me pinned!" Howard said, his
face pale. "Give me a hand."

As Quincy went to help Howard, Murdoch handed
his empty rifle to Ulysses and pulled a brace of pistols
from behind his belt. The range was a little far for pistols, but the awe-inspiring sight of the huge frontiersman stepping out from cover and blazing away at his
foes made the Indians' charge falter. Clutching the

now-empty pistols, Murdoch whirled around and snapped, "Inside!"

Quincy got hold of Howard's left arm and pulled as hard as he could, and there was a tearing sound as the fabric of the older man's coat gave way. Howard stumbled forward, and Quincy guided him toward the door. They hurried inside with Murdoch and Ulysses right behind them. The blacksmith shut the door with a thump and lowered the heavy bar that would keep the Indians from battering it in.

As he helped Howard into a chair, Quincy saw that Mariel and Cordelia had already pulled the shutters closed over the windows and fastened them, and the women were breaking out the extra powder and shot in preparation for reloading the weapons. Everyone was working smoothly and efficiently, but despite the cool, calm façade, Quincy could sense the terror in the air.

"Shawnees, I think, from what I saw of 'em," Murdoch was saying quietly to Ulysses, who nodded in agreement.

"Not like 'em to hit a cabin in the middle of winter," replied Ulysses, "but I reckon the warm weather got 'em to feelin' a mite proddy."

While they talked, they reloaded their weapons using their own powder horns and shot pouches. With that done, they moved aside the little squares of canvas that had been tacked over the gun ports to keep the wind out of the cabin. The men stuck their gun barrels out of the holes and searched for targets. Meanwhile, the sound of arrows striking the walls outside continued without pause. After a moment, Murdoch pressed the trigger of his long rifle, and a few seconds later, Ulysses fired his musket.

"How'd you do?" asked Ulysses.

"Scorched th' pants o' one young buck," Murdoch replied with a grin. "Yerself?"

"Knocked the leg out from under one. Let's keep it up."

They turned to take freshly loaded rifles from Mariel and Cordelia.

Cordelia had just handed a weapon to Murdoch when she noticed Quincy tearing the bloodstained shirt away from Howard's shoulder. "Father!" she cried, hurrying over to him. "I didn't know you were hurt!"

"I'm all right," he assured his daughter in a shaky voice. His face was drained of color.

Another rip of fabric bared the wound, and Quincy took a quick look at it. "The arrowhead didn't penetrate," he said. "It just plowed a nice furrow across your shoulder before pinning your coat to the cabin, Mr. Howard. Pretty messy and I guess it hurts like blazes, but you'll be all right."

"I could tell it wasn't too bad. Tie it up for me, Quincy, so I can get into this fight before it's all over."

"I'll tend to this, Quincy," Cordelia said briskly as she pulled up her dress and tore off a piece of her petticoat. "You help Murdoch and Ulysses."

Despite the calm and efficient manner in which she bound her father's wound, Quincy could hear the fear in her voice. They were all scared, even Murdoch. Quincy had heard the big frontiersman say more than once that only a fool was fearless, and one thing was certain: There were no fools in this cabin.

Mariel was handling the reloading chores by herself, and Quincy glanced at her to make sure she was all right; then he checked on Dietrich. Wearing only a shirt that either his sister or Cordelia had hurriedly pulled on him, the little boy was sitting under the rough-hewn table in the center of the room. His blue eyes were wide with terror as he listened to the boom of guns, the insistent sound of arrows hitting the walls, and the blood-curdling whoops and cries of the attacking Shawnees. Quincy's heart went out to Dietrich, but there was no time to comfort him now. Quincy went instead to another of the gun ports, slid the barrel of his rifle through it, and looked for something at which to shoot.

He caught a flash of red skin through the tiny space above the muzzle of the gun and instinctively pressed the trigger. The flintlock snapped and then boomed as the charge in the barrel ignited. The stock kicked back heavily against Quincy's shoulder, and he withdrew the barrel and leaned over to peer quickly through the hole. He saw one of the Shawnee warriors writhing on the ground some fifteen feet away with a fist-sized hole in his chest. As Quincy watched, the Shawnee grew limp and still—the stillness of death.

Later, when there was more time—if there was more time—Quincy knew he would think about the killing and feel a tightly wound ball of sickness in his belly. He had seen a lot of violence in the last year, but he had never gotten used to it, and he hoped he never would.

But for now, he turned and pressed the empty rifle into Mariel's hands and took the loaded one she had ready for him. For an instant, the eyes of husband and wife met, and Quincy saw the hysteria lurking behind her gaze.

"It'll be all right," he said quietly, trying to sound as reassuring as he could.

She just turned away to start reloading the rifle he had given her.

The deadly accurate fire of Murdoch and Ulysses had taken its toll, and before Quincy got a chance for another shot, the Shawnees broke off their attack and fled into the woods. Murdoch and Ulysses sent a couple of balls after them for good measure, spilling another Indian off his feet. His companions picked him up and dragged him away, just as they carried off their other dead and wounded.

"Reckon they're gone?" Ulysses asked when there was no longer any sign of the Indians.

"Probably," replied Murdoch. "But we had best wait inside for a spell, just t' be sure."

A tense half hour passed before Murdoch and Ulysses unbarred the door and stepped out. Leaving Ulysses to help guard the cabin, Murdoch slipped into the woods and returned a little later to report that the Shawnees were well and truly gone. The danger was over, at least for now.

Quincy took a deep breath of relief and pulled Mariel into his arms. "See," he said softly as he stroked her long blond hair. "I told you it would be all right."

"No!" With a totally unexpected suddenness, she struck him in the chest with both hands, knocking him away from her. "It's not all right!" she cried. "They will just come back and kill us another time! It will never be all right as long as we live out here in this wilderness!" And then she buried her face in her hands and began to sob.

Quincy gaped at her, stunned by her outburst. Gresham Howard looked vaguely embarrassed, as did Murdoch and Ulysses. Cordelia left her father's side and quickly went to Mariel, then led the sobbing young woman to one of the bunks. As she pulled Mariel down beside her, Cordelia wrapped her arms around the younger woman and rocked slowly back and forth, making soft noises just as though she were trying to soothe an upset child. From under the table, Dietrich looked on in confusion.

Recovering his wits, Quincy bent and picked up the boy. "We'd better get some pants on you," he said quietly, "before you catch a chill."

Murdoch, Ulysses, and Howard went outside while Quincy got the youngster dressed. Mariel's sobs had slowed and finally died away completely. Quincy gave Dietrich a slap on the bottom and told him to go outside to play, warning him not to wander off. After what had happened this afternoon, there was no danger of Dietrich straying too far from the cabin. Besides, Quincy reasoned, the three men were out there to keep an eye on him.

Mariel wiped the tears from her face and said softly to Cordelia, "Thank you, my friend. Now I would like to talk to my husband."

"Of course," Cordelia said as she stood up. She cast a glance at Quincy as she left the cabin, but he could not read the emotion on her face.

Mariel stood up, and Quincy held out his arms, ready to embrace her, but she shook her head firmly. "No," she said. "We must talk, Quincy."

"Well, sure. Whatever you want to talk about."

"I . . . I do not know how to say this. Your heart was set on coming out here with your friends. And I knew somehow, from the moment I saw you, that I wanted to be wherever you were. I thought I could live here with you and be happy. Now I know that I cannot."

"You don't want to be married to me anymore?" he asked, feeling as though someone had punched him in the belly. The prospect of losing her chilled him more than any Indian attack ever could.

"*No.* You do not understand. I love you, Quincy. I love you with all my heart. But I . . . I cannot stay here." She paused to draw a deep breath, and when he started to speak she put a hand on his lips to stop him. "You must let me finish. You know I lost all of my family except Dietrich to the Indians back in New York. I could not stand to lose my new family now. Quincy . . . I want you to take me back to civilization."

She took her fingers away from his mouth, but still he was silent for a long moment, turning over in his mind what she had said and pondering how to respond to it. Finally he spoke. "This is good country, Mariel. You've seen it for yourself. And one of these days, when all the trouble is over, it's going to be even better."

"Those days you speak of are far, far in the future. We may all be dead by then. I . . . I cannot risk it, Quincy. I must go back to where a family can live safely, somewhere in the east where the Indians are no longer a threat."

She was being unreasonable, Quincy thought, but he didn't say that. Surely he could talk her into seeing things clearly again.

"But you've got me to take care of you, Mariel. And Murdoch and Mr. Howard, too, and I've got a feeling Cordelia and Ulysses will be getting married, so they'll be around as well. Everything will be all right, I promise you."

Stubbornly, she shook her head.

Quincy's frustration got the better of him. He flung his hands out to the sides and said, "Damn it, I just don't understand—"

"No, you do not," Mariel said quietly. "When I

speak of my family, I am not talking only of you and Dietrich." Her hands went to her belly, her fingers spread and pressing against it. "I mean the life that grows here as well. Quincy . . . I am going to have a baby."

Chapter Thirteen

With the mountains behind them, the going should have been easier for Henry Knox's party. But there were still large hills to cross, and while they did not present as rugged an obstacle as the Berkshires, the trek was difficult and hazardous.

A sudden snowstorm dumped several feet of snow on the Massachusetts countryside, and while the temperature was cold enough to insure that the road did not turn muddy, the snow piled up in such high drifts that the sledges bogged down anyway. Daniel, Penn, and the others spent much of their time trying to clear a path through the drifts, but their progress was maddeningly slow.

January turned into February, and still the caravan pushed on. Henry Knox's optimistic estimate of delivering the cannon to General Washington within three weeks of leaving Fort Ticonderoga had long since been abandoned.

The group had brought few supplies with them, relying instead on provisions they picked up in the small villages they passed along their route. But in the middle of a winter such as this, food was hard to come by. For the past couple of weeks, hunting parties had been sent out every few days to find fresh meat for the men.

"I want you and Sloane and Varley to go out tomorrow and bag some venison, or perhaps a few wild turkeys," Henry Knox said to Daniel one evening as everyone rested around the campfires after a day of backbreaking labor. "Think you're up to it?"

Daniel looked up and grinned. Compared to what he had been doing, the idea of spending a day tramping through the woods in search of game sounded tremendously appealing. "I'd be glad to," he said, trying not to seem too relieved to have been given this assignment.

"You'll tell Sloane and Varley?"

"Sure. We'll get started first thing in the morning, about the same time the rest of you pull out. Maybe we'll be back with some fresh meat by midday."

"I think that would raise everyone's spirits a great deal." Henry clapped Daniel on the shoulder. "Good luck, my boy."

Daniel settled back on his haunches and sipped from his cup of weak tea. They were almost out of tea as well, but there was nothing he could do about that. Tea leaves didn't roam wild through the forest, he thought with a grin.

Then his expression grew solemn as he considered the two men Henry had chosen to accompany him. Tim Varley was a long-faced man with a lantern jaw and jug-handle ears, a farmer who, like Penn Sloane, hailed from the New Hampshire Grants. Daniel knew Varley to speak to, but that was about all. Penn, of course, had been as friendly as ever in recent days, but Daniel had been unable to shake his suspicion of the mountaineer. Penn could have sabotaged that belaying rope, and he could have weakened the ice on that frozen creek.

If Penn knew of Daniel's suspicions, he had given no sign of it, and when Daniel sought him out to tell him that they would be going hunting together the next day, he seemed pleased by the news.

"That'll make a nice change from wrestling oxen and hauling sledges, won't it, Daniel?"

"I hope so," he replied.

Daniel found Varley and told him about the hunting trip, too, and the man just said, "I'll be ready come sunup."

They were all ready before dawn, in fact, and walked out of the camp while the men were still hitching the teams of oxen to the sledges. Henry Knox saw them off with a cheerful wave and a call of "Good luck!"

"I'll let you two decide which way we should go, since you know this country better than I do," Daniel said, his booted feet kicking up puffs of snow. "You're the mountaineers, not me."

"You look about as much like one as we do, Daniel," Penn said. "And I'm not sure we're any more familiar with these woods than you are."

Daniel scratched his beard. Its dark brown hair was shot with gray in places and made him look older than he actually was. He had first grown the beard when he was in disguise in Boston, then shaved it off when he returned to his position as one of General Washington's staff officers in Cambridge, and over the past two months, the beard had grown back. He wore the same type of buckskin pants and jacket as the other two men, and his tricorn had been replaced by a woolen cap. He supposed Penn was right—he did look like a woodsman.

"But if you're willing," Penn suggested, "why don't we split up? We can cover more ground that way and maybe flush out more game."

"Good idea," agreed Daniel. "What do you think, Varley?"

"Whatever you gents want to do is all right by me," Varley replied.

"We don't need to get too far apart. We'd better stay within hearing distance of a gunshot, just in case one of us runs into trouble." Penn rubbed his jaw in thought. "Here's what we'll do. We all have a pistol as well as a rifle. If you get in trouble, fire the rifle first and then the pistol right after it. Two shots close together like that will be the signal for the others to come looking for you. All right?"

"Sounds fine to me," Daniel said, and Varley nodded.

"All right, then." Penn pointed to a thickly wooded hill rising directly in front of them. "I'll take the hill and go straight over it. Daniel, you swing to the west, Varley to the east. We'll rendezvous on the other side and then angle back to the trail so that we can find Knox and the others. That ought to take most of the morning."

Daniel pulled his hat down tight on his head. "Good hunting," he called to the others.

His companions remained in sight for quite a while, and from time to time Daniel caught glimpses of them making their way through the trees. Finally he lost sight of Varley, then paused and looked for Penn, and spotted him moving through a clearing at the base of the hill.

A frown creased Daniel's forehead. Penn had been

quick to suggest that they split up. Had there been a reason for that suggestion other than the one he had given? There had been no further sabotage since the broken belaying rope and the runaway sledge, but now Penn was off by himself, unwatched, able to do anything he pleased.

Was he up to more mischief? Daniel could not answer that question, but he knew that he had to find out. The answer was more important than finding a deer or a wild turkey, and Daniel turned and cut through the woods toward the spot where he had last seen Penn.

Now he would find out just how good a woodsman he was, Daniel thought. It would be easy to track Penn in the snow, but it would be a challenge to do so without his noticing that someone was trailing him.

Daniel moved from tree to tree, angling toward the hill that was Penn's destination. By the time he reached the foot of the slope, Penn had already started to climb the hill, and his tracks disappeared into the dense growth of evergreens. Moving slowly and cautiously, Daniel followed the trail.

For the next half hour he made his way up the hill, but he was unable to tell if he was getting closer to Penn or not. Evidently neither Penn nor Varley had flushed any game, because there had been no shots. Daniel would have heard them easily in the cold, still air, and as it was, he had to take pains not to step on fallen tree limbs, because the sound of a cracking branch would carry just about as well as a gunshot.

He was almost to the top of the hill when he heard the faint sound of voices. He pressed himself against the trunk of a tree for concealment and listened intently. After a moment, he could tell that the voices were not coming any nearer, and he decided it was safe to proceed.

Moving away from the tree, he hurried through a small clearing and entered a stand of evergreens that grew along the ridge atop the hill. Spying something below him on the far slope, Daniel fell to one knee behind a tree and peered around the trunk. What he saw sent a shock coursing through him: Some fifty yards down the hill stood Penn Sloane, leaning on the stock of his long rifle, in earnest conversation with a British officer and a squad of red-coated troops.

Daniel's breath hissed from between his tightly clenched teeth. This was the proof he had been hoping but at the same time dreading he would find. Until this moment, he had been able to hold on to a faint shred of belief that Penn was a decent, honorable man and a loyal patriot, but that belief had just been dashed. Although Daniel could not make out what the men were saying, Penn had a broad grin on his face, and it was clear to Daniel that this was a friendly meeting.

A traitor! A damned traitor just like Dr. Benjamin Church had been in Boston. Daniel wanted to raise his rifle and shoot Penn where he stood. But that would only bring the wrath of the British soldiers down on him, and Daniel quickly reasoned that it would be better for him to return to the caravan and inform Henry Knox of the identity of their saboteur and leave it up to Henry to figure out what to do next.

Daniel stood up slowly and crept away from the tree where he had been hiding, but he had taken only a couple of steps when there was a sudden noise behind him. He spun around in time to see two redcoats lunging toward him.

The soldiers held their Brown Bess muskets low, ready to rip the bayonets up through Daniel's belly, but he was able to fling himself aside from the charge and use the stock of his own rifle to fend off the bayonets. He went down on one knee and then dove forward, rolling into the redcoats and knocking them over.

Daniel's mouth was full of snow, but he struggled to his feet, cocked the flintlock in his hands, and fired from the hip, knowing he didn't have time to aim. There was a tiny, wet sputter of powder from the pan, but not enough to ignite the charge in the barrel. Snow had fouled the lock, and there was no time to fill it again.

One of the redcoats yelled harshly as he leapt up and drove his bayonet at Daniel, and only another frantic leap carried him out of the path of the deadly blade. By now the second redcoat was back on his feet as well, and although Daniel tried to whirl around to meet his threat, he was too late. The butt of the man's musket slammed down between Daniel's shoulder blades and knocked him forward. Then the other redcoat slashed his weapon at Daniel again, and the gun's heavy wooden stock clipped him on the side of the head.

At that moment the second man stepped in while Daniel was off-balance and slammed a fist into his belly. He doubled over and felt his flintlock slipping from his fingers. Another blow from the butt of the first man's musket drove him to his knees. He heard shouting, but it was a vague, faraway sound, barely discernible over the roaring that filled his head as he fell forward and landed face first on the freezing ground.

Snow mixed with the gritty taste of dirt filled his mouth, and cold enclosed him, but he was too tired to fight his way out of its grip. He blinked his eyes, but all he could see was the white of the snow, white that faded away into nothingness as the cold claimed him.

*   *   *

Daniel was still cold when he woke up, but at least it wasn't the coldness of the grave, he told himself. His head hurt so badly he knew he had to be alive.

His eyes flickered open, but he clamped them shut again when he heard British-accented voices nearby. The redcoats had probably taken him to their camp, he thought, and he would have to be careful not to let them know he was awake, so he could find out what they were planning to do.

Not that there was anything he could do about it if he did, he realized bleakly. He was tied hand and foot, and his eyelids were the only things he could move.

"I saw that," a familiar voice whispered close to his ear. "Might as well not worry too much about them knowing you're back among the living. There's not a whole hell of a lot we can do."

Daniel controlled his surprise and slowly opened his eyes. He was lying on his right side on rocky ground that was wet from the snow that had melted underneath him. A foot and a half away, Penn Sloane was also stretched out on the ground, and he was grinning at Daniel from a face that was bruised, swollen, and cut until it was almost unrecognizable.

"Penn? . . ." Daniel gasped.

"Yeah, it's me. They worked me over pretty good. You were lucky. You got knocked out sooner, didn't put up as much of a fight."

"I don't understand." Daniel blinked in confusion. "I saw you talking to them like they were your friends—"

"I was sure as hell trying to convince them they were my friends," Penn cut in. "What did you expect me to do when I stumbled right in on 'em like that, Daniel? I tried to tell 'em that I was loyal to old German George, and I might've worked them around to believing it . . . if that fight between you and those two sentries hadn't broken out."

"You mean . . . you tried to help me?"

Penn managed to shrug his shoulders. "Wasn't much else I could do, now was there?"

"You could have saved yourself!" Daniel hissed, feeling guilt surge through him. "You could have pretended you didn't know me!"

"Might've worked for a little while, but it still wouldn't have saved my bacon. Not after Varley showed up."

"Varley?" Daniel repeated in amazement.

"Yeah, Varley," said a harsh voice as a toe roughly prodded Daniel's side. "I see you're awake, boy. You been fillin' this youngster's head with lies about me, Penn?"

"Just the truth, Varley," Penn said, his voice as cold as the snow.

Rough hands grasped Daniel's shoulder and turned him onto his back, and he looked up into Tim Varley's face. For a change, the farmer was smiling instead of frowning, but it wasn't an improvement. If anything, Varley was even uglier than usual.

He spat off to the side and then said, "I figured you gents'd wake up soon. Wanted you to know what's goin' to happen to you."

A British officer strode up beside Varley. "Are they awake?" he asked.

"Yeah, both of 'em," replied Varley.

"Good. We can go ahead now with our plan and leave a couple of men to dispose of them, eh?"

"Thanks for humorin' me, Major." Varley sneered. "I really wanted to see the expressions on their faces when they found out the truth."

"I can see the truth," Penn said calmly. "You're nothing but a goddamned traitor, Varley."

"Say what you want, Sloane. I'm bein' well paid, and when this war is over, I'll still have my land. I reckon the Crown'll take away everything that belongs to you rebels."

Daniel was almost overcome with revulsion for the man. "You were the one responsible for the sabotage, weren't you, Varley?" he asked.

"That's right. I was supposed to slow down them sledges and cause as much damage as I could so that maybe Knox would give up on the idea of gettin' the cannon to Washington. He's too damn stubborn, though. That's why we're goin' to have to wipe out the whole bunch of 'em."

"That's enough," the major snapped. "I want to get to Potter's Bluff before Knox and his men reach the pass below. That's the best spot for an ambush between here and Springfield."

"You're right, Major," agreed Varley. "We'd best be movin'." He lifted a hand in a wave of farewell. "So long, boys. Won't be seein' you again." Chuckling, he turned and walked off with the British officer.

"Son of a bitch," Penn breathed. "They're going to kill everybody."

"Including us," said Daniel. He saw two grim-faced, red-coated troopers striding toward them, their muskets held at the ready.

The other soldiers were pulling out quickly, marching toward the southeast with the major and Tim Varley in the lead.

"Wot'll we do wi' yer bodies?" the guard asked Daniel and Penn. "Should we just leave 'em 'ere? Food for the wolves, they'd be."

"Maybe we could find a place to 'eave 'em," replied the other redcoat. Daniel realized they were the two men he had struggled with earlier on the crest of the hill.

"There's a gully over there," said the first soldier, pointing off to the left. "Got plenty o' snow in it. We could dump 'em in there and push some more snow in on top of 'em. That's about the closest we're goin' to come to a decent burial, I'd say."

"Aye, and then we can catch up to the major and the rest o' the lads. Well, we might as well get it over with, 'adn't we?"

In unison the troopers lifted their muskets.

Daniel tugged at his bonds, but they were too tight for his hands and feet to slip free.

"Got anythin' to say?" one of the troopers gibed at his victims.

"Just one thing," Penn Sloane rasped. "Go to hell." And then he kicked out as hard and fast as he could, and the soles of his boots smashed into the breech of the redcoat's Brown Bess and knocked it aside. Penn doubled over and then lunged upward, his hands free. He was awkward but fast; his feet were still tied together as he tackled the nearer guard, and together they crashed into the other one. All three of them spilled to the ground, and the two redcoats dropped their guns.

Daniel ignored his amazement at the fact that Penn had gotten his hands free. There was no time to wonder how the mountaineer had managed the feat. Instead, Daniel rolled desperately toward one of the fallen muskets. The gun still had its bayonet in place, and the sharp blade would slice through the ropes binding his wrists—if only he could reach it.

As Penn's fists rose and fell steadily, battering one of the redcoats, Daniel stretched his arms behind him

as far as he could and fumbled for the bayonet. His
fingertips touched cold steel, and he scooted closer and
sawed blindly at his bonds. He felt the sharp bite of the
blade and knew he was cutting his wrists as well, but he
felt the ropes give even as they grew slick with blood. A
heave of his shoulders parted the bonds and his arms
came free. They were numb, but he forced his clumsy
fingers to work as he rolled over again and fumbled for
the stock of the musket.

A few feet away, he saw one of the guards kick
Penn in the head, and Daniel picked up the weapon,
cocked it, and prayed that snow hadn't fouled the priming charge. There was no time to check.

"You bastards!" he shouted, then pressed the trigger.

The musket boomed and jumped in his hands, and
the ball it spat out along with a gout of smoke and
flame caught the redcoat in the chest. The impact
slammed the man backward, and he sprawled in the
snow, his arms outflung at his sides. His feet kicked
once, and then he was still.

The other trooper had scrambled to his feet and
pulled a pistol from under his scarlet coat. He was trying desperately to cock it when Penn scooped up the
other musket and thrust it up from the ground. The
bayonet ripped into the man's belly and lifted him onto
his toes. He gave a high, thin scream, dropped the pistol, and plucked feebly at the bayonet buried in his
body. Penn shoved it in to the very end, then released
the musket and let the redcoat topple over to the side.
A huge crimson stain spread quickly on the white snow
beneath the man's body.

Daniel used the bayonet on the musket he still
held to cut through the ropes around his ankles, then

reached over and sawed through the bonds tied around Penn's feet.

"Are they both dead?" Daniel asked.

"Close enough," Penn grunted. He stood up and staggered as he tried to get his balance back, along with the feeling in his legs and feet. Daniel used the musket to support himself until he felt steady enough to walk.

"How did you get your hands free?" Daniel asked and grinned. "I couldn't believe my eyes when you came up off the ground that way."

"Rawhide stretches when it's wet, my friend, and that's what those ropes are made of. I reckon those Englishmen didn't know that, though. I kept my wrists under me as much as I could, letting the rope soak up the melted snow. I finally got enough play to be able to slip a hand out." He laughed humorlessly. "It was almost too late, though."

"Well, we're alive, and that's what counts." Daniel stiffened as a thought occurred to him. "We've got to warn Henry and William."

"There's not enough time for that," Penn said. "We can't reach them before they get to Potter's Bluff. I know the place."

"Then what can we do?" Daniel asked, frustration gnawing at his belly. "We can't let the men walk into that ambush!"

"Got to stop the British somehow," Penn muttered. "Come on. They don't have too big a lead on us, and they won't be expecting us to follow them. They probably heard the shot, but they'll just figure those boys shot one of us and bayoneted the other one."

They appropriated the powder horns and shot pouches as well as the muskets from the two dead redcoats and set off at a fast walk after the British patrol. The British were taking a risk just being in the Massachusetts countryside, but Daniel supposed they figured it was a chance worth taking if they could stop the caravan of artillery pieces from reaching Cambridge and General George Washington.

The brisk walk got Daniel's blood moving again. "What's this Potter's Bluff the major mentioned?" he asked. "I've never heard of it."

"It's a few miles farther on, a spot where the road travels for about half a mile along the base of a steep bluff that shelves out from the side of a hill. There's a fairly deep gully on the other side of the road, so it's a perfect spot for an ambush. There'll be no place for our boys to hide when the British open up on them."

"What are we going to do?"

"I haven't figured out that part yet. I'm hoping to come up with a plan when we get there."

Daniel kicked through a deep drift of snow and frowned in thought, an idea forming in his mind. "That bluff sticks out from the side of a hill, you said?"

"That's right. I don't know how it got its name. Probably some fellow named Potter called it after himself."

Daniel was anxious to get to the bluff and find out if the nebulous plan that had suggested itself to him had even a chance of working.

The two young men did not waste their energy talking as they pursued the British soldiers. Their breath plumed in front of them in the cold air as they stalked through the snow.

Finally Penn paused and pointed out one of the craggy, wooded hills that rose in front of them. "That's the place," he said. "Potter's Bluff is just on the other side of that hill."

"Let's go straight over the top," Daniel suggested.

"Might be just as fast to go around."

"I haven't been in the army very long," Daniel said firmly, "but I've learned the importance of having the advantage of high ground on your side."

Penn smiled and said, "Aye, there's that to consider. See, you're even starting to think like a mountaineer, Daniel."

"Come on," Daniel said grimly.

Daniel's legs felt as heavy as lead as he and Penn slogged up the steep hillside. Their path was littered with trees and boulders, and the snow had drifted thickly in many places. The going was maddeningly slow.

At last they reached the top and dropped to their stomachs on the rocky summit, which had been swept almost clear of snow by the wind. Thick gray clouds scudded by overhead, and Daniel knew there was more snow on the way.

He and Penn edged forward until they could peer down at the bluff some two hundred yards below. As Penn had said, it stuck out from the hillside like a shelf. Farther down was the road, although Daniel and Penn could not see it from where they lay.

Daniel could see the road back to the west of the hill, though, and what he saw there chilled his blood even more than the snow and wind. The last three or four sledges were in sight, which meant that the rest of the caravan was already on the road just below the bluff. And plainly visible against the snow on the bluff were the red coats of the British ambushers, crouching behind rocks and waiting for the order to open fire on the unsuspecting patriots.

Penn lifted his stolen musket. "I'll down at least one of them," he muttered. "That'll give Knox and the boys a little warning."

Quickly Daniel reached out and closed his gloved

fingers over the barrel of the musket and pushed it down. "Wait!" he said urgently. "I've got another idea."

"Better make it quick," Penn said. "That major is about to give the order to open fire."

Daniel laid his musket on the ground and scrambled to his feet. "Come on," he said as he hurried over to one of the boulders just below the crest of the slope. He placed his shoulder against the massive rock, which stood taller than his head, and pushed.

The ground was icy, which made it difficult for the soles of his boots to find any purchase, but he braced himself as best he could and kept shoving. Suddenly, Penn was beside him.

"I hope this works," Penn grunted as he threw his weight and strength into the effort.

Daniel hoped so, too, but the boulder didn't budge.

Then, abruptly, there was a faint grinding sound, and the rock shifted slightly. Daniel redoubled his effort. Both he and Penn were grunting from the strain, and the pounding of his pulse seemed so loud in his head that he thought surely the British must hear it, too.

"Roll . . . damn you . . . !" Penn breathed between gritted teeth, and Daniel silently echoed the plea.

When the boulder finally moved, it happened so quickly that Penn's feet slipped on the ice, and he fell forward, out of control, but Daniel lunged toward him, reached out, and managed to snag his jacket. Holding on tightly, Daniel scrabbled for a grip on the rocky ground and caught himself in time to keep Penn from tumbling down the slope after the boulder.

Once the huge rock was moving, it gathered speed and bounded down the hillside as though it were a massive ball thrown by a gigantic child. Along the way, it picked up a coating of snow and crashed into other boulders, starting them rolling as well. With a roar, one lone boulder turned into an avalanche, and the rock-slide raced toward the British at a terrifying speed.

They must have heard it coming, but there was no time to run, no place to hide. Although Daniel could not see them through the miniature blizzard caused by the avalanche, he knew the redcoats would be staring in horror at the doom crashing down on them. He was pleased to think that Tim Varley and his friends would pay for their treachery.

Daniel and Penn gulped down lungfuls of the cold air and watched as the avalanche they had started engulfed Potter's Bluff. The angle of the bluff, which was almost perpendicular to the hillside, slowed the progress of the avalanche, but the boulders crashed down on the bluff and stayed there—along with the grisly remains of the British soldiers crushed beneath them.

"We did it," Penn finally said.

Daniel was too tired to do anything but nod; then he said, "Henry's going to be disappointed when we get back, though."

Penn looked at him in amazement. "Disappointed?" he repeated.

"We didn't bag any game," Daniel said with a grin.

Henry and William Knox greeted them excitedly when they rejoined the caravan an hour later.

"There was an avalanche!" William said, looking more animated than Daniel had ever seen him. "I thought we were going to be crushed by it!"

"It came down a hillside right behind Potter's Bluff," Henry explained. He was calmer, at least on the surface, but his eyes shone brightly. "The bluff stopped it before the rocks actually reached the road, or we might have been in a spot of trouble."

"Any idea what started it?" asked Daniel.

"None at all," Henry replied. "Probably a drift of snow shifted when it got too deep. Hard to say what might set off an avalanche in these hills." He frowned suddenly in consternation. "Where's Varley?"

"We had some excitement of our own," Daniel said. "I'm afraid I have some bad news, Henry. Varley's dead."

"Dead! My word, what happened?"

Daniel exchanged a glance with Penn, then said with complete sincerity, "He fell into a ravine and broke his neck while we were hunting. He was already gone by the time Penn and I got to him. The ground was frozen too hard to bury him, of course, but we made a cairn for him out of rocks."

"How terrible," muttered Henry. "But I suppose that was the only thing you could do."

"I'm sorry we didn't get a deer or a turkey," Penn said, "but we headed right back to the road after Varley's accident."

"Of course. I can understand why you were upset." Henry sighed. "Ah, well, another hunting party can go out tomorrow. A little shortage of meat doesn't mean much in the face of a man's senseless death."

Daniel made no reply. Only he and Penn knew just how senseless Tim Varley's death had been. Varley had given in to greed and misguided zeal, and he had paid the price.

No one seemed to notice that Daniel and Penn had returned with British Brown Bess muskets, rather than the long rifles with which they had left, and neither of them brought up the subject.

"There'll be more snow tonight," Henry Knox went

on, echoing Daniel's earlier thought. "We'd better be moving again while there's still some daylight." He turned and boomed out the command. "Let's go, men! Get those sledges moving!"

The caravan was on its way again, and with every step, the big guns were that much closer to General George Washington—and their appointment with destiny.

Chapter Fourteen

The ice was thick in places on the Charles River, and many of Boston's Tory citizens feared that the patriot troops in Cambridge would cross the river on foot and launch an invasion of the city. It was a groundless fear, Elliot Markham thought as he made his way over the ice on a dark, moonless night in late February. He moved carefully, testing each step before he put his weight down. At times the ice shifted and made crackling noises, and each time he stopped where he was, backed up, and advanced at a different angle, hoping to find a path where the ice was thicker and stronger.

Elliot felt certain that an invading army could not march across this ice without cracking it and winding up in the frigid waters of the Charles; it was nerve-racking enough for a lone man to attempt to slip across the river.

But this was the first chance he'd had to get to Cambridge to find Daniel and tell him that Roxanne Darragh had been taken to England.

Elliot did not doubt the validity of what Faye had told him about Roxanne. The patriot intelligence network was highly efficient. Elliot had no idea what Daniel would do once he found out, but he was sure Daniel would do something, and Elliot stood ready to help in any way he could.

Finally, he reached the far side of the river and stepped up onto the bank. The trip across the ice was not something he wanted to do again soon—although he would have to do just that later that night. But for now, at least, he was on solid ground and glad of it.

"Hold it right there! Don't move, mister, or I'll blow you clear back to Boston!"

Recognizing the menace in the voice, Elliot stood still, his hands slightly raised.

"Take it easy, friend," he said in calm, quiet tones. "I mean no harm."

"How do I know you ain't one of them bloody lobsterbacks?"

"Take a look for yourself," Elliot invited. "I'm no redcoat. I'm just a citizen on an errand."

The man came closer, but Elliot could still see only a vague shape in the darkness. The shape was plain enough, however, for him to tell that the man was brandishing a musket.

"Are you a smuggler?"

The question held an undertone of excitement, and Elliot could tell now that his captor was probably still in his teens. A boy patrolling the river, taking it on himself to forestall any British troop movement across the

Charles. It was a foolish idea . . . but a brave one, Elliot thought.

"That's none of your business," he said in reply to the youngster's question. "But I promise you I'm not a redcoat, nor do I have any connection with them. All I want is to go on my way in peace."

"You swear you're alone?"

"I'm alone," Elliot said.

The boy jerked the muzzle of the gun in a curt gesture. "Go on, then. I won't interfere. But you'd better be telling me the truth."

"I am." Elliot lowered his arms. "Thank you, *sir*. By the way, do you know where I can get a horse around here?"

"There's a stable up the road there. Check with old Deakins. He'll rent you a mount."

"Thanks again." Elliot strode away hurriedly before the young man grew suspicious again.

A lantern was burning inside the stable, and an old man was forking some straw for a couple of nags. He was more than happy to rent one of them to Elliot at an exorbitant price, and although he asked no questions, he had to be curious about a young man showing up late at night looking for a horse.

The mare had a slow but steady pace, and Elliot was glad to be on the road to Cambridge. Surely he could find someone there who could get a message to Daniel.

Elliot was challenged by a couple of men at a guard post where the road entered Cambridge.

"I'm looking for Lieutenant Daniel Reed," he explained. "He's a member of General Washington's staff."

"And who might you be?" one of the sentries wanted to know.

"I'm his cousin, Elliot Markham, and I have some important family news for him." It was almost the truth, Elliot thought. Daniel and Roxanne were practically married, and that was close enough to family as far as Elliot was concerned.

"Go ahead," the sentry told him. "But it's a busy night, so try to stay out of the way."

"Thanks." Elliot heeled the horse into a walk and rode into Cambridge, noticing as he did so that there were many lanterns burning and men wearing the blue coats of the patriot army were hurrying about. Something was definitely up, he realized.

He knew where Washington's headquarters were, and as he rode up to the courtyard in front of Vassall House, his eyes widened in surprise. In the courtyard sat two dozen artillery pieces being cleaned and readied for use. Officers strode back and forth supervising the task, and off to one side stood George Washington himself, plainly visible in the light of the torches and lanterns.

Elliot angled his horse toward the general and lifted a hand in greeting. As he did so, an ironic thought struck him. Here he was, the son of one of Boston's leading Tories, a supposed loyalist who ought to despise Washington. Yet he could not help but be impressed by the man who stood tall and straight in a greatcoat that flapped around his calves in the cold wind.

"Hello, General," Elliot said. "I'm looking for an officer of yours, Lieutenant Reed—"

"Elliot!" someone cried before Washington had a chance to respond.

Elliot turned in the saddle and looked behind him but failed to recognize the figure running toward him. The shaggy-haired man wore buckskins and sported a dark beard, and he was accompanied by another buck-skin-clad man and a tall, massive officer.

"Daniel?"

Now, at closer range, he recognized his cousin, even though Daniel looked just like a ridge-running mountaineer. Elliot jumped down from his saddle, and the cousins embraced in a rough, back-slapping hug.

"What are you doing here?" Daniel asked.

"I could ask you what in the world you've been doing, too, you know," Elliot countered.

Daniel grinned. "I've been to Fort Ticonderoga and back with Henry Knox here. Colonel Knox, I should say, since he's not a civilian anymore."

"And that'll take a little getting used to," Knox said, reaching out to shake Elliot's hand. "But I suppose a commander of artillery ought to have a rank. You must be Elliot Markham. Daniel's mentioned you."

"We just got back late this afternoon," Daniel explained. "We brought these cannon back from Ticonderoga. We left the heavier guns in Framingham and hurried on with the lighter pieces. By the way, this is another friend of mine, Pennington Sloane."

"Call me Penn," Sloane said as he shook hands with Elliot.

Elliot felt an instinctive liking for the rugged-looking mountaineer, and he was not surprised that Daniel and Penn had become friends.

Now that the introductions were over, Daniel said, "You haven't told me why you're here, Elliot. There's not any trouble with the family, I hope?"

"Well, that depends on how you look at it, I suppose," Elliot said. "Could I talk to you in private, Daniel?"

"Of course." Lines of concern appeared on Daniel's face. "Come with me."

They walked off to one side, leaving Henry Knox and Penn Sloane standing with General Washington. When they were out of earshot of the others, Daniel stopped and asked, "What's this all about, Elliot? Have you had news about Roxanne?"

Elliot knew that Daniel was expecting bad news, and to ease his mind a little, Elliot said quickly, "I'm pretty sure she's alive, Daniel."

"Alive?" Daniel's hands shot out to grasp Elliot's arms. "Are you certain?"

"No, but nothing else makes sense." Elliot took a deep breath and then went on, "She's in England, Daniel. She was put on a British ship and taken to England."

"My God! Do you have any idea where?"

"I'm sorry. I don't."

"It doesn't matter," Daniel said, excitement growing in his voice. "I'll find her. Wherever she is, I'll find her." He turned and hurried toward General Washington.

The patriots' commander-in-chief coolly met Daniel's agitated gaze and asked, "What is it, Lieutenant?"

"I'd like to request that you temporarily release me from my duties as a member of your staff, sir," Daniel said, making a visible effort to calm himself.

"That's an irregular request, Lieutenant. You'd better have a good reason for it."

"Yes, sir, the best one of all. I need to go to England to rescue the woman I love from the British."

"What?" Henry Knox and Penn Sloane said at the same time.

"This is my cousin, Elliot Markham, sir. Tell the general what you told me," Daniel said, turning from the general to Elliot.

Feeling somewhat awkward, Elliot quickly ex-

plained the situation to Washington, but he could not
tell from the general's expression how he was reacting
to the story. The general had a reputation for being a
stern commander and a believer in firm discipline. Yet
he was rumored to have a compassionate side to his
nature, too, and that was what Daniel would have to
count on now, Elliot thought as he concluded his expla-
nation.

Washington mulled it over in silence for a few moments, then said, "So, Lieutenant Reed, you want to go
to England to try to find Miss Darragh, is that correct?"

"Yes, sir," Daniel replied, a slight tremor in his
voice betraying the depth of his emotions.

A faint smile plucked at Washington's broad
mouth. "I believe there's a ship sailing from Portsmouth the day after tomorrow for the purpose of harry-
ing what little trade the British are still engaged in
across the North Atlantic, as well as perhaps capturing
some munitions for us. I'll write a letter for you to give
to Captain Jones explaining your mission."

"Mission, sir?" Daniel asked.

"That's right," Washington said. "Our friend Benjamin Franklin has been in contact with individuals in
France who support our cause. There has been talk of
the French providing medical supplies for us, as well as
other aid. I need someone to go to France to conclude
the negotiations."

"But, sir—" Daniel began.

"Of course, England is only some thirty miles
across the Channel from Calais. An enterprising young
man could easily slip across there in a small boat and
spend a few days in England . . . but only a few. Do
you understand, Lieutenant?"

Elliot certainly understood. Washington was giving

Daniel a chance to look for Roxanne. A slim chance, but better than none.

Daniel understood as well. He saluted and said, "I'd be happy to carry out that mission, sir, to the very best of my ability."

"That goes without saying, my boy." Washington's expression warmed a bit more. "After all, you were with Henry here every step of the way, and he tells me you came in quite handy a few times."

Elliot hesitated, then spoke up. "Sir? . . ."

Washington looked at him. "What is it, Mr. Markham?"

"What are you going to do with those cannons?"

"I think you know the answer to that as well as I do."

"Yes, sir. I thought so."

The artillery pieces were going to be moved onto the Charlestown peninsula, Elliot knew, and perhaps onto Dorchester Heights as well, and from there, they could bombard the entire city of Boston.

Boston . . . his home, and the home of his parents.

"I'm sorry, Mr. Markham," Washington said quietly. "I'm aware of your situation, of course. Mr. Tallmadge and Mr. Townsend have told me about you in the past. But this is war, and personal considerations play little part in it."

Elliot took a deep breath. "Yes, sir, I understand."

"Oh my God—Uncle Benjamin and Aunt Polly!" Daniel exclaimed.

"Perhaps it would be wise for you to stay here in Cambridge, Mr. Markham," the general suggested.

Without even pausing to think about it, Elliot said firmly, "No, my place is there, beside my parents. I'll be heading back now."

"Take care of yourself, young man," Washington told him sincerely.

Daniel caught his arm. "You've got to go?" he asked.

"I don't really have any choice," Elliot said quietly. "Just like you have to go to England."

Daniel embraced his cousin again and then said, "We'll meet again."

"Damn right we will," Elliot said, his cocky grin reappearing. "Good luck, Daniel. Good luck to us all."

I fear we're going to need it, he added silently.

"Cordelia Howard Faulkner, do ye take this man to be yer lawfully wedded husband?"

"I do."

The preacher, a thick-bodied man with a bald head and a full beard, had ridden out from Wheeling to perform the wedding ceremony. Now he turned to Ulysses and asked, "And do ye, Ulysses Gilworth, take this woman to be yer lawfully wedded wife?"

"I surely do," Ulysses replied, holding his voice down to a dull roar due to the solemnity of the occasion.

Murdoch and Quincy were standing up with Ulysses, and the men smiled broadly. The big blacksmith was pale and nervous, but getting married could do that to a man, thought Quincy. He'd been a mite nervous himself on his wedding day.

But not for a single instant had he ever regretted marrying Mariel. She was more beautiful than ever, he thought, as she stood on the other side of Cordelia. He was a lucky man, even if he was going to have to leave the frontier, but he was going home again, and he couldn't complain about that.

Once Mariel had told him she was going to have a

baby, there was no question in his mind that he was going to do whatever he could to make things easy for her. If she did not want to settle out here on the frontier, that was all right. Maybe later, once the war was over and the Indian threat had been dealt with, they could come back, but in the meantime, they were heading east to Virginia, the home of Quincy's parents, Geoffrey and Pamela Reed.

It would be good to see them again, and Quincy was sure they would not mind taking in Mariel and Dietrich and him. He knew his mother would be thrilled when she heard the news that she was going to be a grandmother. Although the war would likely spread to the south and affect Virginia sooner or later, Quincy had to admit that the plantation would be a lot safer for his wife and unborn child than this wild Ohio River valley that he had grown to love.

It was a beautiful late-winter afternoon, with blue skies overhead and a faintly warm breeze from the south heralding the approach of spring. The ceremony was being held in the clearing between the two cabins, one of which would now be occupied by Gresham Howard and the other by Cordelia and Ulysses. Ulysses was going to build a new blacksmith shop, he had decided, and move his equipment from Wheeling. There were enough settlers up and down the river now so that he would have plenty of business, he said. Besides, he had added with a grin that made Cordelia blush, they were going to need plenty of room for their young ones to grow up in.

There were two dozen people in attendance at the wedding; all the families from the surrounding farms had shown up. A sense of community was important in this sparsely settled land, and after the wedding there would be a party that would last far into the evening.

Quincy was sorry he and Mariel were going to miss that part of the celebration, but they had a long way to go, all the way across the Blue Ridge Mountains into Virginia. Gresham Howard had given them one of the wagons for their journey, and Quincy hoped it would be a shorter, easier trip than the one out here from Massachusetts.

The preacher read a passage of Scripture from his Bible about the holiness of matrimony, then looked up and said, "Seein' as how the two of ye have pledged yer love for each other 'fore God and these folks gathered here, it's my pleasure to say that by the power vested in me by the Almighty, I pronounce the two of ye man and wife! Now kiss 'er, Ulysses."

"I'd be glad to!"

A cheer rose from the gathering as he swept Cordelia into his arms and gave her a sound kiss. Murdoch waved his coonskin cap in the air and let out a loud whoop, and Quincy applauded, then stepped over and slipped his arm around Mariel's shoulder. She rested her head against him and took his other hand in both of hers.

Yes, sir, marriage wasn't too bad, Quincy thought. Cordelia had been through a great deal of trouble in her life, and now she deserved some happiness. He hoped she and Ulysses found it together in this fertile valley. It was hard to believe that he had been attracted to her himself at one time; she was more like an older sister to him now.

Cordelia's face was flushed, and she wore a joyous smile as she turned to Quincy and Mariel. "You'll stay long enough for a toast, won't you?" she asked.

"Indeed," Quincy said.

Gresham Howard tapped a keg of ale that had

been brought from Wheeling, and cups were passed around to everyone.

"To my daughter!" Howard lifted his mug. "May her life with Ulysses be a long and happy one!"

"To the bride and groom!" Quincy said, and Murdoch echoed the toast. Then everyone drained their cups, and the three men who had brought their fiddles launched into a merry tune. Ulysses swept Cordelia into his arms and they danced, moving together with surprising grace despite the fact that he was so large and she was so petite. They fit together well, Quincy thought.

Soon nearly everyone was dancing, and Quincy regretted that he and Mariel could not swing through a few reels, but it was time to be going. When he looked at Mariel, she smiled her agreement and tightened her grip on Dietrich's hand. This was what she wanted, but it was still going to be hard for her to leave Cordelia behind, Quincy knew. The two young women had become good friends in the months they had traveled together.

Mariel put her free arm around Cordelia's shoulders and hugged her, and tears ran down their cheeks. Quincy shook hands with Ulysses and said, "You treat Cordelia right, you hear?"

"Don't worry about that, Quincy," Ulysses said with a grin. "I reckon she's just about the most important thing in my life now. She'll be just fine."

"I know. So long, Ulysses."

"Take care, now."

Cordelia threw her arms around Quincy's neck and squeezed hard. When trouble had closed in around her and her life had been at its lowest ebb, Quincy had been her only friend.

"I really do love you, you know," she said to him.

"I love you, too, Cordelia. We'll be back one of

these days to see you and Ulysses." He smiled. "I expect you'll have a whole passel of kids running around by then."

"I expect so." She leaned closer and kissed him on the cheek. "And one of them is going to be named Quincy."

He was so touched he did not trust himself to speak, so he just grinned at her and stepped over to shake hands with her father.

"So long, Mr. Howard," he said. "We can't thank you enough for this wagon."

Howard waved off Quincy's thanks. "Just bring it back out here one of these days when you come to visit. Good-bye, Quincy, and good luck to you and your family."

Quincy looked around for Murdoch then. Where was the big frontiersman? He had been here only moments earlier, refilling his cup of ale from the keg. But now he was nowhere to be seen.

"Where is Murdoch?" asked Mariel, echoing Quincy's puzzlement. "We cannot leave without saying good-bye to him."

The Scotsman came around the other end of the wagon leading his horse. "Ye will'na have to," he said. "I'll be going with ye."

"What?" Quincy exclaimed. "But you didn't say anything before. . . . We just figured you'd stay out here on the frontier."

Murdoch shrugged his brawny shoulders. "'Tis true tha' th' frontier be me home, but I could'na let ye go all th' way back t' Virginny without me. I'll see tha' ye get where ye're going safely, then I'll come back out here in time t' fight Indians with George Rogers Clark."

"Well, if you're sure." Quincy held out his hand. "We'd love to have you come along."

Murdoch grasped the younger man's hand, and
Quincy felt the warmth of friendship spreading inside
him. He was looking forward to this trip a little more
now that Murdoch was coming along. It was going to be
like old times.

If only Daniel could have been here, too. . . .
Quincy wondered in that moment if he would ever see
his brother again.

"Well, let's be going," Murdoch said as he swung
up into the saddle. "We got a lot o' ground t' cover. So
long, everybody!"

Quincy helped Mariel and Dietrich onto the wagon
seat and settled down beside them. He picked up the
reins and flapped them, calling out to the mules to get
them started. The wagon lurched into motion. Shouts
of farewell floated after them, and when Quincy looked
back, he saw Gresham Howard waving, and beside him
stood the newly married couple, Ulysses' long arm protectively around Cordelia's shoulder.

They were good people, and Quincy knew in his
heart that one day he would see them again.

But now . . . now it was time to go home.

Chapter Fifteen

The bombardment of Boston began on March 2, 1776, when General George Washington, using the artillery pieces that had been delivered to him by Henry and William Knox, Daniel Reed, Penn Sloane, and the other men who had made the grueling midwinter trek across New York and Massachusetts, gave the order to open fire from gun emplacements on the Charlestown peninsula. Several units were also sent to Dorchester Heights, south of the city, to prepare sites for the cannon, once the heavier armament arrived from Framingham.

But that proved to be unnecessary.

General Thomas Gage had been recalled to England by Parliament, and General William Howe was now in command in the besieged city of Boston. For a short time, Howe made plans to invade Dorchester

Heights and capture it in order to prevent the Americans from using that strategic location. However, with the lack of supplies, the rising anti-Tory sentiment in Boston, and the open warfare between patriots and loyalists in the streets of the city, Howe finally decided that in this case, the most prudent course of action would be to get out of Boston while he still could. The only question was whether or not to burn the city behind him as he left.

Knowing that such an action would only increase the patriots' fervor for vengeance—and knowing that much of the city was already in flames from the American bombardment—Howe simply ordered his men to evacuate, and on March 17, 1776, two weeks after the shelling had begun, the British army boarded ships and sailed out of the harbor. For a few moments, it appeared that there might be a naval battle, as several American vessels were standing by offshore, but the redcoats were allowed to leave unmolested, and the city that they had held for so long was now officially in the hands of the Americans.

With the troops no longer in Boston to offer them protection and fearing that the patriots would exact a terrible vengeance on them, most of the Tories fled the city as well, leaving any way they could: on horseback or by carriage across Boston Neck, in small boats across the Charles River or Boston Harbor, and in private ships headed for friendlier ports.

The destination for many was New York City, which was neutral at the moment. It was not occupied by either army, and while most of the people there supported the patriot cause, the mayor and some of the city officials were Tories. Whatever the situation in New York, the loyalists from Boston reasoned, they would be better off going there than staying behind.

Several ships belonging to the Markham & Cummings shipping line were among those sailing from Boston Harbor for New York. Elliot and his parents were on one of them; Avery and Sarah Wallingford, Sarah's parents, and old Cyrus Wallingford, Avery's father, were on another.

Elliot had made it safely back into Boston after giving Daniel the news about Roxanne, and he had watched in horror as the nightmare in the city worsened during the American bombardment. The Markham mansion on Beacon Hill had escaped any major damage during the shelling, suffering only a few broken windows, but as they sailed away, Elliot wondered if the house would still be standing the next time he visited Boston.

He was coming back. He had no doubt of that. For one thing, he had his duties as a secret agent for the American cause. However, he also had his loyalties to his family, and he was going to see that Benjamin and Polly were safely settled in New York before he did anything else.

He felt a pang of regret as he stood at the railing of the Markham & Cummings ship that was carrying his family and him to safety. He looked back at Boston and saw plumes of smoke rising from the city in several places, and a gray haze about the same color as the thick clouds in the sky overhead hung over the buildings. Elliot's mind went back to the years he had spent growing up in Boston, good years for the most part. It had been a beautiful city and perhaps one day would be again, once this war was finally over.

Taking a deep breath, Elliot turned away from the rail. The time for looking back was over. Now it was time to look ahead and hope that the future would bring better days.

*   *   *

Daniel Reed knew nothing of what his cousin and aunt and uncle were experiencing in Boston, although he suspected that the patriot shelling had taken a toll on the city and driven the British army out. His thoughts, however, were focused on England—and Roxanne.

Daniel had spent the first week at sea dashing to the railing every few minutes. He had never dreamed that anyone could be so sick and not die. The crew members had been tolerant of his misery and offered him sympathy tinged with the natural contempt they felt for landlubbers. They had assured him that the sickness would pass, and it finally had. After a week, Daniel was able to keep food down again, and he slept better at night. The face that looked back at him in the mirror as he shaved each morning was haggard, but at least the features had some color in them. By the end of the second week he felt considerably better and only became queasy if the seas were rough.

He was standing at the railing one afternoon, looking out over the waves, when the ship's captain strolled up beside him and commented, "You're deep in thought, Lieutenant Reed. Care to share them?"

Daniel turned his head and smiled. Captain John Paul Jones was only a few years older than he, and the *Providence* was the captain's first command. Daniel had felt an instant liking for the handsome young naval commander.

"I was just wondering how much longer it'll take us to reach France," Daniel replied. "It seems that we should be there by now."

Captain Jones laughed. "Give us another four or five days, perhaps a week, depending on the wind. But we'll get there, Lieutenant, I can promise you that."

"I didn't mean to cast doubts—"

"I know that," Jones said. "You're just worried about your missions . . . both of them."

Daniel had told the captain about Roxanne's captivity in England and how he intended to try to rescue her, but he had sworn Jones to secrecy, and he trusted the captain to keep his word.

"I wish there was something else I could do to help besides taking you to France," Jones said now. "If I could, I'd sail right up the Thames to London and fire a broadside right into Parliament. But I'm afraid we'd never get that far."

"Probably not," Daniel commented dryly. "I just hope I'm able to locate Roxanne quickly. General Washington made it plain that I don't have much time to get in and out of England."

Jones put a hand on Daniel's shoulder. "I wish you all the luck in the world, Lieutenant. But you have to remember that your mission to the French is more important in the larger scheme of things than the problems of two people."

"I know," Daniel agreed, his voice grim. "I'll do my job, Captain, don't worry about that."

"I wasn't," Jones told him sympathetically. "Now, come up onto the bridge with me."

Daniel went without complaint. He liked standing on the bridge with Jones, watching as the man issued the orders that kept the ship sailing smoothly and efficiently across the Atlantic. Daniel wasn't a naval expert, by any means, but as far as he could tell from what he had seen, John Paul Jones was a good commander, intelligent and respected by his men.

He was lucky, Daniel thought, that Washington had sent him to Captain Jones and the *Providence.* So far they had not encountered any British ships, and there had been no battle at sea. The vessel was making good time, and each hour brought him closer to Roxanne, he mused, peering out over the restless, majestic sea.

Bramwell Stoddard leaned against the cushioned seat of the coach and closed his eyes. The vehicle rocked and swayed gently along the road between the estate and the nearby town of Ilford, from which the great house had taken its name. Bramwell had spent the afternoon in consultation with the officials in the town, and he was tired. He had never enjoyed dealing with the government, even though its local representatives were eager to help him make the arrangements he desired—whether those arrangements were totally legal or not. After all, Lord Oakley was the area's most influential resident, and no one wanted to offend him. Especially not when it came to something as important as his wedding.

Bramwell felt a little breathless, and he could tell that his pulse was faster than usual. Keeping his eyes closed, he willed himself to calm down. There was no reason to worry; although it had taken longer to arrange than he had hoped, everything was in place for Roxanne to become his wife. Not only that, but as far as the church and the Crown were concerned, the child she was carrying was his and would become his heir as soon as it was born. That was as it should be; otherwise the estate would pass into the hands of Cyril Eldridge when Bramwell died, and he hated the thought of that, knowing what he now knew about his cousin.

Cyril had been sulking around the estate ever since the violent confrontation with Bramwell over his treatment of Roxanne. He'd had little to say to Bramwell over the past few weeks, which was perfectly all right with the lord of the manor.

Bramwell had had the distinct feeling that the officials to whom he had talked felt that he was daft to be marrying a colonist. They would have been even more shocked, he thought with a chuckle, if they had known Roxanne was not only a colonist but a spy for the patriot movement and a prisoner at the estate. Well, that would soon change. Soon Roxanne would be the mistress of Ilford Grange.

Bramwell smiled when he heard Hamish Mac-Quarrie call out to the horses from the driver's seat of the coach. Hamish and Moira had heartily congratulated him when they found out about the impending marriage. They had grown quite fond of Roxanne in the time she had been at the estate, and the two young women had become good friends.

He owed Moira quite a debt, he reflected. Had it not been for her intervention, neither he nor Roxanne might have known the truth about each other. And knowing the truth was what had allowed them to come to an understanding about getting married. It was a union of circumstance—some of the most convoluted circumstances Bramwell could have imagined, in fact.

But he felt a genuine fondness for Roxanne Darragh, and in another time, another place, he would have truly loved her. At least in this time and place they could be of help to each other, and that was worth a great deal, he told himself.

The road wound through a thick stand of trees, and Bramwell smiled as he looked out at the forest. Spring would arrive soon, and it would be more than welcome after another cold, dank winter. The gloomy overcast that lasted for weeks at a time always dampened Bramwell's mood, and he was looking forward to seeing the sun again. Already, the trees were beginning to bud, and soon the leaves would appear.

The miracle of life, he thought. He could see it in the trees, and he could see it in Roxanne's gracefully swelling belly and glowing cheeks. He loved life, and at moments like this he felt a bittersweet regret that he would be leaving it sooner than he should have. But there was nothing he could do but see the facts for what they were and accept them. Death came when it chose and would not be denied.

Bramwell nestled farther back into the seat and closed his eyes, but he jerked upright when a gunshot suddenly boomed nearby.

With the sound of the team's hoofbeats and the clatter of the coach's wheels to confuse things, it was hard to tell where the shot had come from. But the cry of alarm he heard in the next instant definitely came from Hamish. The young Scotsman shouted encouragement to the horses, and Bramwell heard the pop of the whip as Hamish urged the animals on to greater speed. The coach leapt forward with a lurch.

The abrupt jerk threw Bramwell back against the seat again. He recovered his balance, settled his hat more firmly on his head, and leaned forward to thrust his head out the window. As he did so, a shot sounded, and a pistol ball slammed into the elaborate scrollwork of the coach. The shot had passed less than two feet from his head, and Bramwell flinched as a splinter sliced a shallow cut on his cheek.

"Hamish!" he called over the rolling thunder of the team's racing hoofbeats. "What is it?"

"Highwaymen!" Hamish shouted, wielding the whip again with a sharp crack. "They were hiding in the trees!"

Bramwell looked back along the road behind them

and saw four mounted men galloping after the coach. They were brandishing pistols, and as Bramwell looked at them in wide-eyed surprise, one of the men drew a bead on him. Realizing the danger at the last instant, Bramwell ducked inside the coach even as the would-be robber fired. The ball missed the vehicle itself but passed on to burn the flank of one of the horses. The animal let out a whinny of pain.

Grim-faced, Bramwell reached under his coat and yanked out his pistol. He took a deep breath, then leaned out the window, twisted around, and tried to get a clear shot at the pursuers.

The four riders were some fifteen or twenty yards behind the coach. That was long range for a pistol, but Bramwell was an excellent shot. Rather than bracing himself against the swaying and bouncing of the coach, he went with the motion and concentrated on keeping only the gun steady. When he had the sights settled on one of the highwaymen, he pressed the trigger, and the powder in the pan flared and the pistol spewed flame and smoke from its muzzle.

"You got one, sir!" whooped Hamish from the driver's seat, his neck craned so that he could glance over his shoulder as he kept slapping the reins against the backs of the team.

Bramwell heard another shot as he ducked back into the coach. The ball thudded into the body of the vehicle somewhere near him. He not only heard the impact but felt the vibration from it as he hurriedly reloaded his pistol, spilling some of the powder from his horn when the coach hit a bad bump.

Up ahead, the road took several sharp turns, and Bramwell knew that the coach would be forced to slow down. The men on horseback would probably catch up to them. But he had already downed one of the men, and he would give a hot welcome to at least one more. They would not find him an easy man to rob.

A faint smile plucked at Bramwell's mouth. His pulse was racing again, but instead of feeling breathless and weak, as he had earlier, a seemingly boundless energy filled him at this moment. Life was never so sweet, he supposed, as when one was in imminent danger of losing it. But all he knew for sure was that he felt wonderful, and that he would fight to the last breath in his body if he had to.

But if he died now, a voice of reason warned him, Roxanne would be at Cyril's mercy. Not only that, but she and the child would not inherit the estate.

This attack by highwaymen, if it was successful, was going to be quite a stroke of luck for Cyril, Bramwell realized. Or perhaps luck had nothing to do with it.

He felt the coach slow down as Hamish hauled back on the lines to guide the team into the first curve. Leaning to the side to balance himself, Bramwell thrust his pistol out the window and aimed at one of the thieves. He fired, then said, "Blast!" when he realized that none of the men had fallen or even jerked in their saddles. A clean miss, he thought, but there was another sharp turn coming up.

The coach slowed even more, but the highwaymen pounded on relentlessly. Bramwell settled back on his seat and reloaded. The sound of hoofbeats grew louder, and he looked up to see that one of the highwaymen had drawn even with the coach, and the man was aiming a pistol through the window at him.

In the instant before Bramwell threw himself to the side, he realized that something strange was going on. The robbers who plagued travelers in these woods were more interested in stopping the coaches than in killing the occupants. The man riding alongside the coach should have been aiming at Hamish. It suddenly struck Bramwell that *he* was the target—and only one man had a strong motive for wanting him dead.

The highwayman fired, and the ball whipped past Bramwell's head to bury itself in the seat cushion. He had his pistol reloaded by now and lifted it smoothly as the coach swung into the next turn. The rider was crowding the vehicle, almost touching it, and the shot was point-blank as Bramwell blew the man right out of his saddle.

At that same instant, as Hamish whipped the team through the tight turn, the coach began to tip over. Bramwell was so deafened by the gunshots that he could not hear Hamish's cry of alarm, but he felt the coach going. He leapt toward the door on the far side of the vehicle, slapped it open, and jumped clear as one of the wheels came off and the coach rolled over twice before coming to a stop on its side.

Bramwell landed hard, but he had the presence of mind to tuck his shoulder under and roll with the fall. When he came up on his hands and knees, he saw the wrecked coach and the writhing tangle of legs and harness and heard the horses screaming in fear. Bramwell was sure some of them had been mortally injured in the accident. He just hoped Hamish had had a chance to jump clear before the coach went over.

There was no time to look for the young Scotsman, though, because the two remaining highwaymen were reining in their mounts frantically in an attempt to avoid the wreckage in the road. The hooves of one man's horse almost trampled Bramwell as he scrambled out of the way. The rider tried to bring his pistol to bear, but Bramwell surged to his feet, grabbed the man's arm, and tore him violently out of the saddle.

As he fell the thief's head was dashed against a

sharp rock by the side of the road, and Bramwell heard the unmistakable, sickening sound of a neck snapping. The highwayman's pistol slipped from his lifeless fingers.

"Look out, sir!"

It was Hamish's voice, and Bramwell dove forward instinctively when he heard the warning. A gun fired and the ball plucked at the hem of Bramwell's coat as he threw himself to the ground. He spotted the pistol dropped by the dying brigand and deftly scooped it up. The last highwayman was several yards away, still mounted but with his hands full as he tried to control his horse. From his position on the ground, Bramwell angled the barrel of the pistol up, cocked the weapon, and pulled the trigger, trusting instinct and luck to guide his shot.

The ball hit the man's chest and spun him off his horse. Bramwell got up quickly and looked around to see if there were any enemies he had overlooked. He was the only one standing, however, until a moment later when Hamish hurried around the side of the wrecked coach.

"Mr. Bramwell!" he called anxiously. "Are ye all right?"

Bramwell was breathing heavily, and now that the violence was over, he felt his hands and knees beginning to tremble.

"I'm fine, Hamish. Really, I am."

"Are ye shot?"

"No. I was very lucky, I'd say. Not a scratch."

Hamish could not say the same. His face was bloody from a gash on his forehead, and he was limping. But he grinned as he looked at Bramwell and said, "Well, no' quite, sir. Ye've one scratch there." He pointed at Bramwell's cheek.

He lifted his hand to his face and looked in surprise at the blood on his fingertips. Then he remembered the flying splinter that had cut his cheek, and he
laughed. "If that's the worst that happened in an attack
by four highwaymen, I still consider myself very lucky."
He looked at the bodies sprawled in the road and
asked, "Are they all dead?"

"I'll check, sir," Hamish offered. A moment later
he stood beside one of the bodies. "This one's still
breathin'. No' very much alive, though, so if ye want t'
talk t' him, sir, ye'd best hurry."

"Why did you attack our coach?" Bramwell asked,
kneeling beside the man. "You might as well talk and
make things easier for yourself." Not that it would
really do any good, he added silently. The wounded
man had only minutes to live. From the sound of his
breathing, the ball had clipped a lung.

The man's pale, haggard features contorted, and
he said in a bubbling voice, "We was . . . well
paid . . . not to talk . . . damn you!"

"That money will do you no good now," Bramwell
pointed out. He leaned closer, and his voice took on
added urgency as he demanded, "Was it my cousin?
Did Cyril Eldridge pay you to kill me and make it look
like a robbery?"

The dying highwayman blinked rapidly as he
growled, "Go to . . . 'ell. . . . You've killed me . . .
you and that cousin of yours both."

"Then Cyril did hire you?" Bramwell insisted as he
grasped the man's shoulders, trying to keep the life in
him until the man had told him what he needed to
know.

For a few seconds, he thought he had failed, that
death had already come. But then a hoarse whisper

filtered out of the man's throat. "Aye," he managed to say. "It was . . . him."

The last word was almost drowned out by a rattling cough. A spasm shook the man, blood welled from his mouth, and he fell back limply.

"Good Lord!" exclaimed Hamish. "Why would yer cousin try t' have ye killed, Mr. Bramwell?"

"It's quite simple, really," Bramwell replied grimly as he got to his feet. "Cyril wants me dead before the wedding with Roxanne can take place." His breath caught in his throat. "Roxanne!"

Cyril was nothing if not thorough; Bramwell knew that from experience. If Cyril had worked up the courage to try to have Bramwell killed, it was possible he might strike against Roxanne, too.

Bramwell swung toward the team. "Find one of those horses that can still run or at least walk and cut him loose from the others," he barked at Hamish. "And put the others out of their misery, then follow me to the estate as fast as you can."

"Wha' are ye goin' t' do, Mr. Bramwell?" asked Hamish as he contemplated the grim task before him.

"I'm riding to Ilford Grange," Bramwell said, "and I pray to God I'm not already too late."

Roxanne and Moira were in the upstairs bedchamber that had been Roxanne's room the entire time she had been at Ilford Grange. She was not confined to a single room anymore, of course; she was soon to be the mistress of the entire house and could go wherever she chose . . . within reason. Bramwell Stoddard, for all his lack of interest in politics, was loyal to his king, and Roxanne had been brought here as a prisoner of the Crown. Bramwell was not ready to give her free rein just yet, perhaps fearing that if he did so she would leave and try to return to the colonies.

That was what Roxanne intended to do eventually. But now that she was past the seventh month of her pregnancy, she was in no shape to be traveling. No, she decided, it would be safer for her to marry Bramwell and enjoy his protection until after her child was born. Then she could figure out what to do next.

Roxanne stood on a chair while Moira pinned up the hem of the wedding gown Roxanne was trying on. Moira had made the dress, putting long hours of work into the yards of white silk and lace until she had fashioned a beautiful garment that would have made any bride proud. Roxanne looked down at the gown and smiled wistfully.

"Somehow I don't think this is quite appropriate," she said ruefully, her hands gliding over the silk that covered her rounded belly. "A bride so obviously with child in a white wedding gown, I mean."

"'Tis yer first wedding, is it not?" asked Moira around the pins in her mouth.

"Well, yes, but . . ."

"Then ye ha' th' right t' wear white, as far as I be concerned. Now, I dinna want t' hear any more about it no' bein' proper, do ye ken?"

Roxanne smiled. "All right. And thank you, Moira. You've been awfully kind to me."

"Ye've been good for Mr. Bramwell," the housekeeper said, looking up at her. "Ye deserve any kindness Hamish and me can do for ye." She straightened and put her hands on her hips. "I'm out o' pins. I'll run down to me room and get some more. D' ye mind waitin' there on the chair for me?"

"Not at all. Go right ahead," Roxanne told her.

Moira hurried out of the room and closed the door

behind her. Roxanne's hands still rested on her belly, and she flinched suddenly when the baby kicked. The child had been quite active for two months now, and sometimes it felt as if it was stomping through Roxanne's insides wearing gardening boots. She smiled a little at that thought. She could put up with any amount of discomfort as long as it meant that the child she and Daniel had made would be born healthy and grow up happy.

The door opened and closed again behind her, and she said, "You got back quickly with those pins, Moira."

There was no answer but harsh breathing.

Feeling the blood in her veins turn to ice, Roxanne jerked her head around, then threw her arms out to the sides to catch her balance. She was horrified to see Cyril Eldridge standing there, his narrow eyes filled with hate as he stared at her.

Without taking his eyes from her, he reached behind him and twisted the key in the lock.

"Don't do that!" Roxanne said sharply. "You'd better get out of here, Cyril, before Bramwell returns. You know he doesn't want you to bother me."

A hideous semblance of a smile passed over Eldridge's face. "Dear cousin Bramwell won't be returning," he said. "I hate to tell you this, Miss Darragh, but Bramwell was attacked and killed by some highwaymen on his way back to the estate from Ilford earlier this afternoon. There will be no wedding."

"No!" The cry ripped from Roxanne's mouth, mingling shock, pain, and disbelief.

"Oh, yes," Cyril said smugly. "In fact, we should be hearing all about the dreadful tragedy . . . quite soon."

The meaning of his words sank into Roxanne's

stunned brain, and anger welled up within her. "You!" she all but spat. "You're responsible!"

The ugly smile on Cyril's face widened. "Indeed I am. But you'll never have a chance to tell anyone. You see, you're going to . . . slip while you're standing up there and fall to the floor. You're going to lose your baby and in the process bleed to death. It was very convenient of you to climb up there like that, Miss Darragh. You've saved me all the trouble of making up a suitable story. Now your death will truly look like an accident."

"No one will believe you," she said hotly, concentrating on her anger so that her growing fear would not overwhelm her. "Moira and Hamish will know the truth."

"Unfortunately, MacQuarrie died in the same ambush as Bramwell. And no one is going to listen to the ravings of a grief-stricken Caledonian woman, not over the testimony of a respected member of His Majesty's government."

Eldridge was right, Roxanne thought miserably. If Bramwell and Hamish were truly dead, then Eldridge could kill her, too, and make the murder appear to be anything he chose. Her only chance was to fight him off.

As if he had read her mind, he slipped a small knife from the pocket of his coat. "So much blood," he murmured. "It's going to be difficult to tell what really happened here, what with all the blood."

Roxanne felt helpless, balanced on the chair, with Eldridge advancing slowly toward her. She had to do something.

Suddenly the doorknob rattled, and Moira called anxiously, "Miss Roxanne? Is something wrong? Why is th' door locked?"

Roxanne screamed as loud as she could.

Cursing, Eldridge sprang forward and lifted the knife. Roxanne jerked away from him, but her balance deserted her, and she felt herself falling backward. Time seemed to slow down as she hung suspended in the air, and outside the room heavy footsteps sounded in the hall. Something crashed into the door, then hit it again and yet again.

Roxanne cried out in pain and desperate fear when she landed on the floor. Eldridge loomed over her, the knife upraised, but before he could strike, the door of the room slammed open under the onslaught of Bramwell and Hamish, who spilled through the opening as the doorjamb splintered. Hamish stumbled and went to one knee, but Bramwell kept his feet. As Cyril spun toward him in surprise, Bramwell's left hand closed over his cousin's wrist and wrenched hard. The knife fell from Cyril's fingers, and before it even hit the floor, Bramwell's bunched right fist crashed into Cyril's face. Cyril staggered, then folded up like a puppet whose strings had been cut.

Bramwell knelt beside Roxanne, lines of fear and concern etched on his face.

"Roxanne!" he said urgently. "Are you all right?" He caught one of her hands in his.

She was breathless, and her heart was pounding wildly in her breast, but as Bramwell helped her into a sitting position, she took stock of herself and found no pain other than an ache in her hip where she had landed on the floor.

"I . . . I'm all right," she whispered.

Bramwell put his arms around her and crushed her to him for a moment, then placed his hands on her shoulders and looked intently at her.

"You're sure?" he asked.

"I'm fine. I was just so frightened when Cyril . . . when he told me you were dead."

"That was his plan," Bramwell replied grimly. "He hired men to ambush me, but they were the ones who met with the bad end."

"Speakin' o' bad ends, sir," said Hamish, "what would ye ha' me do with this 'un?"

Roxanne saw that the young Scotsman was holding a pistol in one hand and had it trained unerringly on Cyril. Hamish's other arm was around Moira's shoulders in a reassuring hug.

"Keep an eye on him while he packs his things, and then make sure that he's off the estate by nightfall," Bramwell said coldly.

Cyril had a hand on his swollen jaw, but he took it away and said thickly, "You can't do that, Bramwell! This is my home, too."

"Only by my sufferance, which is at an end." Bramwell stood and turned so that he loomed over his cousin. His hands clenched into fists, and Roxanne could tell that he was fighting off the murderous impulses that must be running through him.

"I renounce the bond of blood between us, Cyril. You're no longer welcome here, and if I see you on my land again, I'll not be responsible for what happens."

"I'm an agent of the king—" Eldridge sputtered.

"This is a private affair, and no business of the king," Bramwell cut in. "An English lord still has certain rights, and the king will not interfere in this matter. If you seek his aid, I'll make you a laughingstock in London, Cyril, as well as see that you are relieved of your duties in the Ministry of War."

"You can't—"

"Oppose me, and you'll see what I can and cannot

do," Bramwell said, his voice cold and hard with menace.

Cyril swallowed nervously and dropped his angry gaze. He had been defeated, at least for the moment.

Bramwell turned to Roxanne, helped her to her feet, and put his arm protectively around her shoulders.

"When you've seen to putting Mr. Eldridge off the estate," he said to Hamish, "take the coach to the village and fetch the vicar. There's going to be a wedding. Tonight!"

"Bramwell!" Roxanne gasped. "But we're not ready."

He looked at her determinedly. "I'll not wait any longer. You shall be Lady Oakley before this day is over, Roxanne, so that Cyril will no longer have any motive for his villainy." His attitude softened a little. "Is that all right with you?"

Roxanne had been prepared to take this step, and now she would just be taking it a little sooner than she had intended.

"It's fine with me," she said softly.

Bramwell's embrace tightened, and he bent his head and lightly kissed her hair. She closed her eyes and sighed. Finally, after all the terrible things that had happened, fortune had smiled on her again, and she had found a good man to help her. She wondered fleetingly if Daniel would have liked Bramwell. She wanted to think so, but she would never know, because Daniel was part of her past, and from now on, her eyes would be on the future.

Cyril Eldridge burned with shame, humiliation, and rage as Hamish prodded him down the stairs. No one could be allowed to thwart his will like this, no one, and especially not Bramwell!

"Mind ye remember wha' Mr. Bramwell said," Hamish warned him at the front door of the mansion. "Dinna come back here, ever. I've saddled ye a horse and loaded yer things in th' coach. I'll deliver 'em t' th' inn in town when I go t' fetch th' vicar. Now get goin', Eldridge."

"You'll regret talking to me like that when I return to claim the estate." Cyril looked at the Scotsman coldly. "Bramwell is a fool, and a dying fool at that. His ruse in marrying that traitorous commoner will fail, you'll see."

Leaning close to him, Hamish said quietly, "If ye dinna shut yer mouth and get on tha' horse and ride out o' here, I'll save Mr. Bramwell th' trouble o' killin' ye."

Trembling with outrage, Cyril clamped his mouth shut, awkwardly mounted and turned the animal, then banged his heels against its flanks and galloped away from the great house.

Bramwell might have won this round, Cyril thought, but just as he had told Hamish, Bramwell was a fool. He might have placed another obstacle between Cyril and the estate, but that obstacle could be overcome. Once Bramwell was gone, if that redheaded slut and her whelp were to die, the estate would still go to its rightful inheritor—Cyril Eldridge.

No, Cyril thought with an icy smile, he was not through with the Stoddard family just yet, not by a long shot.

Chapter Sixteen

D aniel pulled his horse to a stop and leaned forward in the saddle to ease his aching muscles. He had ridden long and hard, and he would soon reach the great estate called Ilford Grange.

He had asked for directions to the estate in the village of Ilford, and the stout yeoman of whom he had inquired had been happy to oblige. If the man wondered about Daniel's American accent—which Daniel had tried to minimize as much as possible—he'd said nothing about it. Besides, Daniel supposed, many Englishmen had spent some time in the colonies and then returned to the mother country with a trace of an accent.

Ah, but if the villagers had known he was really a lieutenant in the patriot army and a member of George

Washington's staff . . . well, then things might have been different.

It had been a little over a week since Captain John Paul Jones and the *Providence* had dropped anchor at Le Havre. Daniel had found representatives of the French government waiting for him, and they explained that they had been expecting an emissary from Benjamin Franklin and George Washington. Even if the matter of rescuing Roxanne had not arisen, Daniel realized, there was every chance General Washington would have sent him here anyway.

The negotiations were hampered somewhat by Daniel's less than perfect command of the French language, but luckily the diplomats from Paris spoke English fairly well. In less than two days, it had been agreed that the French would prepare a shipload of medical supplies for transit to the rebelling English colonies in North America. When it was decided that Daniel would sail back to America on the supply ship, Captain Jones was free to return to sea in hopes of finding some British vessels to harry. Daniel had spent another day wrapping up his official business with the French, and then he had broached the subject of the real reason he was there—Roxanne.

He supposed that his dilemma appealed to the romantic nature of the Frenchmen, because they could not do enough to help him in his effort to rescue the woman he loved. It was quickly arranged for him to be smuggled across the Channel into England. The French diplomats also agreed to have a small boat waiting offshore in the same place each night for a week, as Daniel figured it would take him at least that long to locate Roxanne and free her from captivity.

It had been an optimistic estimate, even with the names of several supporters of the patriot cause to use as contacts. He had found the names, along with a note from his old friends Benjamin Tallmadge and Robert Townsend, in the dispatch case Washington had given him before he left Cambridge. It didn't surprise him that Tallmadge and Townsend knew of Roxanne's plight. Nor was he shocked that the two patriot spymasters had contacts in England itself.

But even with that unexpected assistance, the trail had been long and difficult. Daniel had spent the better part of three days just locating someone who could tell him something about the British ship that had brought Roxanne to England.

A minor functionary in the harbormaster's office at Liverpool had seen a beautiful woman with red hair being taken off a warship a couple of months earlier. The description fit Roxanne, and Daniel, elated at the confirmation that she was indeed alive, could not imagine another lovely redhead being brought in by a warship. The woman had left in the company of a certain major who was known to have rented a house near the town. In return for a healthy bribe, the office worker told Daniel where to look.

The trail had gotten cold after that, until Daniel found a farmer who had noticed a coach traveling through the area with a military escort and a beautiful young woman inside. He had pointed Daniel in the proper direction, and after that it was a simple matter of asking the right questions in the towns and villages he came to. It was a tracking job even Murdoch would have been proud of, Daniel thought.

Finally, as he drew nearer and nearer to London, he found someone who remembered that the coach belonged to Cyril Eldridge, a government official who lived on an estate some twenty miles away, near the village of Ilford. That had been at midmorning of this very day, and Daniel had ridden hard ever since, not stopping except to ask in Ilford where he might find Cyril Eldridge's estate. There he learned that the place was called Ilford Grange and that it belonged not to Eldridge but to one Bramwell Stoddard, Lord Oakley.

And now he was almost at his destination. He knew he could not ride right up to the front door of the mansion and inquire about Roxanne. He would have to be more cautious than that. So when he reached the path leading through the rolling lawns to the great house, he reined his horse off to one side and tied it out of sight in a thick stand of trees.

From what he could see of the mansion and the property, Ilford Grange was an impressive place. Bramwell Stoddard must be a rich man indeed, Daniel thought, and he wondered why Roxanne had been brought here.

For the next half hour, Daniel worked his way closer and closer to the house, taking his time and being careful to stay out of sight. His nerves were stretched taut, and even though he had no proof that Roxanne was here, every instinct in his body told him that she was.

Finally he was within twenty yards of the house, and the cover had gotten quite sparse. He crouched behind a low row of shrubbery, peered through the growth, and tried to figure out a way to cross the open ground next to the mansion. A quick dash might have to suffice, but there were quite a few windows in the wall facing him, and if anyone inside happened to glance out, they would see him immediately. It was a chance he had to take, he decided, and he tensed his muscles for action.

"I would'na be makin' any quick moves, me friend, else I'm liable t' pull th' trigger o' this gun."

Daniel froze as the menacing voice spoke behind him. For one insane moment, the man's accent made Daniel think that Murdoch had just spoken to him, but he realized right away that the voice was different from that of the frontiersman.

"I'm not looking for any trouble."

"Is tha' so? Ye could ha' fooled me, skulkin' around th' way ye been doin'. I been watchin' ye, mister, and I ain't in no mood t' be lied to. Wha' do ye want here?"

"Can I at least stand up and turn around?"

There was a moment of silence, and then the man said, "Slowly, me bucko, slowly. And keep them hands where I can see 'em."

Following orders, Daniel straightened and lifted his hands to the sides as he turned around. He saw a young man standing about ten feet away with a cocked flintlock pistol in his hand. The man was a few years older than he and had reddish-brown hair and a broad face. He wore boots, brown whipcord pants, and a brown coat over a homespun work shirt. A black tricorn was pushed back on his thatch of hair.

"Are you Bramwell Stoddard?" asked Daniel.

"Not hardly." The man laughed. "Do I look like th' laird o' th' manor?"

"Now that you mention it, no. You're Cyril Eldridge, then?"

This time the man grimaced as if there was a sudden bad taste in his mouth. "Since ye be a stranger hereabouts, ye dinna ken how much ye're insultin' me," he said. "Me name is Hamish MacQuarrie, and I'm th' groundskeeper o' Ilford Grange. And it seems t' me tha' ye be askin' a lot o' questions, considerin' tha' I'm th' one holdin' th' gun!"

Well, he had found out a little bit, Daniel thought

as he stood there tensely. Obviously Cyril Eldridge was not well liked around here, at least not by Hamish Mac-Quarrie.

"Look," began Daniel, "as I said, I'm not here to make trouble. My name is Daniel Reed, and I'm looking for either Bramwell Stoddard or Cyril Eldridge."

"Eldridge does'na live here anymore," MacQuarrie replied. "And Mr. Bramwell is busy these days. Th' lord just got married a couple o' days ago."

"I'm sorry, but I must see him and speak to him," Daniel said. Maybe Stoddard could help him. From what the Scotsman was saying, there might have been some trouble between Stoddard and Eldridge. And Eldridge was the one who'd had Roxanne as his prisoner.

"Oh, ye must speak to Mr. Bramwell, must ye?" responded MacQuarrie. "A wee bit high an' mighty, ain't ye?" Suddenly he frowned. "Now I know where I heard tha' same sort o' accent. Ye be an American!"

Daniel just looked stoically at his captor. There was no point in denying the accusation.

MacQuarrie gestured toward the house with the barrel of the pistol. "All right, get on in wi' ye. I hate t' disturb Mr. Bramwell, but this is goin' t' need a smarter brain than mine t' figure it all out."

Well, he was getting what he wanted, Daniel thought, even though he had not expected to be taken into the house at gunpoint. All he could do now was try to make the best of the situation. He was fairly confident he could get away from Stoddard and MacQuarrie if he needed to, although they would arouse the countryside against him and he would have a much more difficult time following Roxanne's trail.

With MacQuarrie directing him, Daniel went to a side door and opened it. Inside, the house was luxuriously furnished, even the small corridor in which Daniel found himself. MacQuarrie prodded him into a main hall.

"They be in th' study, I reckon," the Scotsman said. "Move along now."

Daniel went to the door that MacQuarrie indicated and grasped the knob.

"Knock on th' door," MacQuarrie snapped.

Daniel rapped his knuckles on the gleaming hardwood panel, and a voice from inside asked, "What is it?"

"'Tis me, sir," MacQuarrie replied. "I found a gent skulkin' around outside, and he says he wants t' speak t' ye."

"Come in," Bramwell Stoddard replied.

Daniel stepped into the room, and his eyes darted from side to side, quickly taking in everything he saw. The room was lined with bookshelves and had a large window that overlooked the grounds and a massive fireplace to one side. A tall man with a commanding presence stood there by the mantel, one hand on the back of a wing chair in which a woman sat. The woman was young and lovely, with a cascade of red hair—

Daniel's brown eyes met her green ones across the room. Her hands flew to her mouth, and she screamed. As she started up out of the chair, Daniel and Stoddard cried out at the same instant, "Roxanne!"

And then her eyes rolled up in her head and she fainted dead away.

It had been a nightmare, Roxanne thought as consciousness stole back into her head, nothing but a nightmare. She had only dreamed that she was in the study with Bramwell when the ghost stepped into the room. She knew it had been an apparition, a figment of a disturbed imagination, because Daniel was dead. He had been dead for months. Just a nightmare, Roxanne told herself again, and when she was fully awake, she would find herself in her bed, safe from any cruel phantoms that forced her to remember the pain and loss she had suffered.

Then her eyelids flickered open, and she gazed up into his face again, the features she remembered so well now etched with lines of concern.

"Roxanne?" Daniel whispered as he leaned over her. "Roxanne, are you all right?"

A hysterical laugh burst from her lips. There was no denying the evidence of her own eyes. Daniel was alive, but that meant everything else—Major Kane, Cyril Eldridge, her long captivity, Bramwell—all of that had been the fiction. She must have dozed off in the hay in Lemuel Parsons's barn and had a long, horrible dream.

"Is she coming around?" Bramwell asked, peering anxiously over Daniel's shoulder.

Roxanne wanted to scream again, but she forced down the impulse. Both men were here, leaning over her, and she gradually realized that she was lying on a sofa in Bramwell's study. It was all real.

"Daniel?" she whispered.

He caught her hand. "I'm right here," he said earnestly. "And I'll never leave you again, Roxanne."

"Help me up. If I'm to lose my mind, I don't want to do it lying down."

"You're not losing your mind, my dear," Bramwell said grimly as Daniel helped her into a sitting position on the sofa. He stayed close beside her, holding her hand, while Bramwell stepped back, crossed his arms on his chest, and regarded them with a solemn, worried look.

"How . . . how did you get here, Daniel?"

"I've been looking for you for months," he told her, "ever since that British patrol raided Lemuel's farm and knocked me out. When I came to, I discovered that they'd carried you off!"

"But you were dead!" Roxanne exclaimed, still struggling with disbelief. "They checked your body and said you were dead."

"Then they were either mistaken or lying, because I'm very much alive." Daniel glanced up at Bramwell. "At least for now."

"You had best start at the beginning and explain the whole thing," Bramwell said. "I'm afraid I'm quite confused."

The story tumbled out of Daniel then, how he had searched for Roxanne first in Boston and then here in England. He revealed without hesitation that he was a member of the patriot army; the shock of seeing Roxanne had left him stunned and unable to come up with a suitable falsehood.

Bramwell nodded occasionally as the story was pieced together, and his stern look softened slightly, and when Daniel was finished, he said, "Well, we seem to have something of a dilemma here. You're aware, Mr. Reed, that I could summon the authorities and have you taken away?"

Roxanne clutched Daniel's hand tightly. "Bramwell! You wouldn't do that."

"But you certainly could," Daniel admitted.

"However, I won't. I'm a Whig, Mr. Reed, at least officially—although I have to admit politics usually do not interest me in the least. I've never supported the idea of going to war against the colonies, and I won't betray you to the army. You have my word on that."

"Thank you," Daniel said sincerely.

"But we still have the problem of what to do with you. And there's the matter of Roxanne being my wife."

She saw Daniel look at her sharply, and she tried to read what was in his eyes. Anger? Disappointment? Disbelief? Roxanne could not be sure, but she knew he was surprised. His expression was equally unreadable as his gaze dropped momentarily to her stomach. She was clearly pregnant, and he had to at least suspect that the child was his.

But all he said was, "I'd say the next move is up to you, Lord Oakley."

"Indeed," murmured Bramwell. "You shall have sanctuary here, Mr. Reed, until we can make arrangements for you to be smuggled out of England. Then you can return to the colonies or go wherever else you might wish. But Roxanne will not be going with you."

Daniel stiffened at Bramwell's words. "I don't agree," he said flatly.

"I was not giving you a choice, sir. I am merely telling you how things are going to be."

"I won't leave without her."

"As I said, you have no choice."

Daniel stood up, and Roxanne had the horrible feeling that violence was about to erupt in the room. Some women might have been flattered by the idea of two men coming to blows over her, she thought, but she just wanted them to stop this madness.

Then Hamish MacQuarrie stepped back into the room and said, "Beggin' yer pardon, Mr. Bramwell, but there's a wee problem tha' needs yer attention."

"What is it?" Bramwell snapped.

"Yer cousin is outside," Hamish said, "and he's got some men with him who look like right louts, sir. Highwaymen, I'd say, like tha' bunch he hired t' try t' kill us."

"Cyril? What the devil does he want?"

Hamish leveled a finger at Roxanne. "He says he wants Lady Oakley—and he means t' have her, one way or another."

Daniel still didn't fully understand what was going on. It was almost more than his mind could comprehend that Roxanne was not only here at Ilford Grange, but also that she was married to the lord of the estate—and pregnant. Who was the baby's father?

Bramwell Stoddard had stiffened angrily at the news Hamish had brought.

Daniel saw his reaction and took a chance on a question. "This man Eldridge," he said, "who is he, and what does he want with Roxanne?"

"He's my cousin, and he's also an assistant deputy minister in the Ministry of War," Bramwell replied. "I suspect he has something to do with espionage."

There was the connection between Eldridge and Roxanne, Daniel thought. Someone in the British army who knew of her activities as a patriot agent had gotten hold of her after she was captured and sent her over here to Cyril Eldridge, who was probably connected with the British intelligence apparatus. The circuitous trail that had led Daniel to this estate now made more sense.

"You can't let Eldridge have her," he said to Bramwell.

"I don't intend to." Bramwell put a hand on Roxanne's shoulder. Daniel suppressed an angry reaction at the possessiveness of the gesture, and Bramwell went on, "I suspect Cyril really wants more than Roxanne. You see, he expected to inherit my estate and title, until Roxanne and I were married. Before that, I banished

Cyril from the estate because he tried to have both of us killed."

Daniel tensed. "You're saying he wants to murder both you and Roxanne?"

"That's right, Daniel," she said before Bramwell could reply. "But he doesn't know anything about you. You can still slip away."

"And leave you here to Eldridge's mercies? No, I would never do that, Roxanne." He faced Bramwell squarely. "I'll do anything I can to help. It seems that fate has cast us in the role of allies."

"Yes, it does, doesn't it?" Bramwell smiled ironically and turned to Hamish. "Tell Cyril that he can come in, but his bully boys will have to stay outside. I'll speak to him in here."

"I'll tell him. But he's got a wild look in his eye, Mr. Bramwell. I would'na trust him if I was ye."

"Don't worry, Hamish. I don't intend to."

The Scotsman hurried out of the study, and Bramwell said to Roxanne, "Why don't you go upstairs, my dear? You'll be safer there."

"I'd rather stay here," Roxanne said stubbornly.

"Well, I didn't really intend for Mr. Reed to be a party to this discussion—"

"I'm staying," Daniel interrupted.

"There's no time to argue with either of you," Bramwell said. "Just be quiet and let me do the talking with Cyril."

A moment later, a short, slender man with narrow, unpleasant features stalked into the room. He gave Daniel a curious glance, then turned his attention to Bramwell and said, "I don't suppose you expected me to return this soon, did you, cousin?"

"I told you to stay away from Ilford Grange or be

prepared to suffer the consequences," Bramwell replied, his voice taut with anger.

Cyril Eldridge laughed humorlessly. "I'm afraid you're the one who is going to suffer, Bramwell, unless you come to your senses. I have eight men outside, more than your Caledonian there can handle. Unless you agree to sign the estate over to me immediately, neither you nor your blushing bride, nor your unfortunate friend here, whose identity is unknown to me, will leave here alive." Eldridge spread his hands and added, "I hate to be so blunt about this, but you've left me no choice. I intend to have what I want, Bramwell, and if you oppose me, I'll kill you and everyone else in this room."

For a long moment Bramwell said nothing. Then, in a voice that grated between clenched teeth, he uttered, "You insufferable little bastard! How dare you, Cyril?"

"Great men dare whatever is necessary for greatness," Cyril said smugly. "And I *will* be Lord Oakley, Bramwell." He slid a hand underneath his coat. "I've already had a solicitor draw up all the necessary papers—"

"Look out!" Daniel cried. "He's got a gun!"

Daniel leapt toward Eldridge, but Bramwell moved faster. "Protect Roxanne, Mr. Reed!" he called, then got between Daniel and Eldridge. He reached for his smaller cousin, but Eldridge darted away from him.

Eldridge cursed bitterly and pointed his pistol at Bramwell, Roxanne, and Daniel. "Stay back!" he warned. "MacQuarrie! Get over there with the others. Where's that wife of yours?"

"Moira's gone into th' village t' do some marketin', thank th' Lord," he said, slowly walking over to join the others. "'Tis glad I am she's not here t' see what a sorry pass things have come to."

Eldridge's thin lips quirked into an ugly smile, and he said, "She'll have quite an unpleasant surprise waiting for her when she comes home, won't she?" He looked from Daniel to Bramwell and went on, "I'm withdrawing my offer of clemency, since it was made before I knew you were harboring an American spy, Bramwell. The name Reed struck me as familiar, and now I know where I've heard it." He glanced at Daniel again. "You're Daniel Reed, aren't you? Miss Darragh's lover and her partner in treasonous schemes against the Crown? Oh, yes, I've heard all about you."

Daniel's mind was whirling. He had no idea how Eldridge knew about him and his connection with Roxanne, but such things no longer mattered.

"I don't know what you're talking about, Cyril," Bramwell was saying. "Mr. Reed is an old friend from Northampton—"

"Don't bother lying to me, Bramwell," Eldridge said with a sneer. "The man's voice will condemn him. Why don't you say something else, Mr. Reed? Well?"

"Go to hell," Daniel growled, not bothering to try to conceal his American accent.

"Ah, there you are, proof of my supposition." Eldridge lifted the pistol slightly and continued, "I'm going to summon my men and have one of them bring the authorities to place all of you under arrest. Control of the estate will pass to me, and once you and your bride are behind bars, all sorts of accidents can be arranged so that the situation will be permanent. Yes, indeed, everything is going to work out just fine."

The smug grin on Eldridge's face was as maddening as his oily voice, Daniel thought. Fear for Roxanne's life—and the life of the child she was carrying—warred inside him with anger and a fierce desire to thwart Eldridge's scheme. Bramwell had retreated to take up a position on the other side of Roxanne, who still sat on the sofa, her face pale and drawn. Hamish stood off to the left of Bramwell.

Daniel felt his heart thudding heavily in his chest. One of them had to stop Eldridge. His muscles tensed. A quick leap, Daniel thought, a fast blow to knock Eldridge unconscious before he could fire. It was a slim chance, but the only one they had. He got ready to move—

Bramwell acted first.

The nobleman shouted, "I'll see you in Hades first!" and threw himself at his cousin.

Eldridge jerked the pistol toward Bramwell and fired. The ball took Bramwell in the body, but his momentum carried him on into Eldridge, and his fist smashed into Eldridge's face and drove the small man backward. Eldridge collapsed, out cold.

But the shot he had managed to get off before Bramwell hit him would have alerted the men waiting outside.

Bramwell staggered, one hand pressed to his midsection, but he stayed on his feet. Daniel leapt forward and caught his arm to support him, while Hamish held his employer on the other side.

"Bramwell! You're hurt!" With tears running down her cheeks, Roxanne hurried to his side.

"Don't worry," Bramwell said in a firm voice, straightening and shaking off Daniel's and Hamish's grip. "It's not a bad wound. But those men will be here any moment, and we've got to stop them. Hamish, come with me. Mr. Reed, if you'll stay here and care for Roxanne—"

"No!" Roxanne said. "I can handle a gun. I'm coming with you."

There was no time for arguing, and they knew it.

"Come along, then," Bramwell said with a smile of admiration.

All of Daniel's protective instincts were in full flower, and he wanted Roxanne to stay where it was safe, too. But he knew she could fire a gun, and she could reload for the rest of them if that was what was needed. Bramwell and Hamish ran toward the foyer at the front of the house, and Daniel and Roxanne were right behind.

"I barred th' door when I let Eldridge in," Hamish said breathlessly, "but it sounds like they're already tryin' t' break it down."

"Here," Bramwell said, yanking open a gun cabinet of beautifully polished hardwood. He handed muskets to Daniel and Hamish, along with powder and shot, then took a pistol for himself and after a moment's hesitation handed one to Roxanne as well.

"Whatever happens, my dear," he said quietly, "you know that . . . I truly did love you."

"I know," she whispered.

Daniel forced down the bitter taste of jealousy that surged up into his throat. They would have to work this out later—if they were all still alive.

The sound of something—probably several shoulders—thudding against the front door of the mansion had gotten louder. Daniel tried to ignore it as he poured powder in the barrel of the musket, rammed a ball and wadding home, then primed the weapon with more powder in the pan. When it was ready to fire, he turned toward the doorway. Beside him, Roxanne, Bramwell, and Hamish stood ready.

The heavy door splintered and crashed open, and

several men stumbled through. More were waiting just outside. They all carried pistols, and as one of them spotted the four people waiting on the other side of the foyer, he yelled, "Look out!"

The defenders of the house fired as one.

The murderous volley ripped into the attackers, spilling a couple of them with mortal wounds and sending the others scurrying for cover.

"Upstairs!" Bramwell called, and the four of them backed hurriedly toward the broad staircase that led to the second story of the mansion. Working feverishly, they reloaded on the way.

"Charge 'em!" shouted one of the men outside. "We got to get in there and find Mr. Eldridge!"

Naturally reluctant to face another volley like the first one, the attackers hesitated, and that gave Daniel, Roxanne, Bramwell, and Hamish time to get halfway up the stairs before more of the highwaymen ducked through the smashed door, guns up and ready. Daniel fired and saw one of the men knocked backward by a ball that shattered his collarbone. Beside him, Roxanne's pistol cracked and another man staggered. Hamish fired next, the sound of his shot blending with a blast from below. The highwayman's ball hit the banister of the staircase and sent splinters flying through the air. Hamish's shot was more accurate and burned a path along a man's forearm and then smashed his elbow.

"Back!" Bramwell panted. "Back down the hall!"

They reached the second-floor landing and started along the corridor. Hamish dropped to a knee and finished reloading. From where he was, he could still aim down the stairs at the foyer. He fired, then grunted and rolled backward as one of the return shots clipped his upper thigh. Grimacing as blood flowed between the fingers of the hand he clutched over the wound, Hamish scuttled backward down the carpeted hallway toward the spot where Daniel, Roxanne, and Bramwell were reloading their weapons.

Daniel glanced at Roxanne. Her hair was disheveled, and where she had brushed it back from her eyes, she had left a streak of black from her powder-smoke-grimed fingers. She stood there—pregnant, resolute, pistol in hand—and Daniel thought she had never looked more beautiful than at that moment. If they were to die here, at least it would be together. At last, after all the months of separation, they had been reunited. She met his eyes, and he knew she was thinking and feeling the same thing.

"Here they come again," Bramwell said, and calmly strode toward the head of the stairs to meet the attackers.

"Stay here," Daniel said to Roxanne, "just in case they get past us." Without waiting to see if she did as he said, he hurried after Bramwell and reached him in time to see the final three raiders bound through the foyer and start toward the stairs. Daniel and Bramwell fired as one, even as the men below fired up at them. Bramwell grunted but stood his ground. Daniel saw two of the attackers fall; then a third shot sounded beside him. The final man spun crazily off his feet and pitched lifelessly to the floor. Daniel saw Roxanne beside him, smoke curling from the muzzle of her pistol. She had disregarded his order . . . which, knowing Roxanne, was not surprising at all.

The foyer and the floor at the base of the stairs were littered with bodies, some dead, some still alive but passed out from their wounds.

Bramwell surveyed the gruesome scene and said in a peculiarly thin voice, "I expect that will do it, then."

At that moment his legs folded at the knees, and he fell forward, dropping the empty pistol as he tumbled down the stairs toward the carnage below.

"Bramwell!" Roxanne screamed, letting go of her own gun and hurrying recklessly down the stairs after him, heedless of her own safety. Daniel went after her, ready to grab her and steady her if she fell.

Bramwell came to rest several steps above the bottom of the stairs. His head was above the rest of his body, and his eyes were open as Daniel and Roxanne knelt beside him. At the top of the stairs, an anguished-looking Hamish MacQuarrie hobbled awkwardly toward them, his wounded leg still bleeding.

"Bramwell . . ." Roxanne said softly as she lifted his head and pillowed it in her lap. "Oh, dear God."

Daniel looked at the two large bloodstains on Bramwell's shirt. The first wound had been worse than he had admitted, and both together would undoubtedly prove fatal within minutes. It was a miracle, a testament to the man's iron will, that he had stayed on his feet and fought for so long.

He managed to lift his hand and close his fingers on Roxanne's as tears rolled down her cheeks. "Don't cry," he said hoarsely. "You know . . . that I had very little time . . . so little time . . . left to me . . . but I spent it . . . so well."

"But you can't die now!" Roxanne said raggedly. "This isn't right! It wasn't supposed to be this way!"

"Things are . . . the way they are . . . my dear. . . . You learn that . . . when you face death as . . . as I have." A great shudder went through Bramwell's body, and Daniel could almost see the life racing out of him. But the Englishman forced himself to go on, "This is . . . all yours now . . . Roxanne . . . or should I say . . . Lady Oakley? Lady Oakley . . ."

His bloodless lips smiled, a smile of infinite weariness as his eyelids began to droop closed. "Good-bye . . . milady."

Roxanne's tears came even more freely now. Bramwell Stoddard was dead.

But they were alive, Daniel thought, and he wanted to make sure they stayed that way. Otherwise Bramwell's sacrifice would have been for nothing.

To Hamish, he said, "Stay here with Roxanne while I go check on Eldridge."

"Aye, sir."

Daniel went down the stairs and grimaced as he stepped over the sprawled, bloody corpses of the killers Eldridge had hired. He hurried down the hall to the study and gripped his musket tightly as he stepped through the door. The musket was unloaded, but it would make a perfectly good club if Cyril Eldridge was lying in wait for him. But no one was lurking inside the study. Eldridge was gone.

Eldridge must have come to while his men were attacking the house, Daniel reasoned. And seeing that the battle was going badly, he had slipped out of the mansion. Right now he was probably on his way to Ilford to summon help. He could tell any sort of story he wanted, and no doubt everyone would believe him.

Grim-faced, Daniel returned to Roxanne and Hamish, who were still waiting with Bramwell's body.

"We've got to get out of here," Daniel said to them. "Eldridge is gone. He'll come back here with soldiers, and when he finds Bramwell dead, he'll claim that one of us killed him. He'll raise a hue and cry about an American spy being here, and there won't be a safe haven for us anywhere around here."

Hamish looked up at Daniel and asked, "Then wha' can we do?"

"Get out of England," Daniel answered bluntly. "We can take the coach I saw outside and head for the coast. There is a ship waiting in the Channel each night to take us to France. We can rendezvous with it tomorrow night, if we can manage to avoid the pursuit that long. It's our only chance."

"Yes, you're right," Roxanne agreed. "But it's hard to leave Bramwell here. . . ."

"That's what he would have wanted, Roxanne," Daniel told her gently.

"I know." She took a deep breath and squared her shoulders. "What about Hamish?"

"You'll have to come with us," Daniel said. "Otherwise Eldridge will see that you're blamed for this, too. You'll probably be hanged if you stay behind."

"Aye, ye be right. But wha' about me wife? I can no' leave wi'out Moira."

At that moment there was a terrified scream from the front door of the mansion, and Daniel saw a red-headed young woman standing there, her hands clapped over her mouth in horror, her marketing bag fallen to the ground and forgotten as she stared at the bodies of the dead and unconscious men.

"Moira!" Hamish called urgently as he got to his feet and began limping toward her. "Moira, 'tis all right! I'm right here, lass!" He reached her and folded her into his arms, letting her bury her face against his chest so that her eyes would be shielded from the awful sight before her.

"We have to go," Daniel said to Roxanne, putting a hand on her arm.

"I know." She looked down at Bramwell's oddly peaceful face for a moment longer, then turned her gaze to Daniel. "I'm ready. I brought little here with me, and I'll take nothing. Nothing except memories."

Chapter Seventeen

Four days later, Daniel and Roxanne, as well as Hamish and Moira MacQuarrie, boarded a French ship in the port city of Le Havre. The vessel was loaded with a cargo of medical supplies bound for the warring colonies, and Daniel and his companions were the only passengers.

When he walked up the gangplank next to Roxanne, Daniel took her arm. She looked lovely in a dark green gown bought in a local dress shop, but there was a wistful expression on her face, and Daniel knew she was thinking about Bramwell Stoddard.

He told himself, not for the first time, that there was no reason for him to feel jealous. When Roxanne had agreed to marry Bramwell, she had been convinced that Daniel was dead, and she had been doing the only thing she could to protect herself and their unborn child. She had assured him that he had no reason to resent Bramwell, that in fact he ought to be grateful to the Englishman for helping her. But it was still difficult to look at her and know she was thinking about another man.

Daniel took a deep breath and forced those thoughts out of his mind. The captain of the French ship, a man named LeMonde, was waiting for them at the head of the gangplank. He smiled and took Roxanne's hand, bowing over to kiss it. Then he straightened and said, "My vessel is yours to command, M'sieur Reed. Where would you have us sail?"

Daniel had been thinking about that, practically since the moment they had fled Ilford Grange, through the desperate night and day and night again as they made their way to the English Channel and were picked up by the small boat waiting at the prearranged spot. Once they were safely off British soil, his mind had worked more clearly, and he had reached his decision.

Roxanne was no doubt expecting him to tell the French captain that their destination was Massachusetts, but instead Daniel said, "I want you to take us to Virginia, Captain LeMonde. Norfolk, Virginia. I can point it out to you on your charts."

"Very good, M'sieur. We sail within the hour."

As LeMonde hurried away, Roxanne turned to Daniel and said in surprise, "Virginia? I thought we were going home."

"We are," Daniel told her. "My parents have a plantation in Virginia, as you know. I think it will be the safest place for you. The war is only going to get worse in Massachusetts."

Roxanne's jaw tightened, and Daniel recognized

the stubborn glint in her eyes. "You should have told me that's where we're going," she said.

"I know. And I'm sorry. But we've both had so much on our minds."

"I suppose you're right." She rested her hands on her belly. "This baby will be born on American soil, in a land that will one day be free."

"I'm glad you understand. I just want what's best for you and the child."

Roxanne returned his smile and said, "And I'm sure your mother will enjoy having a grandchild around. Just make sure the captain of this ship knows we have to reach America before I give birth."

Daniel laughed. "I'll pass along those orders."

Hamish and Moira came up to them, Hamish still limping from the wound on his leg, which had been cleaned and bandaged properly when they reached Calais. Moira smiled at Roxanne and asked, "Ha' ye decided where ye'll be headin'?"

"Virginia," answered Roxanne without hesitation. "We're going to the plantation where Daniel's parents live."

"A large estate, is it?" asked Hamish.

"Not as large as other plantations in Virginia, like Thomas Jefferson's home, Monticello," Daniel said, "but it's a pretty good-sized place."

"Do ye think yer father might have some use for a groundskeeper?"

With a laugh, Daniel clapped Hamish on the shoulder. "I'm sure he can always use another good man." His face became solemn as he went on, "But I have to warn you. I don't know what the situation in Virginia is. I don't think the war has extended into the Piedmont region yet, but it could. There could be fighting there, just like anywhere else in the colonies."

"We're goin' t' a new land," Moira said, "and a new land is worth fightin' for, isn't it?" Hamish nodded in agreement.

"New beginnings are always worth fighting for," Daniel said, and his arm tightened around Roxanne's shoulders.

But there was more than the war to worry about, he knew. Cyril Eldridge was still alive, and as long as Roxanne and her child were living, Eldridge could not inherit his cousin's estate and the title that went with it. With his position in the British government, Eldridge probably had a long reach, but was it long enough to stretch all the way to Virginia?

Time would tell, but for now, Daniel told himself as he turned his face toward the sea breeze, he and Roxanne were together again, and that was all that mattered.

"New beginnings," he whispered. And wasn't it strange how the breeze from the sea smelled like freedom?

PATRIOTS—*Volume VI*

STARS AND STRIPES
by
Adam Rutledge

In the early summer of 1776, safely back on American soil, Roxanne Darragh Stoddard and Daniel Reed are reunited with his family at their ancestral home in Virginia.

Brothers Daniel and Quincy are thrilled when the women they love become mothers on the same day, but while a healthy son is born to one, tragedy awaits the other.

In New York City, Elliot Markham and Avery Wallingford forge an uneasy alliance in order to bring food by ship from Canada to relieve the starvation facing the Tories who have fled from Boston.

Having shadowed Roxanne to America, Major Alistair Kane wants her for himself, but her dead husband's cousin, Cyril Eldridge, wants only to insure that she and her child die.

And the birth of a nation is jeopardized when a band of cutthroats intends to kill Thomas Jefferson. Can Daniel, Quincy, and Murdoch Buchanan stop the threat in time?

Look for *Stars and Stripes,* Volume VI in the PATRIOTS series, on sale in spring 1994 wherever Bantam paperbacks are sold.